INTO THE GLEN

JON ATHAN

Copyright © 2019 Jon Athan
All Rights Reserved.

This is a work of fiction. Names, characters, businesses, places, events and incidents are either the products of the author's imagination or used in a fictitious manner. Any resemblance to actual persons, living or dead, or actual events is purely coincidental.

For more information on this book or the author, please visit www.jon-athan.com. General inquiries are welcome.

Facebook: https://www.facebook.com/AuthorJonAthan
Twitter: @Jonny_Athan
Email: info@jon-athan.com

Title page font (Horroroid) by Daniel Zadorozny: http://iconian.com/commercial.html

Book cover by Sean Lowery: http://indieauthordesign.com/

ISBN: 9781686333569

Thank you for the support!

First Edition

WARNING

This book contains scenes of intense violence and some disturbing themes. Some parts of this book may be considered violent, cruel, disturbing, or unusual. This book is *not* intended for those easily offended or appalled. Please enjoy at your own discretion.

Table of Contents

Chapter One 1
Chapter Two 19
Chapter Three 29
Chapter Four 35
Chapter Five 43
Chapter Six 57
Chapter Seven 65
Chapter Eight 71
Chapter Nine 79
Chapter Ten 91
Chapter Eleven 101
Chapter Twelve 109
Chapter Thirteen 115
Chapter Fourteen 119
Chapter Fifteen 141
Chapter Sixteen 149
Chapter Seventeen 157
Chapter Eighteen 169
Chapter Nineteen 187
Chapter Twenty 195
Chapter Twenty-One 203
Chapter Twenty-Two 209
Chapter Twenty-Three 223
Chapter Twenty-Four 229
Chapter Twenty-Five 233
Chapter Twenty-Six 257
Chapter Twenty-Seven 269

Chapter One

November 15, 1996

"So, what's the plan this weekend?" Brooke Page asked, thumbs hooked under the straps of her baby blue backpack. "Are you *finally* going to go out with Eric?"

Carrie Klein giggled and shook her head, her wavy, dark brown hair undulating with the breeze. Bright with unbridled passion, her honey brown eyes glowed with the sunshine. In her young, naïve mind, her first crush felt like her first love, and she couldn't hide it. Like Brooke, she was a fourteen-year-old high school freshman.

She said, "I don't know what you're talking about."

"Really? *Really,* Carrie?" Brooke asked, smirking. "Everyone knows you guys like each other. When's the first date? Come on, tell me."

"I told you: I have no idea what you're talking about. Who's Eric?"

Allison 'Allie' Klein ran forward, caught up to her sister and her sister's friend, and she kicked a tin can on the side of the road. She skipped beside the older girls.

"Eric!" Allie exclaimed. "You don't remember him anymore? In your diary, you–"

"Hey! Shut up, Allie! I said we weren't ever going to talk about him or anything you saw in my diary. You promised, remember?"

Allie sucked her lips into her mouth, frowned, and

nodded. She said, "I'm sorry."

"Whatever. Just mind your own business."

Brooke winked at her and said, "Allie, you can tell me about it later."

Carrie chuckled and said, "Stop it. Jeez, you guys are so annoying."

The girls laughed together as they made their way home. They lived in the small town of Montaño in northern New Mexico, away from the hustle and bustle of Albuquerque and Santa Fe. To their left, a dense woodland stretched into a mountainous region—a sea of trees. To their right, across a wide road, there was a seemingly never-ending meadow, grassland as far as the eye can see.

A rusty, red pick-up truck with a coughing, sputtering engine drove past the girls, chugging along on its last legs.

Carrie looked at Allie and said, "Seriously, don't tell mom and dad about Eric. Not one word, okay?"

"Okay," Allie said, capering about between the pavement and the dirt footpath beside the road. She said, "I won't say nothing if you don't tell mom and dad about *my* boyfriend. Deal?"

Carrie and Brooke looked at Allie with their brows furrowed, as if to say: *what the hell did you just say, kid?* They huddled together and giggled.

Brooke said, "Allie, come on. There's no way you have a boyfriend. You're in, like, the second grade."

"I'm in the *third* grade," Allie said, holding three fingers up to the older girls. "And I do have a boyfriend."

"Oh, really? So, who are you dating, Little Allie? Please don't say Mr. Ramos or some sick, perverted teacher. I don't wanna hear that."

"Perverted? What does that mean?"

Carrie responded, "A pervert is a pig. Forget about it. Who's your boyfriend, brat?"

"John."

"John who?"

Allie looked straight ahead and said, "John Stamos."

Carrie and Brooke burst into an uncontrollable guffaw, holding their hands over their stomachs and bumping into each other. Their laughter echoed through the woodland, creating a jovial mood in the desolate area. Allie snickered along with the girls. They laughed at her, she was the butt of the joke, but she enjoyed the attention. She wanted to entertain them because she wanted to be one of them.

As she caught her breath, Carrie said, "If mom ever asks… just tell 'em my boyfriend is John Stamos, too."

"Don't leave me out," Brooke said. "We can share him."

A white sedan—its exterior decorated with black smears, yellow blotches, and dozens of scratches and scuffs—drove past them.

Brooke said, "So, we've got no plans this weekend, right? Let's go to the movies."

Carrie's eyes widened and she hopped forward. She said, "Hey! I think *Romeo & Juliet* just came out."

Brooke leaned in closer to her, she moaned playfully, and she shouted, "Aww, Leo!"

"I wanna watch *Space Jam!*" Allie yelled.

Carrie said, "Nope, no, no way. You're not tagging along again. I don't want to watch any stupid kid movies, and I don't want to come home at eight because you're too sleepy to stay up. Stay at home and watch movies with dad."

"But I wanna watch Space Jam!"

The sisters argued while Brooke watched and giggled from the sidelines. Carrie loved her little sister, but she believed in boundaries—'me time' not 'her time.' Allie resembled her mother: soft brown hair, glasses over her eyes, and cheeks speckled with freckles. Yet, she only ever wanted to be like her older sister. She loved Carrie and she wanted to spend every waking moment with her. Brooke didn't care about the argument. She saw them both as close friends. Their fights were innocent and humorous.

A white windowless van cruised past them. The van rolled to a stop about a quarter mile ahead of the girls. They didn't notice it.

Carrie said, "Listen, brat, I'm already doing you a favor by letting you walk home with us. I could have left you–"

"No, you couldn't!" Allie yelled. "Mom said you can't leave me alone!"

"Yeah, well, mom is wrong. I can and I will if you don't–"

She stopped as she spotted the van from the corner of her eye. The van reversed slowly towards the girls. Allie stopped screaming as soon as she spotted it, too. The girls stopped at the side of the road, eyes sparkling with curiosity. Five seconds, ten seconds, twenty seconds—the van crawled towards them in what felt like slow-motion, its dead backup lights giving no warning.

One minute and twenty-five seconds. The van reached them and parked beside them in exactly one minute and twenty-five seconds.

"What the hell?" Brooke muttered.

Two men sat in the van, one in the driver's seat and the other in the passenger's seat. The driver wore a silicone werewolf mask with a gray face and a head of beautiful, voluminous dark brown hair. The hair stuck out from the top, the sides, and the jaw of the mask. His beady blue eyes could be seen through the eye holes, along with parts of his crows' feet.

The passenger wore a silicone pig mask. The mask appeared lifelike, its pale pink color blending with his neck. This mask had painted eyes that looked human. The eye holes were puny, barely revealing the man's dark brown irises. Like the driver, he wore navy coveralls. They didn't wear nametags, though, and they didn't look like plumbers or janitors.

Due to the high quality of the masks, gullible kids could have easily mistaken the men as crew members on a production team working on a big Hollywood movie.

Carrie and Brooke weren't gullible kids, though. The men rolled their windows down, the glass rattling and the crank handles squeaking. The engine kept humming.

The driver hung his arm out the window as he leaned against the door. He said, "Well, well, well. Look what we've got here: three little pigs. You must be running away from the barn, right?" He chuckled inwardly. He asked, "Where are you headin' this fine evenin'?"

Allie grinned at the man in the pig masked and shouted, "Look, it's a pervert!" She giggled, then she said, "We're going ho–"

Ow!—she yelped as Carrie pinched her arm.

"What did you do that for?" she asked, frowning.

"Shut up, brat," Carrie said. "You remember what mom said."

Allie was an impulsive but well-behaved child. She often acted without thinking, but she wasn't stupid or ill-natured. She listened to *everything* her mother said. She already knew the lesson her sister referenced: *Don't. Talk. To. Strangers.* She nodded at her sister, puckered her lips, and rubbed her arm. She still felt some pain from the pinch.

She looked at the men and said, "Sorry, mom said not to talk to strangers."

As the passenger chuckled, the driver said, "Oh, I see. Your mama is a smart woman, isn't she? Oh, how I would love to dissect her brain, mmm-mmm-mmm. But, here's the thing, little pigs: we're not strangers. Look who I've got with me." He pointed at his passenger. He said, "It's Uncle Oinks from the barn. Say 'hello,' Uncle Oinks."

The passenger leaned forward in his seat. He waved at the girls and oinked like a pig, emitting one deep, nasally grunt after another. Allie giggled and hopped in place. Brooke huffed and rolled her eyes. Carrie stepped in front of her sister, ready to protect her. The older girls were not amused by the strange men.

With a steady facial expression, not a twitch of her eyelids or her nose, Carrie said, "You're very funny, but we have to go now. Bye."

The girls walked forward. Carrie held Allie's left hand while Brooke held the young girl's right hand. They were taught about staying safe around strangers at school and home.

Carrie leaned closer to her sister's ear and whispered, "Don't look back at them, okay? Just keep walking."

"Is something wrong?" Allie asked, pouting.

"Just do what I say."

Their shoulders raised, they took ten steps, then fifteen, and then twenty. The van rolled beside them and matched their pace. The Wolf and Uncle Oinks leered at the girls, disrobing them—*molesting them*—with their eyes. Their heavy breathing could be heard through their masks.

Carrie and Brooke shuddered as soon as they spotted the van. They tightened their grips on Allie's hands and sped up, their stroll turning into a brisk walk. Yet again, the van accelerated to match the girls' speed.

The driver said, "Piglets, don't you run away from us. Mr. Wolf and Uncle Oinks, we're close friends. We work at the barn together and we want to take you back home with us. We want to take care of you. I certainly don't want to eat you, you hear me? Hmm? Okay, okay... maybe we want a little taste. Just one bite for me, one bite for Uncle Oinks. How's that sound?" He howled like a wolf while Uncle Oinks continued to oink. He said, "Come on, let's have some fun."

Brooke yelled, "Stay away from us, you freaks!"

The girls dashed into the woods. Carrie followed Brooke's lead, grabbing her little sister's hand with both of hers and pulling her into the woodland with them. Allie mewled and complained: *ow, you're hurting me.* The older girls didn't hear her words, though. They only heard the van's engine behind them.

The old vehicle's engine emitted a soft, normal sound, but it sounded *monstrous* to them, like the roar of an animal. The van cruised down the road with the men leering at their prey from afar.

The girls lurched through shrubs, hopped over detached branches and fallen trees, and stumbled through makeshift walkways paved with crunchy autumn leaves. They ran for a quarter mile until the road was no longer visible, until the trees looked the same from every angle. They weren't lost, but they were in danger.

In the woods, no one could hear them scream.

Allie tripped over a branch and fell to her knees. Carrie accidentally dragged her a foot across some rocks, scraping her sister's bare knees. Allie yelped and cried. She broke free from her sister's grip, grabbed her scraped knees, and grimaced in pain. Carrie stopped beside her sister, breathing heavily. Brooke slid to a stop in front of the siblings, glancing every which way.

"Oh shit," Carrie said. "Allie, I'm sorry. I'm so sorry. But it's okay, you're going to be alright. We just can't stop running, okay? Come on, please, let's go."

Allie yelled, "I don't wanna go! I'm tired and my legs hurt! It hurts real bad, Carrie!"

"I know, I know. It was an accident. Don't worry, mom will spray some Neosporin on it and it'll be better by tomorrow morning. I promise, Allie. Okay? Let's just get home already."

"It really hurts."

Brooke ran up to the girls and said, "Okay, Allie,

we'll try to carry you. Put one arm over my shoulder and the other one over Carrie's. But please *try* to walk a little. We can't stay here forever."

Allie pouted and shrugged, then she asked, "Why? What's the big deal?"

Brooke didn't know how to explain the situation to an eight-year-old. *Serial killers, pedophiles, rapists—* those words weren't common to children.

Carrie asked, "Who were those guys? Psychos? Jocks?"

"I don't know," Brooke responded. "Not jocks. They sounded way too old. I mean, I know we didn't see their faces, but they didn't look so young, either. They were creeps."

As she struggled to her feet, Allie said, "They were kinda funny."

"They weren't," Carrie said. "Those guys... They were trying to take advantage of us, Allie. You know what I mean? They wanted to, um... They wanted to win our trust so they could hurt us later. They're–"

The sound of a *snapping* twig interrupted her.

One-by-one, the girls turned their heads to look into the woods behind them. A gust of wind swept a blanket of autumn leaves across the ground. Tree branches groaned while some shrubs shook. The area was desolate, not a soul in sight. Yet, they felt someone watching them, eyes glued to their young, unblemished bodies.

Although her younger sister clearly wasn't incapacitated by the fall, Carrie threw one of Allie's arms over her shoulders and helped her walk. Brooke jogged a few meters ahead of them and scanned the area.

Oink, oink!

Brooke slid to a stop. She fell to her ass, then she crab-walked in reverse until she bumped into the other girls. Carrie and Allie were already frozen with fear.

Uncle Oinks jumped out from behind a tree and startled them. He oinked and squealed and laughed, his arms away from his body as if he were welcoming a hug. A large duffel bag hung from his shoulder. The girls glanced over their shoulders, ready to run, but they found Mr. Wolf waiting for them. He held his hands up in a peaceful gesture.

The girls could have ran into the woods. The woods were vast, after all, and the girls outnumbered the men. They could have split up while screaming at the top of their lungs. They were young, though, and they weren't prepared for such a dark and disturbing situation. Their parents lectured them about dangerous perverts, but they didn't teach them how to fight—*how to survive.*

Carrie pushed Allie behind her, using her own body as a shield. She looked at the van's passenger, then at the driver.

Breathing shakily, she said, "Don't come any closer. My dad, he–he's a cop." Mr. Wolf stepped forward. Carrie shouted, "I said don't!"

Brooke jumped up to her feet. She kept her eyes on Uncle Oinks, who leaned against a tree behind them. Mr. Wolf took a knee in front of the sisters.

He said, "Daddy's a cop, is he? Well, little piglet, I've got some news for you: I'm a cop, too."

"You're not a cop, you're a wolf," Allie said, peeking from behind her sister.

Ow, ow, ow, ow!—she yelped as Carrie pinched her arm and backed up into her.

Mr. Wolf chuckled, then he said, "Well, I'm a part-time cop, part-time wolf."

Brooke asked, "What the hell do you want from us?"

"Straight to the point. I like that about you. You're young but fierce. I think you're going to be a problem for us, so I'll–"

"Just tell us what you want and leave!"

The girls couldn't see the men's faces because of the masks, but they could *feel* their emotions. They knew when they were happy, smiling and amused. They also knew when they were angry, scowling and growling. Brooke's defiance—*her insolence*—infuriated Mr. Wolf.

He stood up slowly and, in a stern voice, he said, "I want to play cops and robbers. We're the cops and you're the robbers. We've got you cornered now, so it's time for y'all to get down on the ground, face-down with your hands behind your backs. No, no. Let's do this the right way. Get on the ground on your stomachs and interlock your fingers behind your heads. You understand me?"

"In–In–Inter-*what?*" Allie stuttered. She furrowed her brow and asked, "What's that mean?"

"These older girls know what it means. Follow their lead. Come on, get to it before I get angry."

Brooke shouted, "As if, dickwad! We're not doing it! Leave us alone!"

Mr. Wolf walked up to her. He towered over her, his six-three stature easily dwarfing her five-foot-one figure. He looked at her with his sharp, burning eyes, then he chuckled. He patted her head. Brooke shook her head and swiped at his arm. With the soft slap, she felt his firm, muscular forearm. He wasn't the creepy, old, out-of-shape child predator her mother had warned her about. And that terrified her.

Mr. Wolf said, "You know, by resisting arrest, I am *legally* authorized to use force to apprehend you." He looked at Allie and said, "In this case, little piglet, force means violence and violence means pain."

He drew a handgun from his pocket—*a sleek, new Ruger P90*. He aimed the pistol at Brooke, a steady arm giving him pinpoint accuracy. Uncle Oinks followed his lead. He pulled a handgun out of his duffel bag. He slid the safety off and then he aimed it at Carrie. He kept leaning against the tree, unperturbed by his own actions. Aiming loaded weapons at children was second nature to him.

Carrie panicked, sobbing and wheezing. Allie had seen her father's handgun before, she had been warned about playing with it, but she didn't understand the severity of the situation. Brooke smiled, frowned, and smiled again. She laughed and shook her head, trying to play it cool, although tears gushed from her eyes and rolled down her rosy cheeks.

Taking a deep breath between each word, Brooke said, "This... isn't... real. No... it's..." She stomped and shouted, "It's not real! This isn't real! We have to go home! We have to get your dad! They can't catch us all. Let's just... let's... let's run already! Come on, Carrie, let's–"

Mid-sentence, just as she took a step towards her friends, Mr. Wolf shot Brooke in the stomach. The bullet entered her torso above her belly button at an angle and exited through the small of her back, tearing through her small intestine. Her pink shirt, soaked in blood, hung away from her stomach. The blood stained the sleeves of her jacket and the waist of her jeans, too. It was everywhere.

Brooke grimaced, wrapped her arms around her stomach, and staggered. She collapsed in front of her friends, hitting the ground face-first. She whined, panted, and snorted, her pained cries echoing through the woodland. She squirmed on the mud, unable to lay still due to the pain emanating from her torso. The burning pain raced across her body, entering her limbs and her skull, as if her blood were replaced with acid.

"Oh my... Oh my God," Carrie said weakly.

Her eyelids flickered and her legs wobbled. The violence shocked her while her best friend's cries devastated her. She fainted and landed in the bush behind her. Puffy-eyed, lips quivering and teeth chattering, Allie looked at Brooke and then at Carrie. Death and violence weren't part of her world yet. She was innocent.

She stuttered, "Wha–What did you do? Why are you hurting us?"

Mr. Wolf said, "Shut up and get on the ground. I'm done playing with you."

"I don't... I'm..."

"Get on the ground and put your face in the mud. *Now,* piglet. If you don't, I'll shoot this little bitch again and then I'll shoot your other friend."

"She–She's my sister," Allie cried as she pointed at Carrie. "Please don't hurt her."

"Then follow my instructions. You have five seconds. One, two, three..."

Allie dropped to the ground, her chin sinking into the mud as she gazed into the woodland. Uncle Oinks dropped his bag beside her. He oinked and patted her head.

Two minutes later, Carrie awoke. She stared up at the sky, a canvas of blue dappled with white clouds. The tree branches waved at her and a few birds watched the violence from above. She heard her sister's muffled voice. Uncle Oinks was silent, but Mr. Wolf had a lot to say. He was scolding Brooke.

As he circled her, Mr. Wolf said, "You see? This is why you shouldn't resist arrest. Now you're dying, kid. A slow, painful death. You could have bought yourself sometime. Tell me: what's it feel like knowing you're going to be dead soon? Huh? Knowing it's over and you can't do anything to stop it? I've always wondered what death felt like."

"It–It hur–hurts so much," Brooke stuttered. "I–I–I need to–to go to a–a doctor. Pl–Please, mister, I'm sorry. Don't... Don't let me die. Please, sir..."

Carrie peeked over at them. She saw Uncle Oinks hog-tying her sister. Allie's wrists and ankles were tied together behind her back while a strip of duct tape covered her mouth. Mr. Wolf knelt beside Brooke and examined the girl. Brooke's cheeks and lips were now discolored, and a cold sweat drenched her body.

Carrie's fight-or-flight response took control of her body. Before she knew it, she found herself running away from the group. She vaulted over a bush between two trees and lurched into the dense woodland. She stopped a mere twenty meters away from them. The *boom* of a second gunshot roared through the area.

Brooke screamed in pain. She was shot in the leg. The bullet was lodged in her thigh. A string of bloody saliva hung from her lips and pooled under her face. She rocked from side-to-side.

Mr. Wolf aimed the gun at Brooke and stared into the woodland. He couldn't see Carrie from his position, but he knew she stopped running somewhere behind the trees in front of him.

He said, "Girl, if you don't come back here this instant, I'm going to kill your friend and your little sister. You hear me?"

Carrie swallowed the lump in her throat. She trembled and sniffled as she stared down at herself. She continued walking forward, away from the group, but she felt like she wasn't in control of herself. Someone else was piloting her body, leading her to safety.

Mr. Wolf heard her slow footsteps. He huffed at her. He stepped on Brooke's stomach, his heavy boot crushing her hands and aggravating the gunshot wound. Once again, Brooke shrieked in pain. More blood oozed out of the wounds on her stomach and back. The burning pain returned with full force.

"Carrie!" Brooke cried, her voice breaking. "Please, Carrie! Don't leave me! I don't want to die! Help me! Ahh, God! Please!"

Carrie closed her eyes and whimpered. She took another step forward. A third gunshot sent the birds flying skyward. Mr. Wolf shot Brooke in the other leg. The bullet went straight through her right thigh. He didn't take his boot off her stomach, either. He wanted her to squeal. Guilt was a powerful weapon.

"Stop! It hurts!" Brooke shouted. Out of breath, she said, "Please... Carrie... please..."

Carrie let out a shaky sigh. She swiped the tears and mucus off her face. Although her mind told her to run, her heart wouldn't allow her to abandon Brooke or Allie. Dragging her feet, she returned to the group. She emerged from behind a tree with her hands up.

"Attagirl," Mr. Wolf said.

Carrie responded, "I didn't... I didn't mean to run. I don't know what happened, but, um... I'm sorry, okay? Please don't hurt my–"

Without looking at her, Mr. Wolf pulled the trigger and shot Brooke in the head. The bullet entered her skull through her left temple and exited through the right. Bits of her brain splattered on the mud underneath her. Her eyes hemorrhaged and blood rolled out of her ears. She twitched for twenty seconds after her death, saliva foaming out of her mouth.

Carrie asked, "Why? Why did you... Wha–" She choked up, her throat tight and chest heavy. She asked, "Why? Why? Why? Why? Why?"

She couldn't say another word. She kept repeating herself as she listened to the *plop* of Brooke's blood and the pain in Allie's cries.

Mr. Wolf said, "Because she didn't follow my instructions. Because she got on my bad side. Now you know the consequences of disobedience. The next time you think about running away, I want you to remember this moment."

He stepped on Brooke's head, pushing half of her face into a mound of mud, then he twisted his foot left-and-right as if he were crushing a cigarette. Blood came out of her nose and leaked from her eye sockets. A *crackling* sound came from somewhere on her head.

"You could be next," Mr. Wolf said. "Or maybe—*maybe*—if you try something stupid again, I'll shoot your sister next."

"You're a monster," Carrie croaked out. "My dad is go–"

Uncle Oinks hit the back of her head with the butt of his pistol. Carrie was instantly knocked unconscious by the blow.

Chapter Two

A Regular Day on the Beat

Keith Klein stood beside the driver's seat of a cherry-red muscle car, a driver's license in one hand and the other hovering over his handgun holster. The name on the driver's license read: *Andrew Hernandez.* Keith's eyes drifted upward. He stared at the awkward seventeen-year-old in the driver's seat, watching him smile and fidget.

Andrew glanced at the cop, then at the rearview mirror, and then at the steering wheel. He puckered his lips, smiled, and shrugged. His body language said something along the lines of: *I'm playing it cool, but I know I fucked up.* A cloud of tension hung over them. From the outside looking in, it looked as if one false move could have led to a fatal shooting.

Keith cracked a smile and chuckled. He said, "Your mama taught you how to drive, didn't she? That woman, *that* woman, she drives with both feet flat on the floorboard. Pedal to the metal. Brakes? I don't think she's ever used 'em. I've been telling her for years now: someday, she's going to drive off-road and onto hell's highway. Now she's got her son speeding, too."

Andrew sighed, then he said, "I'm sorry, Officer Klein. I just lost track of time at Angela's house and I'm trying to get home before my mom. That's all." He smiled and said, "She really did teach me how to drive, by the way."

(Andrew lied through his teeth. He taught himself

how to drive, but he wanted to humor the cop to win some brownie points.)

"You were at Angela's? The Garcias' house?"

"That's right."

"Does her dad know you were there?"

Andrew bit his bottom lip and nodded. His eyes darted to the left and his nose twitched. His face betrayed him. Yet again, he was lying and it was obvious.

Keith smirked and said, "And just like your mama, you're not a very good liar." He placed his hand on the roof of the car and bent over, nearly matching the teenager's eye level. He said, "Be careful with that girl, Andrew. I'll be blunt with you, kid: her father is an asshole, and he's been to jail before. He *will* kick your ass. Get on his good side before his bad side gets on you. Alright?"

"Yeah, alright."

To Andrew—and to many of the locals—talking to Keith was like talking to a funny, experienced uncle. He was an honest, caring man who served his community with honor and courage. Andrew wasn't sure if Keith would let him off the hook, though. He held his breath in anticipation, begging for mercy with his eyes.

Keith knocked on the roof of the car and said, "Alright, I'm going to let you off with a warning today, Andrew." Andrew breathed a sigh of relief as the cop handed him his driver's license. Keith said, "*But* this is the last one. I know Officer Cooper has let you off the hook before. Don't go around thinking you're going to get a break from all of us."

"I won't, sir. Thank you. Thank you so much."

"Yeah, yeah. Slow down, alright? Is your speedometer working? Hmm? Do you even know how to read it?"

Andrew snickered, then he said, "Yes, sir."

"Good. Keep your eye on that thing and follow the speed limit. I know it's safe and boring, you've heard it all before, but... Listen, I used to be a daredevil when I was younger, too. I'm thirty-three now and I know from experience that it's not worth it. Going fast, speeding through life, riding like lightning... You know the rest. Take it slow. You've got a lot to live for. The last thing I want to do is scrape your body off the pavement, kid."

"I understand."

"That's what I like to hear. Tell your parents I said hi."

Keith took a step away from the car, then he stopped. He bent over near the driver's door again, slid his sunglasses down to the tip of his nose, and gazed at the teenager.

He said, "And don't go around telling people that I'm some sort of pushover, alright? You know me, kid. I'm not afraid to push back."

Andrew smiled nervously and said, "I won't. I promise."

"Attaboy. Get home safely."

Keith moseyed over to the police cruiser parked behind the muscle car on the side of the residential street. He watched as Andrew cruised away, he jotted down some notes on a pocket notepad, and then he headed back to the police department to finish some paperwork and end his shift. It was a regular day on the beat.

***

Keith drove his police cruiser up a dirt driveway, leafless trees to his left and right. In front of him, the sun fell behind his two-story house, rays of golden sunshine ricocheting off the slate roof. He parked in front of the garage and climbed out of his car. On his way to the porch, he took a deep breath through his nose and glanced around, cherishing the fresh air and the quietude of the region. He lived in the outskirts of town, not a neighbor in sight.

"I'm home!" he shouted as he entered the house. He hung his coat and tossed his wallet and keys on a console table. He said, "As usual, no red carpet for the old man."

He heard his wife's voice from the front door, but he couldn't make out her words. He entered the kitchen through the archway. He found Lisa Klein, his wife, sitting in the bound angle pose on a counter and speaking to someone on the phone. Lisa had beautiful gray eyes that changed in intensity with her mood. Usually, her eyes were bright—*almost blue.* In the kitchen, on that grim day, her eyes were hollow and dim. Keith didn't notice the concern in her eyes or the fear in her voice.

He kissed her, then he opened the fridge and asked, "What's for dinner, babe?"

Lisa continued talking on the phone: *uh-huh, hmm, oh, okay.*

Keith glanced around the kitchen until his eyes stopped on the dining table. He didn't see or smell any food. He looked up at the ceiling. He didn't hear his daughters either. He leaned back against the kitchen island in front of his wife and watched her, eyes glinting with curiosity.

A minute passed, then three.

Lisa said, "Okay, yeah. Yeah... Thank you, Lynn. Please call me back as soon as you hear anything. Love you, too."

She hung up the phone. She stared at it for a few seconds, then she looked at her husband. *Devastation*—it was written on her eyes.

Keith smiled and shrugged. He asked, "What? What is it?"

"The girls aren't home."

Keith nodded at her. He stood in silence for ten seconds, waiting for her to continue. He gave off another uncertain smile along with a shrug, as if to say: *so what?*

Lisa asked, "Do you know what time it is?"

"Dinnertime?"

"I'm serious, Keith. It's already past seven. They're not at Brooke's or Evelyn's or any of their friends' houses. They're not at school, either. I checked, I called. So, where are they?"

Keith said, "Alright, let's try to calm down a little. So, they're not home, they're not with the usual suspects, and they're not at school. I'm going to assume they, um... hmm..." His eyes widened as a likely possibility popped into his head. He said, "They snuck off to watch that new DiCaprio movie. You know, *Romeo & Juliet?* Come on, Lisa, you know what that boy does to girls. Hell, he even gets *you* fired up."

Lisa chuckled and sniffled. She found some relief in her husband's sense of humor, but she couldn't stop worrying about their daughters. Her mother's intuition told her something had gone terribly wrong.

She said, "We're talking about our girls here. I need you to be serious."

"Okay, I understand. And I seriously believe they went to the movies."

"On one hand, I hope they did, too. At least they'd be safe there. On the other hand, I'm furious. *Fucking. Furious.* They should have came home to drop off their bags, they should have called us or told someone. I mean, I don't even think they have enough money for one movie ticket? What if they snuck in?"

Keith opened the refrigerator again, as if cooked food would magically appear the second time. He grabbed a stick of string cheese. He ate it without peeling it.

He said, "If they snuck in, I'll arrest them myself."

"Come on, Keith. Stop it with this whole... nonchalant bullshit. This is serious."

"Okay, okay. I'm sorry. I'm just trying to keep you calm. I know how your overactive imagination works. It consumes you. You can't eat, can't sleep, can't operate. I need us to both think rationally. We can't do that if we're both upset, right?"

Lisa nodded.

Keith continued, "I'm giving Carrie and Allie the benefit of the doubt. Don't ask me how, but I know for a fact *Romeo & Juliet* was starting at 5:15. It should be ending soon, so they should be home soon. So, if they're not home by eight, I'll hop into my car and start looking for them myself."

"Fine. But I can't cook right now. Not like this."

"I told you, babe: you can't operate like this. I get it, though. Try to get your mind off things. I'll order pizza."

***

Keith sat on a recliner in the living room, watching the Chicago Bulls play against the Charlotte Hornets. Lisa stood near the front door, peeking out the window from behind the curtains. She looked at the clock on the wall above the console table.

Five, four, three, two, one. The clock struck eight.

Lisa said, "It's time. They're not home yet and you'd said you'd search for them. It's eight, Keith. Please, find our babies."

Keith drew a deep breath and nodded. He wasn't annoyed or frustrated. Truth be told, he was terrified. He tried his best to bury his emotions to protect his wife. He kissed Lisa, then he prepared himself to leave. As he put on his coat and grabbed his keys, the phone rang. The couple looked at each other with wide, hopeful eyes. Lisa dashed into the kitchen.

"Lynn," she answered the phone.

"Hey, Lisa, it's Janice."

"Janice! Oh, thank God, I've been waiting for your call. Did you hear anything?"

"Well, that's what I was calling about. I haven't heard from Brooke and I'm getting a little concerned. She hasn't shown up at your house, has she? I know she loves going over there unannounced. Your daughters, they're like sisters to her."

Lisa began to shake. She opened her mouth to speak, but she couldn't utter a sound. Her cheeks reddened and her jugulars bulged from her neck. She was holding her breath involuntarily—fear itself wrapping its spindly fingers around her neck and crushing her throat.

Keith asked, "Hey, what's wrong? Lisa, are you

okay?"

She didn't say a word. He took the phone out of her hand. Staring vacantly ahead, she leaned back against the wall near the archway and she slid down to the floor.

Keith held the phone to his ear and said, "It's Keith. What's going on?"

"Keith, it's Janice. Um... Okay, now I'm getting a little scared. I was just trying to ask Lisa about our daughters. She called me earlier and told me Carrie and Allie weren't home yet. We thought Brooke might have joined them, but, well... I haven't seen my little girl, either, and it's getting late. Is she there? Please tell me she's with you."

"Janice..."

"Hey, tell me she's there or tell me you've heard from them. I'm... Oh God, Keith, I'm about to have a panic attack. I'm really–"

"I'm going out to look for them. Okay? I'll find Carrie, Allie, and Brooke. I want you to do me a favor. Tell your husband to head over to the east side of town to look for them. Mark knows that area well. I'll look in the west side. I'm guessing they're at the theater watching a movie. Maybe they got caught sneaking in or maybe they're at the arcade chatting with boys. Don't panic, okay? Panicking won't get us anywhere."

Janice stuttered, "O–Okay. Sh–Should I call the police?"

"I'll call it in. Just wait there until we bring them home."

"Okay, I understand. Thank you, Keith."

"I'll call you if I hear anything," Keith said before

hanging up the phone.

He glanced over at his wife, who sat on the floor with her knees up to her face and her arms around her shins. She was pale now—*ghostly.*

Keith knelt down in front of her and said, "Hey, *hey.* They're just watching a movie, sweetheart. It's nothing. Come on, sit down in the living room and wait for me. I'll be back in an hour, maybe two. I'll find them, I promise."

Lisa didn't say a word. The absent look in her eyes—the eyes of a corpse—stayed. Keith led her to the recliner. He put a pillow behind her head, kissed her forehead, and he promised to find their daughters. He hopped into his police cruiser and headed to town, gritting his teeth and muttering to himself every mile of the way.

Chapter Three

Disposal

Brooke's nude corpse lay face down on the basement's concrete ground. Rivers of blood flowed from her body to a drain at the center of the room. Her throat was slit from ear-to-ear and her Achilles tendons were snipped. Most of her blood was siphoned through those wounds as well as the injuries she had sustained in the woods.

Her body emitted a sour stench. It seeped into the cracks on the ground and stained the brick walls. Like a loud, obnoxious actor, it had a dominant *presence* in the room—the center of attention.

Dale Hill stood in the basement, only wearing a pair of boxer briefs, gloves, and chukka boots. His fat, pale body was exposed for the world to see, but he was covered in blood. Some of the blood even landed on his beach blonde hair. His face was covered by a gas mask, something soldiers would use to protect themselves against chemical and biological agents. But his deep brown eyes were visible.

Dale was Uncle Oinks.

He grabbed a hacksaw from a duffel bag. He sat on her back, grabbed her shoulder in one hand, and began sawing into her right arm below her shoulder joint. The sound of skin *shredding* tore through the room. The *crackling* of her weak muscles and the *crunching* of her bones dampened the sound of her ligaments tearing. The hacksaw constantly came to a sudden stop between strokes, jammed in her flesh.

Blood poured out of her shoulder, heading down to the drain in waves. It took him five minutes to sever the arm.

Voice muffled by the mask, he said, "Damn, girl. How much blood you got in ya?"

He moved on to the other arm and repeated the process: sawing until the arm was severed. He cleaned the hacksaw, scrubbing the blood, gummy muscle, and skin off the blade.

Then he turned around and worked on her legs. He placed one hand on her hip, his thumb on her ass, and he sawed into her leg at the upper thigh. Her thighs were thicker than her upper arms and her femur bones were durable. He used a hammer and a chisel to shatter the bones. He was prepared for everything. He had been in that situation numerous times before. It took him nearly ten minutes to sever each leg.

Dale piled the legs near a table at the other end of the room. He took a five-minute break, then he returned to Brooke to finish the job. With the hacksaw, he cut into her neck starting at her nape. His goggles were foggy with sweat and dew. From the fingertips of his gloves to the crooks of his elbows, his arms were covered in blood. The blood landed on his upper arms, his neck, his torso, and his legs, too. His boxers were soaked in blood, hanging away from his body like a baby's full diaper.

Her spine *snapped*. The hacksaw's teeth ate away at her throat, ripping through her esophagus and her trachea. More blobs of blood fused with mucus, along with her tongue, came out of her mouth. Within five minutes, she was beheaded. Her head rolled away from the torso until it stopped two meters to the right.

Dale was tired, but he wasn't finished with his job. He went over to the table with Brooke's head. He put her head in a vise installed on the edge of the table. As he grabbed the crank handle, he heard a door open upstairs.

Allen Cooper walked down the basement stairs, the steps creaking under his boots. His wavy black hair was combed back and stubble covered his face. He wore coveralls.

He was Mr. Wolf.

Allen glanced around, holding an indifferent expression effortlessly. Despite the young age of the victim, the blood and gore couldn't rattle him. With two decades in the business, he grew accustomed to the violence. He understood that the victims of senseless crimes came from all backgrounds: young and old, black and white, male and female, and everything in between. When he wasn't capturing vulnerable people through extravagant and even theatrical chases, he was a stern, disciplined, and pragmatic man.

He said, "The kid will be arriving earlier than expected. Just after midnight."

"Yeah, so?" Dale responded, standing there in his underwear with a gas mask covering his face and a child's decapitated head in a vise.

"So I want you to put this mess away as soon as possible. If you can't get it out of here by midnight, at least have it packed up before he gets here. Then I want you to prep 'The Room' and call Curtis and a cameraman. Oscar or Lawrence will do. They have strong stomachs. Get the movie into production, and we'll show the boy what we can offer. Got it?"

"I got it. I'm almost done here anyway."

"Dandy. Fuckin' dandy. Let's get this money."

As Allen turned to leave, Dale asked, "How are the girls doing?"

Allen stopped, his back to Dale. He stood in silence for a few seconds, then he blew out a loud exhale. He glanced over at his partner, emotionless.

He said, "Stay away from them."

"What? Hey, brother, I was just asking. If no one takes them, maybe I can–"

"You can't. *You won't.* You remember what I told you a few years ago? I said we'd run this like the gangs run their businesses. We don't get high on our supply. Those girls, they're for *customers.* You want one? Hmm? Then you pay for her like everyone else. And there ain't no damn employee discounts around here, alright? Pay in full and follow the rules. You understand?"

"Yup."

"Say it right."

Dale rolled his eyes, coughed to clear his throat, then he said, "I understand."

Allen said, "Good. Save your payday after this next job and maybe you can afford one. Until then, follow my directions. Don't get sloppy." As he walked up the stairs, he said, "This boy, he's going to bring us a lot of money. He comes from a rich family—filthy rich. Who knows? He might buy those sisters as a set. That's a lot of money, man. Think about it."

Dale listened as the basement door closed behind Allen. He sneered and muttered to himself—*ah, whatever.* He turned the crank handle—once, twice, thrice. The vise crushed Brooke's head slowly. Her skull collapsed into itself with a loud *crack.* Her left eye popped out of her head while the other was crushed in its socket. He turned the crank handle again, using all the energy he could muster.

His plan was simple: flatten the six severed body parts as much as possible; spray the body parts with pepper spray to mask the smell and keep the animals away; double-bag the pieces in durable black bags; place the bags in separate luggage cases; and then bury the luggage in holes in different parts of the woods. Six feet deep wasn't enough, either. He always went for eight.

Dead body disposal was his specialty.

Chapter Four

A Night on the Town

The New Mexico town of Montaño was small and quiet, but it was growing rapidly thanks to new business investments and a recent surge in real estate development. New apartment complexes and business offices sprung up every month. A twenty-story building was under construction, hoping to restructure the city's flat skyline. There were other new buildings, too, sheathed in large curtains and awaiting completion.

Keith drove around town in search of his daughters and their best friend. He had already visited the movie theater. He learned no tickets were sold to minors without guardians after six in the afternoon, so the girls weren't there. Some teenagers hung out at the neighboring arcade. None of them saw the missing girls that afternoon.

He pulled over in front of a diner and climbed out the car. He found a group of community college students celebrating something inside—a birthday, maybe. He didn't see his daughters or Brooke. He approached the homeless man sitting in the alley beside the diner—*Dwight Rodgers*. The old man's frizzy, grizzled hair matched his long beard. He ate a banana and drank a Coke. It was an odd combination, but he wasn't picky.

"How's your night going, Dwight?" Keith asked.

Dwight sneered and said, "I'm eating a banana with soda sitting in a cold alley by myself while listening to a bunch of *assholes* laughing and cheering and all that happy bullshit. How does it look like it's going?"

"Well, it sounds like a regular day for you."

"Yup, a regular motherfuckin' day. What do you want? You come to sit with me? You want to share my banana? Or you want to arrest me for trying to live?"

"You know I'm not here to arrest you."

With a furrowed brow, Dwight watched Keith pacing back-and-forth in front of him. He had known him for years, even before he was outcasted to the streets.

He smiled and asked, "So, how's *your* night going, officer?"

Keith stopped in front of him. He turned his head slowly until he met eyes with the homeless man. He liked Dwight, he trusted him and his sources, but he was momentarily muted by his own doubt—*his own fear.* By asking him for help, he felt like he was accepting the worst possible outcome: his daughters were in trouble. He only went to Dwight for information when violent crimes occurred after all.

In a soft voice, he asked, "Have you seen my daughters, Dwight? My daughters, Carrie and Allie, and their best friend Brooke. You seen 'em?"

"Oh, those angels... Are they in trouble?"

"I'm not sure. Can you tell me anything?"

Dwight continued to grind the banana against his teeth and gums. He took a sip of his Coke, then he let out a long, satisfying *ahh.*

He said, "Nope. I haven't seen them all day."

"You hear anything? You see anything suspicious in the area?"

"*Well,* I did see an ice cream truck out west."

"Okay, so? Why is that suspicious?"

"I'm talking *west,* kid. You know Green Street, don't you? Every house on that street has been abandoned and condemned and beat-up and *fucked up* for years. I heard they were supposed to be tearing 'em down and building new, fancy apartment buildings out there. Hell, why not a homeless shelter, huh? I could use a place to sleep."

Keith stayed quiet. He digested Dwight's information, trying to link the abandoned neighborhood, the ice cream truck, and his daughters. Dwight could see he was having trouble.

He said, "For crying out loud, there ain't no reason for an ice cream truck to be out there at noon on a school day. There ain't no customers, right? The wrong 'clientele,' right? Shit, if I can figure that out before you, maybe I should be the cop. Damn it, man."

Keith responded, "I get it. I'll look into it. Thanks."

As he took a step to leave, Dwight lunged forward and grabbed his leg, like a dog welcoming his owner home with a good humping.

He said, "Come on, officer. I gave you something, so you should give me something, too. Don't be like that, son. You know I ain't up to no good. Just a little cash. Please?"

Keith handed him a ten-dollar bill, thanked him again, and then he went on his way.

***

Keith headed west, driving down alleys and cruising past abandoned buildings. He searched everywhere for his daughters—parked cars, backyards, cafés, bars—but he didn't look inside the dumpsters. Dumpsters stored trash and corpses. He refused to believe his daughters were killed. He didn't find anything suspicious.

He stomped on the brakes, flinging himself forward. He stared into an alley to his left. His eyes, wide and zany, said something along the lines of: *what the fuck?!*

A middle-aged man stood beside a dumpster, his pants around his ankles. A young woman squatted in front of him. Her skirt rode up to her waist, exposing her bare crotch. The man thrust his dick into her mouth—fast and hard. Slimy saliva poured out of the woman's mouth and hung from the man's dick. On the verge of vomiting, she gagged and coughed. Streaks of tearful mascara stained her cheeks. She slapped the man's stomach, his hips, and even his ass, but he didn't stop.

To most people, it looked like rape—*brutal.* Although his daughters were his primary concern, he couldn't drive off and ignore the attack. He vowed to protect his community. He jumped out of his car, jogged into the alley, and drew his handgun and a flashlight. He aimed the pistol and light at them.

He barked, "Get away from her! Put your hands up and step back!"

The man glanced over his shoulder, squinting as he held his hand over his face. He kept thrusting his cock into the woman's mouth, although he slowed down. Keith wasn't wearing his uniform, so he resembled a good Samaritan.

The man shoved his dick into his pants and asked, "Who the hell are you?"

The woman spit and retched as she stood up and

adjusted her skirt.

Keith shouted, "Put your hands up and step away from her! Now!"

"What the fuck, man? I paid for–"

"Montaño PD! Get away from her! Don't reach for anything!"

The woman staggered forward and yelled, "What the hell?! I'm working here, you pig!"

Keith lowered his weapon, baffled by her reaction. He was the knight in shining armor, but she wasn't looking for rescue. He recognized her as a prostitute—*Vanessa Arellano.* And her anger was sincere. The man was a high-paying customer who paid her to dominate her. Police weren't good for business.

The client said, "Wait a second, wait a second. This guy's really a cop?"

Vanessa sighed and nodded as she swiped at the saliva and pre-ejaculate on her lips. The client looked at Keith, then at Vanessa. He sprinted down the alley.

"Hey! Get back here! Don't move!" Keith shouted. The client didn't stop. Keith muttered, "Goddammit. I don't have time for you, you pervert."

He turned his attention to Vanessa. Like Dwight, she was down on her luck. She was one of the town's nocturnal faces—the local prostitute.

He said, "So you're still working."

Vanessa spit a loogie, then she said, "And you're still bad for business. Shit, back in high school, you'd tell on me whenever you'd catch me with my boyfriends. Everyone thought you were jealous. Turns out: you were just a goody-goody who couldn't mind his own business. Still can't, can you?"

Boyfriends—in Vanessa's world, the word meant 'clients.' Even at a young age, she traded her body for money. Her high school 'boyfriends' treated her a lot better, though.

Keith said, "I'm not here to bust you. I'm not going to take you in. To be blunt with you, you can suck a million dicks tonight and I wouldn't give a fuck."

Sensing the fear and frustration in his voice, Vanessa asked, "What's wrong with you? Did you finally snap?"

"No, but I think I'm about to. Look, my daughters didn't come home from school today. I can't find them and no one has seen them. I'm beginning to suspect... the worst. Have you seen or heard anything?"

"Haven't heard of any missing kids."

Keith lowered his head and muttered indistinctly. The world came crashing down on him, his conscious reality morphing into a nightmare. Shame and guilt attacked him. He protected his community, but he couldn't keep his daughters safe. He blamed himself for everything. *Lisa was right,* he thought, *every second mattered, and I threw time away.*

Vanessa said, "Hey, I've got a tip. Something you might want to stick your nose in." A sparkle of hope glimmered in Keith's eyes. The prostitute said, "I, um... I ran into a 'suspicious' John recently. I guess 'suspicious' is the right word."

"What do you mean? How was he suspicious?"

"There are a lot of different types of Johns out there. Some of them can't get hard and just want some company for the night. Someone to make them feel loved. Others want a quick fuck for a buck. No passion, no emotion. Then... Then there are those that really want to *dominate* a woman. No, they want to… They want to *punish* us for some reason."

Keith nodded at the alley, as if to say: *him?*

Vanessa chuckled, then she said, "No, hun, that's a regular. He just wanted to shove his four-inch dick into my throat to make himself feel big. These other guys… they're violent. I'm talking *real fuckin' violent*. I don't run into those guys often around these parts, but one of them picked me up this week. Picked up some of my friends, too. He fucked us up. He's a monster. He pays well, but he's a *real* monster, Keith."

"Did you get a name?"

"No."

"What did he look like? Where'd he pick you up?"

"He was a white guy. Tall. Strong. Black and gray hair. Mostly gray. Green eyes. Kinda handsome. He picked me up a few blocks that way, near those abandoned houses. Fucked me in his van. *Raped me* in his van. The guy loves anal and he doesn't take 'no' for an answer. But at least I got paid. I'd rather be paid and miserable than poor and miserable. I guess that makes me crazy, right?"

Keith's nose wrinkled and his eyes narrowed in disgust. The hope in his eyes turned into a fiery fury. He wasn't disgusted by Vanessa, though. Her story made him sick. *Rape*—it was like taking a person's life away without killing them. He hated her John just like he hated all rapists.

He said, "Call me if you see him or if you hear anything about him."

"He was suspicious, Keith, but I don't think he has anything to do with your daughters. I just thought you'd want to, you know, know about him. Your girls, they're good, smart kids. They'd stay away from a guy like that, handsome or not."

"I know, but someone has to look out for you. I'll look into it after I find my girls. Just call me, alright?"

Vanessa nodded and said, "Yeah, sure. Thank you." As Keith went to his car, she shouted, "Good luck! I mean it!"

Keith waved at her without looking back. He headed home, ready to admit defeat and call his boss for help.

Chapter Five

Shopping

Riley Watts sat on a dusty recliner. The blue of his eyes glowed through his sunglasses. His button-up shirt was open down to his chest and the sleeves were rolled up. He combed his platinum blonde hair back, styled to appear perpetually windblown. His chiseled face, strong and angular, was clean shaved. He was a handsome young man—twenty-six years old, to be exact.

He yawned out of sheer boredom. He stood up and walked around the living room, which was illuminated by lanterns and candles at regular intervals. The floorboards squealed under his boots. All of the furniture—tattered sofas, creaky tables, damaged paintings—was old and rotting. The fireplace was boarded up, dust and other particles flowing past the planks of wood. An archway led to the kitchen, a door led to the basement, and a staircase led to the second floor.

He fell into the recliner again. A strong, burly man stood behind him with his arms crossed—wearing black from head-to-toe. His name was Chuck Russo, and he was Riley's personal bodyguard.

"How much longer?" Riley asked, sinking into the seat.

With a deep, brooding voice, Chuck responded, "I don't know. You want me to go find them?"

"I'm bored."

"I know."

"If I don't get some action soon, I might burn this—"

The creaking stairs interrupted him. Allen came down from the second floor, wearing his wolf mask. Riley stared at him with a deadpan expression, then he burst into a belly laugh. His laughter was unique—*maniacal,* like a clown's in a cartoon. Every *'ha'* was distinguishable, sharp and loud. Like a boy on Halloween, he was amused by Allen's costume.

As he recomposed himself, he asked, "Now what is this? I know you have a reputation, but I'm not one of your products. I'm a customer. A high-paying customer."

Allen sat down in the recliner across from him. He said, "Your father is a high-paying customer. He asked me to wear this during our introduction so you'd know who I am—so you'd know this isn't daycare. You're here to have some fun because your causing too much trouble for your dad. He wants you to get it out of your system. That's where I come in. Me and all of my *wonderful* resources. You know who I am, right?"

Riley smirked and said, "Of course. You're the big bad Wolf. Mr. Wolf, right? And this..." He looked around the living room again. He said, "*This* is the Wolves' Den."

"That's right. One of many I operate across the country."

"I've heard a lot about your business. From my dad, from friends... It sounds like a lot of fun, and I've been itching for some fun. Why don't you take that mask off so we can get started?"

Allen was the boss, so he didn't like a younger

man—*a customer*—telling him what to do. But Paul Watts, Riley's father, was a powerful, wealthy man. He was a multimillionaire thanks to his real estate business, stock market investments, and a string of new business investments. The man was even trying to break into the movie industry. He offered a cache of cash, gold, and property deeds in exchange for his son's stay at the Wolves' Den.

Allen removed the mask and said, "Let's get down to business. First of all, I believe we sent y'all a list of rules." He pointed at Chuck and asked, "Who's this? My partner, Dale, tells me you wouldn't come without him."

"That's Chuck, my bodyguard," Riley responded. "It's fine, he's trustworthy. My dad personally hired him when I was sixteen. You know, after that asshole tried to kill me at a bar for talking to his bitch. You remember that? Good times, eh?"

"Yeah, it was all over the news. *'Heir gets his ass beat at a bar.'* Good stuff. For now, Chuck can stay. I'm going to assume he understands the rules. If you're not part of the club, you *never* talk about the Wolves' Den. You got that, Chuck?"

Chuck nodded.

Allen clapped and rubbed his hands together. He said, "Great. So, Riley, let's talk about some of our 'luxury' features."

"Sure, let's talk," Riley responded. "With all those animal masks around, I'm guessing you have a barn around here, right? Do you offer some intimate time with the animals? I've fucked plenty of pigs back in LA and Miami, but never a real one. Wonder what that's like. Don't you?"

He cackled again, his unhinged laughter echoing through the house. Allen and Chuck remained silent.

Unamused, Allen said, "The only animals around here are us and them. Let me show you around."

"I was joking, man. Lighten up."

"I know, I know. Come on."

**

Allen led Riley and Chuck to the second floor. There were three iron doors to the left, three to the right, and one at the end of the hall. The doors were new. The faint sound of a man screaming seeped into the hall from one of the rooms. Allen unlocked the padlock on the first door to the left. The hinges screeched as he pushed the door open.

Riley grinned. The screaming was clear. They were shrieks of pain with a few seconds of heavy, hoarse breathing in between. He peeked inside.

He said, "Well, well, well. I thought I heard someone screaming before I got here."

Jeremiah Ellison sat on a chair at the center of the room—a bedroom renovated into a chamber of torture. Broad strokes of fresh blood painted the walls and floor red. The older blood, from past victims, looked black in the dark room. The window was boarded, and not a slit of moonlight could slip past the planks of wood. A single lantern in the corner lit up the room.

Thick rope kept Jeremiah restrained to the chair, his arms tied to the armrests, shins to the chair's legs, thighs to the seat, and torso to the backrest. He was nude, covered in sweat and blood. His face was swollen, bumpy and purple. His left eye was blocked by the knots. His right eye didn't fare much better.

There was a massive gash over his right eyebrow. Blood from the gash cascaded over his face and entered his eye. His vision was narrow, blurry, and specked with blots of red.

A screwdriver protruded from his abdomen, above his bellybutton. The screwdriver was thrust nearly four inches into him, puncturing his colon. His abdomen was riddled with five other stab wounds. Along with several ounces of blood, some yellow fluid exited the wounds. His intestinal fluids were leaking into his naval cavity and oozing out of him.

Curtis Cox, an employee at the *Wolves' Den*, tortured him. He wore a silicone mouse mask to protect his identity. He wasn't a fan of it, he thought it was cowardly, but he wore it to follow Allen's rules. If it were up to him, he would torture his victims without hiding his identity. He was aroused by the terror he struck into his victims' hearts.

Lawrence Alfaro wore a black hood over his head, but he didn't torture Jeremiah. He stood in the corner of the room, recording the violence with a cassette camcorder.

"How do you like that, boy?" Curtis asked.

"Fuck you!" Jeremiah yelled, saliva spurting from his mouth. He cried, "Let me go! Oh God, what the fuck is this? You're killing me!"

"That's the idea, smart guy."

"*Fuck! You!*"

"Christ, boy, I'm impressed. You got a big mouth and a big set of balls. Let's see what we can do with that."

Curtis pulled a box cutter out of his pocket. The four-inch blade shot out of the handle with a rapid succession of *clicks.* Jeremiah leaned back against the seat and almost fell over. Curtis stepped on his knee and kept him grounded. He shoved his gloved fingers into Jeremiah's mouth to stop him from gritting his teeth.

Then he sawed into his cheeks with the box cutter, one after the other. The blade tore through his flesh like a knife through warm butter. He was sliced from the edges of his mouth to his ears. Blood poured into his mouth and dribbled down his face. His mandible was damaged by the blade, too, leaving his jaw dangling open. He couldn't keep his mouth closed for longer than five seconds.

He mumbled, "Wha–What the… Why a–are you…"

"Shut the fuck up. I'm not finished yet."

Curtis grabbed Jeremiah's scrotum with a tight grip. His left testicle looked like it was about to burst because of the pressure, bulging out from between Curtis' thumb and index finger. Jeremiah was instantly revitalized. He stared down at himself, but it was too late. Curtis had already started cutting into his scrotum with the box cutter.

Jerimiah felt a powerful pinch followed by a burning pain. For a second, he believed his genitals were set ablaze. But he didn't see any flames. He clenched his eyes shut and gasped as he felt another strong pinch *in* his scrotum. It sent a jolt of pain across his entire body, then an unusual numbness spread across his crotch. He tried to scream, but he could only let out some short, raspy breaths.

His crotch was covered in blood. It looked like his scrotum had exploded from the inside. His penis was unscathed.

He asked, "What... did... you... do?"

Curtis held Jerimiah's severed testicles up to his face. He shoved the bloody testicles into Jerimiah's mouth, one-by-one, then he pushed his chin up and forced him to close his mouth. Jerimiah squirmed and snorted. One of the testicles had rolled into his throat. He couldn't breathe. He was suffocating slowly, choking on his own balls.

Curtis laughed at him. He watched him choke, his eyes on the lump—*the testicle*—protruding from his throat. He memorized every gruesome detail.

He asked, "You want me to help you out, boy? Hmm? Want me to help you breathe? If you do, I'm going to need you to speak up. 'Take these balls out of my mouth.' Come on, say it."

Jeremiah's head fell back, limp. He was barely conscious.

Curtis continued, "Don't sleep now, boy. I promise, if you sleep, I'll find your family when *they're* sleeping and I'll wake them up and I'll bring them here. I don't care if they're young or old. You hear me? Now say it! Beg for mercy!"

From the doorway, Riley huffed and muttered, "Amateur."

"You can torture someone here, too," Allen said, watching the violence with a steady, unmoving face. He said, "We can even give you a 'memento.' A home movie, directed by you, starring you... You get the idea. Hell, kid, we have some of the best cameras in the business."

"I know. We donated them, didn't we?"

"Your father did. That's right."

Riley smirked as Curtis sliced Jeremiah's throat

open vertically down the center. The gore didn't affect him. The torturer forced two fingers into Jeremiah's open throat. He tried to pull the testicle out through his neck. Waves of blood poured out of the wound and rippled down the victim's torso.

Allen said, "Listen, I know you want to get your hands bloody. We can have another 'guest' here within the next seventy-two hours and you can have all the fun you want."

"Why couldn't I have him?"

"Because my friend there, Curtis, he already paid for him. We can't take another client's toy away and give it to another kid. That's not how it works. He paid first, so he plays first. Someone else already paid for Jeremiah's 'movie,' too. We couldn't find a role for you that would fit the client's idea for the film. We can–"

"You have too many rules in this damn place," Riley interrupted. He paced back and forth in the hall, swiping his fingers through his feathery hair. He said, "Okay, okay. I won't snap at you again. I'm just, you know, I'm, um... I'm a little 'antsy,' right? I don't want this. I *love* this, but I don't want it. I'm not craving it right now. I want something else. That's why I'm here."

Allen sniffled and nodded, as if to say: *okay, whatever.* He closed the door and secured the padlock. He leaned back against the wall and watched his guest. His erratic behavior caught his attention.

Still pacing, Riley said, "Violence is everywhere. It's easy to get. Maybe it's not as easy as it is out here, but I could get it anywhere. My dad could have sent me to 'vacation' in Thailand, Korea, or China, and I could have slaughtered anyone out there. Hell, those movies you make, I can order them off this thing they call the 'internet.' You've ever been on there? Oh man. *Oh man.* There's some fucked up shit on there. The connections I've made through there... I can get more than murder. Can you get me more than this? More than torture? Or are you small-time?"

Allen drew a deep breath, then he sighed. He said, "You won't find a hands-on experience like this anywhere else in the world. China? You think they're going to hold your hand and walk you through an organ-harvesting factory? You think they're going to let you play with their product? Really? I've found success from California to Florida. If you don't like what you see here, I can always send you to another branch. I'm sure the weather's better in Miami right now anyway."

"That's not what I want. That's not what my dad paid for. Miami, Los Angeles... The cops out there are actually starting to investigate operations like this. You believe that? They're starting to care about 'human trafficking' and whatever other bullshit title they put on it to make themselves feel better. I wish I could, but I can't do it. I told my dad I'd stick to this, I'd fly under the radar out here, so that's what I'm doing."

"Good. So how can I help you? What do you want to do, kid?"

Riley stopped in front of him. He tapped Allen's chest and said, "First of all, don't call me 'kid.' Secondly, I don't need to kill anyone right now. I did that last week. I need... I..."

He stopped upon hearing a faint feminine cry. He turned his head slowly until he spotted the second door on the right side of the hall. He heard the whimper again.

He said, "I want to fuck."

***

A key ring jingling in his hands, Allen said, "You should wear a mask before I open this door."

"Why?" Riley asked.

Allen stopped looking through the keys. He stared at Riley in disbelief. *Why?*—in the Wolves' Den, under those circumstances, it was the stupidest question he had ever heard.

"Are you joking?" he responded. "If they see your face and if they *somehow* get away, you'd be fucked. Your dad wouldn't be able to fix a problem like that."

"I'm not wearing a mask."

"Then wear a bandana."

"No, I'm not covering this gorgeous face," Riley said, snickering. "Listen, you said you have two girls in there. Those girls are scared, right? So they won't trust me if I look like one of you. I need their trust to make this easy. Besides, you're not small-time, remember? You're a professional, so I know you won't let them escape. Right?"

Allen sighed and shook his head. He forced his employees and clients to wear masks or hoods during their escapades. He was powerless in front of Riley, though. Riley's father was too wealthy and powerful to cross. He feared disrespecting his son and his wishes would harm his business. He put on his wolf mask, then he unlocked the padlock and opened the door.

"Thank you," Riley said. He entered the room, a grin on his face and some pep in each step. He said,

"Hello, ladies. How are you doing? Has Mr. Wolf been treating you well?"

Carrie and Allie huddled together in the farthest corner of the room, crying uncontrollably. They were chained to the wall at their ankles. The bedroom was devoid of furniture. The walls and floorboards were dusty, spiders and cockroaches skittering across the old wood. The window was boarded, but there was a centimeter-wide slit between two of the planks. The bedroom wasn't used for torture—at least, not recently.

Riley squatted in front of the girls. In a soft tone, he said, "Don't cry, babies. I'm here on official police business. My name is Steven Carter and I'm investigating a noise complaint. Someone said they heard two precious angels crying. You wouldn't happen to know anything about that, would you?"

Carrie held her sister's face closer to her chest as she sniveled. She was confused and terrified. A part of her told her to trust Riley—*he's not wearing a mask, he sounds nice.* But she wasn't stupid. Her father was a police officer, so she could identify a cop without seeing a uniform or badge. Allie didn't understand a single thing. *Kidnapping? Guns? Men screaming?*—it was all surreal to her. Prior to Brooke's murder in the woods, she didn't even know the definition of violence. Like her sister, however, she knew Riley was lying. She saw him as a clown, putting on a performance for a couple of kids.

"You're not very talkative, are you?" Riley asked. "Alright, how about we start by getting to know each other? Come on, it'll be like the first day of school. What are your names? How old are you?"

"Allison. My name is–"

"Shut up," Carrie snapped at her sister. "Don–Don't talk to them."

Riley giggled, then he said, "*Wow*. I can tell you're sisters. You're the older one, obviously, and she's the younger one. Sweet. So sweet. I'll get straight to the point: I want to take one of you out of here so we can have a good time. I'll be... Well, I'll be *kinda* gentle. Maybe."

A good time—Allie thought about those words, but she couldn't connect the pieces. She wondered if he was one of the good guys. Carrie understood him. Her parents taught her about pedophiles—how to avoid them, how to report them—but they didn't teach her how to fight back. She was weaker than the men, but she only thought about Allie and her safety. She had one plan and one plan only.

She stuttered, "I–I'll go wi–with you. I'm, um... I..." She panted and sniffled. She said, "I'm older and I'm more mature. I've, um... I–I've had sex before, so I, uh... I know what to do. I'll be good, I promise."

Riley removed his sunglasses and gazed into her eyes. He saw something he had only ever seen in children before: *innocence, purity.* He lost that a long time ago.

He tapped her nose with his index finger and said, "You see, baby, that's exactly what I'm *not* looking for." He stood up and began to walk away. As he put on his sunglasses, he said, "The small one."

Allen entered the room, the wolf mask covering his head. Chuck followed his lead, half of his face veiled in a bandana. He hooked his arms under Allie's armpits and lifted her from the floor without a struggle. Allie shrieked and kicked, but she couldn't stop Allen from unlocking the shackles around her ankles.

The young girl yelled, "No! No! I don't wanna go! Carrie, please! Help me!"

"Take me!" Carrie shouted. She grabbed her sister's leg and tried to pull her back to the floor. She cried, "I'm begging you! I'll do anything! Please, please, please! Oh my God! Don't take my sister!"

Allie's leg slipped out of her clammy hands. She reached for her again, her fingertips gliding across Allie's foot. She missed her, so close but so far. She touched her young sister, but she failed to grab her— failed to pull her back, *failed to protect her.* She followed the men as they carried her out of the room, but the shackles stopped her from reaching the door. She scratched at the floorboards until her fingernails cracked. She begged, she offered herself to them, but she was ignored.

Allen closed the door behind him, securing it with the padlock. Allie was carried into another bedroom down the hall.

Carrie heard her sister's faint cries through the walls. She couldn't tell if Allie cried because of fear or pain—or both. She didn't know what would happen to her sister, either. She knew it would be bad, though. She tugged on the chains and tried to free herself. The chains were attached to a floorboard in the corner of the room. To her dismay, she wasn't strong enough to yank the floorboard out. She came up short—again and again and again.

She hit the floor, looked up at the ceiling, and screamed, "Daddy!"

Chapter Six

Helpless

Tracy Farnsworth, reporting for Montaño Local News, stood in front of the Klein house. A white news van, proudly decorated with the organization's logo, and two police cruisers blocked the driveway behind her. A few beat officers stood guard outside of the house.

She said, "Police officers and volunteers have been searching the wooded area outside of Montaño in search of three missing girls, who are believed to have vanished sometime after 5 PM yesterday. And, as you can see behind me, the police presence is expanding. Investigators are going door-to-door, talking to neighbors, transients, taxi drivers, and bus drivers. They are–"

Keith turned off the television. Lisa sat on the recliner, her knees up to her chest and her feet on the seat. She wrapped a blue blanket around herself. Along with her husband, she stared vacantly at the reflection on the TV. They saw two pale, puffy-eyed, sleepless people—walking corpses, *zombies.* They hadn't slept a wink since the previous morning.

"Where did they go?" Lisa asked without taking her eyes off the television. "You said they were at the movies. You told me... You *promised* you'd find them."

"I'm sorry."

"I know. I don't... I don't want to blame you, I just don't know what to say."

"You should blame me. I should have gone looking

for them as soon as I got home, as soon as I knew something was wrong. And I *knew* something was wrong, I *knew* it, but I didn't listen to myself. I lied and I said everything was okay. 'They're at the movies.' It was bullshit. I'm so sorry, Lisa. I'm–"

"Stop it," Lisa interrupted. Her voice breaking, she said, "Just stop it. I can't... I... I can't do this right now, Keith. I'm hurt. I just want my babies back."

She wanted to lash out at him, but she tamed her tongue. *It's your fault, it's all your fault*—she wished she could say those words to him. But she blamed herself as much as she blamed him. She was fully capable of searching for her daughters on her own. Instead, she spent the night at home, waiting by the phone. Carrie had her own house key, so she didn't have to be there to answer the door if they returned home while they were out.

She said, "Tell me the truth. You're the expert. So... what's the likeliness that we'll find them? I mean, they're still alive, aren't they?"

Yes—it was the most optimistic response, but he couldn't say it with confidence. A vast majority of missing children landed in two types of scenarios: they either ran away or they were abducted by a family member. Carrie and Allie weren't the type to run away, and they had no other family members in the area. Therefore, the missing girls would most likely be found in the other less probable case types: lost or injured; nonfamily abductions; or victims of sex trafficking.

Lying through his teeth, Keith said, "I'm sure they're alive. I'm positive. There are... *so* many possibilities. They could be staying at a new kid's house for a sleepover. Maybe they got lost taking a shortcut in the woods. I don't know. Either way, we have hundreds of people combing the area and I know there are detectives going door-to-door right now. They're asking questions and they're getting answers. They're coming home, sweetheart."

"I hope so. I won't be able to sleep until they do. God, we should have saved more money. We could have bought Carrie a cell phone. They're expensive, but we wouldn't be in this situation if she had one. She could have called us if she was in trouble. Christ, she's old enough al–"

Someone knocked on the front door. Lisa stared at the door coldly, as if it were a living person who once betrayed her. She knew her daughters weren't on the porch. If they were, she would have heard a stampede of nosy reporters and the *clicking* of cameras on her driveway before the knocking. *Another cop,* she thought, *more thoughts and prayers.*

Keith rubbed her shoulders, then he answered the door. Captain Eduardo 'Eddie' Martinez, his boss, stood on the porch. He dressed like a modern-day cowboy: boots, jeans, a button-up shirt with a bolo tie, a blazer, and a cowboy hat. A graying mustache sprouted from his lip.

"Martinez," Keith said.

He couldn't think of any other words to say.

"How are you holding up, Klein?" Eddie asked, "Wish I could have gotten here earlier. Been a busy morning. Hope you understand that."

"Yeah, it's alright. Um… What can I do for you?"

"Well, I'd like to have a word in private. You mind taking a walk with me?"

Lisa marched to the door, the blanket falling behind her. She said, "If you have something to say about *our* daughters, you can say it to both of us. These are *our* girls, Eddie. You understand me?"

Eddie chewed on his lip and looked at Keith, as if he were expecting him to give him a different response. Keith was reluctant. If his captain had bad news to share with him, he didn't want Lisa to be the first to hear it. He sought to protect her, but he knew he couldn't stop her from pursuing the truth.

Keith said, "You can say it to both of us. What's going on, Martinez?"

Eddie sighed, then he said, "Alrighty, I don't have *awful* news for you, but I don't have great news, either. Nothing's come up in the search, but I'm using all of our available resources to find Carrie, Allison, and Brooke. The State Police have already joined the search, I'm sure you've heard, and I'll request federal help if we find signs of foul play."

"Foul play," Lisa repeated in relief. "You don't have any evidence of foul play yet. That's good. It's a good thing, right? Oh, thank God. They're still okay."

"We certainly hope so. I'll be moving Detectives James Sullivan and Jose Garcia from Homicide to a Missing Persons Unit to investigate. You might hear about that on the news, so I just want to clarify this: this is *not* a homicide case and we're not treating it like one. We intend on bringing your girls back home safely, so I've put my best investigators on the job. I have an army of cops out there, searching the streets and combing through the woods. We've got some fine citizens giving us a hand, too. Those walkthroughs will continue throughout the week. No stone or acorn will be left unturned out there. Montaño isn't so big, so I figure it shouldn't be too hard to find those angels."

Lisa said, "This might not be Los Angeles, but there are a lot of people out here. There are a lot of *new* people out here, too, with the construction and those new apartment buildings. We don't know where they're coming from. Maybe they're not as friendly or 'fine' as they look. And those woods, Martinez… The woods are endless. You'll need more than a week to even walk through it once."

"You have my word, hun: we're going to find them."

Keith said, "Let me join the Missing Persons Unit."

Eddie gave off a soft smile. He said, "That's what I came to talk to you about. I can't allow that."

"What? Why?"

"Well, for one: you're not trained for it. And two: the chief has already given you some paid time off. In other words… you're on administrative leave. He doesn't want you investigating in any capacity on behalf of the department during your time off. You're just too close, son."

Keith scowled and responded, "Are you kidding me? They're my daughters. I know them best."

"I understand that. If Sullivan and Garcia need anything from you, they'll ask. And I'll keep you updated every step of the way. I won't keep you in the dark. Now, I've got to get going. You're in my thoughts and you've got my prayers. Call if you need anything. It was nice to see you again, Lisa."

Eddie nodded at them, but they didn't respond. He sucked his lips into his mouth and walked away. Keith closed the door while Lisa trudged back to the recliner. They looked at each other, eyes devoid of hope and flecked with sparks of resentment. They were bitter towards one another, but they bottled it up. They only cared about their daughters.

Keith went to Allie's bedroom. A mural of a blue sky dappled with fluffy white clouds and filled with hot air balloons decorated the wall behind her small bed. Lisa painted it for her daughter at her request—*mommy, I want to see your beautiful drawing every morning!* Her desk was covered with coloring books while dolls and toy furniture flooded the floor. She was a messy child, but she was well-behaved.

Keith found a drawing on the desk—a family portrait comprised of stick figures. A doodle of a golden retriever was drawn in the corner, but they never owned a dog.

"We'll get you a pup when you get home, so please come home," he whispered.

He found a VHS on the desk, too—*Toy Story,* her favorite movie. He remembered coddling her after she first saw Sid's mutant toys. The memory brought a smile to his face.

He made his way to Carrie's room. Posters of hip-hop artists and rock bands were plastered on the walls, from the Fugees to Guns N' Roses. She loved music, especially rap. Her textbooks stood along the edge of the desk against the wall, the spines aiming towards her chair. He took the cassette tape out of the Sony Walkman on her desk. The cassette stored about an hour of music. He planned on listening to it until she returned home.

He stopped before he could exit the room. He looked at her bed. He knew about the diary under her pillow. Lisa had told him about it before. He respected her privacy, but he was desperate. He sat down on the bed and pulled a pink journal out from under the pillow. He flipped through the pages, reading each line as if he were reading an addictive thriller. He read his daughter's thoughts on school, celebrities, music, and movies.

He also discovered her dream: *to be an author.* She scribbled her ideas on the corners of each sheet. Some were blatant rip-offs of her favorite movies, others were unique and original. A few sections of her journal were dedicated to fanfiction as well. The stories brought tears to Keith's eyes. They weren't sad stories, though. He was proud of Carrie. He only wished he could have supported her more before her disappearance.

He stopped on a page about a boy—*Eric Soto.* Carrie drooled over him each time she mentioned him in a passage. Keith wasn't concerned about his daughter's innocent crush. He recognized the boy's last name. He had a strong, healthy relationship with the Soto family. He trusted them, and he believed he could find more information about the disappearances if he questioned Eric.

Keith made his way back to the living room. As he slipped into his coat, he said, "I'm going out."

Lisa asked, "Where to?"

The couple locked eyes. The house was silent—not a rattle of the windows, a groan of the pipes, or a creak of the wood. Yet, their eyes spoke volumes about the situation.

Keith said, "If anyone asks, I'm just out for a drive. You should read Carrie's diary. She had a lot of friends. A lot of people worth talking to, I think."

"Yeah, um... *Yeah*, I'll make some calls."

"I'll be back soon."

As Keith went to his police cruiser, Lisa stumbled onto the porch. Tears rolling down her cheeks, she said, "I'm proud of you. Find them. *Please.*"

Keith couldn't make any more promises. He nodded in determination before heading out.

Chapter Seven

Loneliness

The *clank* of the padlock hitting the iron door sounded sonorous—deep, powerful, monstrous. A series of *clicks* and *clacks* followed. Someone was unlocking the door.

"No, please don't come back," Carrie squeaked out as she scooted closer to the corner. "Not without Allie…"

The door swung open. A soft, barely perceptible whimper followed the squeal of the hinges.

Wide-eyed, Carrie said, "Allie?"

The door closed. She snapped out of her contemplation and looked up. She didn't notice him when he entered the room due to the whimper, but Allen approached her. He wore the wolf mask again, refusing to bend the rules for himself. He placed a plate and a can of Coca-Cola in front of her. Two slices of pineapple and ham pizza sat on the plate. The food was cold.

Leaning against the wall, arms and legs crossed, Allen said, "I figured you were the pineapple-and-ham-type rather than the plain ol' pepperoni lovers like the rest of us normal folk. You come off as 'stuck up.' Did you know that, girl?" Carrie scooted again, squeezing herself into the corner—crushing herself like a can against the wall. The man asked, "Aren't you hungry?"

Carrie glanced at the pizza. The cheese was hard, the crust and the pineapple chunks were dry, and the ham looked stiff. Yet, it tantalized her taste buds. She didn't want to eat a killer's food, though. It didn't feel right, especially since she wasn't aware of her sister's condition. *Is she eating pizza, too? Is she okay? Is she alive?*—the questions ran through her mind.

She tried to get her mind off her hunger. She looked at the window. A thin ray of early morning sunshine penetrated the planks of wood, illuminating the dust floating through the air. She cried herself to sleep after Allie was taken from the room. She dozed in and out of consciousness after she awoke. She guessed it had been at least twelve hours since the kidnapping—perhaps four to six hours since she last saw Allie.

Allen said, "Alright. Not hungry, I suppose. So, do you have any questions or concerns, piglet?"

Piglet—that word made her scowl at him. Brooke's desperate cries echoed through her head and her vision turned red. The kidnapper seemed nice and calm in the room, but he was a vicious animal. *That's why you wear that mask,* Carrie told herself, *you're a real monster, you're just trying to trick me again.* She looked away from him, tears welling in her eyes.

Allen snickered. He reached for the food and the soda. Carrie couldn't stop her survival instincts. Her mind told her to eat and drink before she could starve. She instinctively lunged forward and grabbed his wrist. She gazed into his eyes. The man was calm, sure, but he wasn't nice. There was nothing but hatred in his eyes—hatred for life, for people, for himself.

Carrie said, "My sister, Allie... Is she okay?"

Allen stared at her for about fifteen seconds. He sat down cross-legged, causing Carrie to slam herself back against the wall. She breathed heavily, eyes and mouth wide open.

"Do you really wanna know the truth?" Allen asked. Carrie nodded. Allen said, "Really? Really, really?"

Her voice shaking, Carrie stuttered, "I–Is she okay?"

"She's alive. She had some 'fun' last night with my special guest, but she isn't bleeding. I didn't see any bruises on her, either."

Blood and bruises weren't the only signs of pain, and Carrie understood that. She kept thinking about the talk she had with her parents about sexual predators. Although the idea traumatized her, she wondered if her sister had been sexually assaulted by the men. She clenched her fists, driving her fingernails into her palms. She thought about attacking Allen, but she wasn't willing to take the risk.

She asked, "Can I see her?"

Allen shook his head and said, "No. My guest is resting after a long, *long* night of fun. He's going to want her as part of his... 'second course.' But don't worry about her too much, little piglet. She's fine. She's getting the deluxe treatment. She's not fighting back, so she's being treated like a princess. I gave her a toy, she ate some warm pizza, drank some Coke, and finished up with some ice cream. We still have some in the freezer in the basement. It takes a lot of ice to keep it frozen throughout the day out here, but I think good girls like your sister deserve it. Do *you* want some ice cream?"

Carrie frowned and shook her head. It all sounded menacing to her because of the cold, dead look in his eyes. He was a better actor than Riley, but his eyes couldn't tell any lies. There was ice cream in the basement, but it came at a cost. She refused to sell her body for some 'luxuries.' She was only willing to trade herself for her sister.

She said, "Take me instead of her. I can do 'it' better than her. I promise, I–I'll be a good girl. I'll be your princess."

"I'm not looking for a princess. I'm looking for my next star. Maybe you'll get a chance to perform. Until then, be on your best behavior. I'll be back to feed you at lunch, piglet. Enjoy the meal."

"No! Don't leave! Allie! Allie, can you hear me?! Allie, dad's coming! Don't... No, don't leave me!"

Allen exited the room and locked the door behind him. Hysterical, Carrie threw the plate and the soda at the wall. The plate shattered into a dozen tiny pieces and the pizza hit the floor with a soft *thump.* The can burst open and a geyser of soda shot out. She tugged on the chain until her arms trembled from fatigue. She was lightheaded, too.

"Why me? Why us?" she whispered as she lay back and stared at the ceiling.

Her stomach rumbled and squeaked. She glanced over at the broken plate. The pizza landed on a dusty floorboard, cheese-down. The can lost at least seventy percent of its soda. She crawled to the food and picked up one of the slices of pizza. Ants marched across the crust and cheese. She was disgusted, but she was out of options. She tried to blow all the ants off, then she took a bite.

She ate the dirty pizza and drank the rest of the soda while crying in the corner by herself. She had never felt so lonely before.

Chapter Eight

The Hunt Begins

"Thanks for meeting me," Keith said as he sat in the passenger seat of a burgundy 1995 Cadillac Fleetwood. "I would have met you at your office, but, well... it wouldn't look good, you know?"

Gerald Greenwood sat in the driver's seat. He was one year younger than Keith, but he had just as much experience. He only spent two years as a cop, though. He now worked as a private investigator with his own firm located in Montaño. He quit law enforcement because of the money. He didn't see a sustainable future with the low wages, long hours, and difficult work.

The car was parked in an alley behind a multistory car park, which was scheduled for demolition. The area was lonely and quiet.

Gerald coughed to clear his throat, then he said, "I understand. I'm sorry about your daughters. I'm sure they'll turn up soon, Keith. In the meantime, if you need anything, I'm here for you."

"I'm happy to hear that because I need a favor."

"I figured. We wouldn't be meeting like this if you didn't. What is it? What's on your mind?"

Keith stared at the dashboard and said, "I want you to investigate the disappearances of Carrie Klein, Allison Klein, and Brooke Page. I'm making this request as a friend *and* as a customer. This is a... a business proposition, Gerald. That's all. Okay?"

Narrow-eyed, Gerald stuttered, "Wha–What?"

Keith responded, "You heard me. Look, I can't 'officially' investigate because I've been placed on administrative leave. So, I don't have any resources other than a spare pistol, my reputation, and what I've got up here." He tapped his temple to reference his training, his knowledge, and his memories—all valuable investigative tools. He said, "But I need someone with *more* information. I need an extra gun at my side in case things go south. I need... I need someone to talk to so I can *visualize* this thing. Gerald, I need you."

Gerald stared at him with a blank expression, then he smiled and shook his head. He clenched his jaw before he could chuckle. He saw the sincerity in Keith's desperate eyes. His request was genuine.

He said, "Keith, man... If your bosses don't want you investigating, then it would probably be best if I didn't interfere."

"Why? Standing back, watching this circus from the sidelines... That's better than helping?"

"That's not what I meant. I just–"

"It wouldn't be unethical or illegal if you investigated. Like I said, this is private business between two private citizens. Hell, if it makes you feel any better, you can write Lisa's name on the receipts. She's fine with it."

Gerald slid his palm across his bald head and sighed. He looked out the windshield because he couldn't look at Keith. He saw Carrie and Allie in his friend's eyes. He had been meeting the girls at least twice a year since they were born. They called him 'uncle' and he treated them like nieces. He didn't want his emotions to influence his decision. *Business*, he thought, *it's all about the business.*

He said, "I could lose my license."

"You won't. Imagine what the media would do if they found out you lost your license because you helped me find my missing girls. They would eat the department alive, and I'm not just talking local news. And think about it: if you help me, if we find these precious girls together, then you'd receive nothing but positive publicity. You're a businessman, aren't you? Well, this is a business offer you can't refuse. You know it."

He knew Gerald was still reluctant. His silence and lack of eye contact gave it away. He was close to convincing him, though. He pulled a small photograph out of his wallet. The picture depicted Carrie and Allie eating cake during Carrie's twelfth birthday. The girls grinned at the camera, white frosting smeared on Allie's lips.

Upon spotting the picture, Gerald looked away and said, "Come on, man, don't show me that. I know what–"

"Look at them," Keith interrupted. "These girls are innocent, Gerald. They're good, *sweet* girls. Whatever happened to them, they don't deserve it. We need to find them as soon as possible. We both know that… that… that we're running out of time. Please, Gerald. Help me find them before it's too late."

Gerald drew a deep breath. He watched as a homeless man limped towards the car, shaking a tin can filled with coins at them. He waved at the homeless man, as if to say: *not now.* The man sneered and muttered something at them, then he limped away and continued shaking the can at the air, like a baby playing with a rattle.

Gerald asked, "Why me? I catch cheaters, I find runaway wives, I follow men on business trips. I find dirt on people. That's it. I should be working for Jerry Springer, not you."

His voice stern, Keith responded, "I trust you. You know a different side of Montaño. And you're a good shot. I need a man like you, and I need you now. It's been almost twenty-four hours since I've seen my girls. You know what that means... No? *No?* Then let me tell you. After twenty-four hours, the chances of finding them drops dramatically. After a week... They're gone for good. I can't let that happen. Help me."

Gerald struck the steering wheel gently with the bottom of his fist. Tight-lipped, he bounced his leg rapidly and looked every which way. He sighed loudly and shook his head.

He said, "Alright, I'll help you."

"Thank you, Gerald. Thank you so much."

"Yeah, don't worry about it. We'll talk about the 'business' details later. Just tell me what to do before I change my mind."

"Sounds good. Let's go visit a friend of mine. He's like an informant. Maybe he has more information for us."

***

Keith pointed out the windshield and said, "That's him."

Dwight Rodgers shuffled down the sidewalk and searched for shelter, his oversized pants sagging down around his ass. He tried to cover his head with one hand while holding his pants up with the other.

He constantly glanced up at the sky and muttered to himself about the sudden downpour. The rain drenched his clothes and dripped from his wild hair.

The car rolled to a stop beside him.

Keith rolled the window down and shouted, "Come here!"

Dwight glanced at him, looked away, and then glanced at him again. He was hesitant because he didn't recognize the vehicle, but he recognized Keith through the rain.

He asked, "You givin' me a ride to a motel?!"

"I don't have time to take you anywhere right now, Dwight."

Dwight bent over beside the passenger door, like a prostitute negotiating with a John. He huffed upon spotting Gerald. The private investigator looked uptight, stiff and nervous.

"I know," Dwight said. "I heard about your angels while I was 'window shopping.' I can't believe those girls are really missing..."

"Have you heard anything?"

"Nope. I haven't heard a thing about missing girls."

"You're lying."

"What? What the hell's that supposed to mean?"

Keith leaned closer to Dwight's face and gazed into his eyes. Rain hit his hair and face, but he didn't blink. His nostrils flared as he breathed deeply through his nose.

He said, "I can smell the alcohol on you. You've been drinking, haven't you?"

"Yeah, so?"

"So? I told you my daughters didn't come home last night. I expected you to keep an eye out for them, to listen for anything suspicious. I didn't expect you to drink until you were shitfaced. I'll ask you again, and you need to give me something to work with this time. If not, I'm going to get out of this car. You don't want that."

Dwight patted Keith's shoulder and said, "Calm down, son. There's no need to threaten anyone right now."

Keith kept his eyes on Dwight. Dwight leaned away from the car, his face twisted in confusion. The men shared a relationship of 'professional' benefits. Dwight gave Keith information about suspicious people and Keith gave Dwight money. Their relationship grew personal over the years, expanding beyond business. They argued, Keith arrested Dwight more than once a year, but they were never spiteful. Dwight had never seen Keith in such a destructive, dangerous state of mind.

Keith said, "Tell me about the ice cream truck. It was on Green Street, right? What was it doing there? Who was driving it?"

Dwight nodded slowly and responded, "Hmm, the ice cream truck... I don't got the answers to your questions. I don't know who was driving that truck, but I know it was parked there for thirty minutes—*at least*—and there were no kids around. It was parked in front of that three-story house on Green Street, too. I heard it was a drug house. A *crack* house, you hear me?"

"Yeah? Have you told anyone else about this?"

"No. Who do you want me to tell?"

Keith stared at him for fifteen seconds, only the sound of rain *pattering* on the car moving through the empty street.

He said, "No one. You tell no one about this, okay?"

"Fine by me," Dwight responded.

Keith handed him a ten-dollar bill and said, "Do *not* drink until I find my girls. I need you to be reliable, Dwight. You understand me?"

Dwight took the money and nodded slowly, almost as if he didn't trust him. He walked away, constantly glancing back at the Cadillac. He vanished in an alley.

Gerald asked, "You think an ice cream truck is connected to your girls?"

"I think we need to follow every lead. Let's go."

As he drove off, Gerald said, "I could be more helpful if you told me everything. Your suspects, your informants, your leads… Tell me something: have you stolen anything from anyone recently? Have you roughed anyone up?"

"What? You think I'm corrupt?"

"That's not it."

"Then what is it?"

Gerald said, "I heard the way you spoke to that man, saw the way you looked at him… I've known you for years, and I've never seen you act like that. You looked and sounded vicious, Keith. You know who you reminded me of?" He stopped at a red light. He said, "Wife beaters, child abusers, cold-blooded killers. So, I want to make sure that I know where you're coming from so I know where you're going. If you're corrupt, or whatever you want to call it, you're bound to have enemies coming for you from every angle. I need to know where to look. Okay? You got anything to say?"

Keith sat in silence, awed by Gerald's suggestion.

He thought of himself as the cleanest cop in Montaño. His behavior was influenced by his desperation, anger, and sadness. He spoke to Dwight using the same voice he heard in his head—the voice that told him he failed as a father, that he deserved to be punished for losing his daughters.

He said, "I didn't hurt anyone and I didn't do anything to make any enemies, Gerald. You have my word on that. I only want to find my girls. That's all. If I sound angry, it's because I'm mad as hell—*at myself.* So, forgive me if I'm not using my training to interview people properly right now. Forgive me if I sound vicious, like a fucking wife beater. Forgive me if I lose control sometimes. Okay?"

Gerald nodded. His intuition told him to believe every word out of his mouth. He drove through the intersection and headed to the west side of Montaño.

Chapter Nine

Round Two

Sitting in the corner, curled into a ball, Carrie cried as she listened to the moist licking and slurping in the bedroom. Riley sat on the floor in front of her, eating a Nestlé Drumstick. The melted vanilla ice cream rolled down the side of his hand. He licked it as it touched his forearm, running his tongue from his wrist to the tip of his thumb. He kept his eyes on Carrie, waiting for her reaction—*fear? Curiosity? Excitement? Arousal?*

"You want one?" he asked.

Carrie shook her head and sniffled. She flinched as Riley took a bite. To her ears, the *crunch* of the cone sounded like a bomb.

Riley snickered, then he said, "Don't be scared. I'm not going to hurt you. Come on, kid, you look hungry. How about some more pizza? Maybe some tacos? 'Yo quiero Taco Bell.' Right? You want some Taco Bell?" He cackled at his own impression of the Taco Bell chihuahua, his devilish laughter dancing through the home. He said, "Anything? Hmm? Not hungry, are you?"

Carrie shook her head again. Her stomach gurgled and growled, begging for food, but she refused to accept Riley's offer. She could see the deviance in his eyes. Riley ate the rest of his cone, then he sucked the melted chocolate and ice cream off his fingers. He wiped his hands with a handkerchief, then he examined his clothes—*spotless.*

He said, "I came here to help you. I want to be your friend. Can we be friends?" Carrie stayed silent. Riley sighed, then he asked, "What can I do to gain your trust? To prove myself?"

Carrie swallowed loudly, then she stuttered, "Te-Tell me the truth. Is... Is my sister okay? Did you hurt her?"

"Did I hurt her? No, of course not. I pleasured her. I let her feel ecstasy, sweetheart. Do you know what that means?"

Carrie sobbed as soon as she heard those words. She had never heard of 'ecstasy' before, but the context was disturbing. A grown man couldn't pleasure a child. The idea was wrong. It was immoral. *It was horrific.* She believed her sister was living through their mother's warnings. Lisa had always said: *those type of men will hurt you to please themselves.*

Riley asked, "Would you like me to pleasure you, too?"

"I hate you," Carrie cried, tears and saliva dripping onto her legs.

"It's really no trouble for me. I'm not the type to brag, not like this, but I'm a *very* skilled lover. I know how to pleasure a girl. It's all about the foreplay. The kissing, the licking, the touching... Then it's about the stroke. I know how to balance my speed and my power. It's good stuff, really. Tell me: have you ever had sex before?"

"Stop talking."

"What's the matter? I'm just curious. You said you had experience, didn't you? Tell me about your first time."

"I–I lied. I–I'm just a kid."

Riley chuckled, then he said, "I know you lied, and you're lying again. Allie, your sister, she's a kid. I can agree with that. You? You're practically an adult, sweetheart. What are you? Thirteen? Fourteen? You've got breasts, your pussy gets wet for boys, and you know all about sex. You're a young adult. I'm okay with that. Fourteen, thirteen, twelve, eleven, ten, nine, eight, seven, six… five, four, *three… two… one.* I'm okay with all of it."

"Oh my God," Carrie cried out, horrified. "What is wrong with you?!"

"Nothing, honey. Nothing at all. I'm only embracing what we all try to hide. You know your old man has thought about fucking you before, right? He has. He's probably jerked off while thinking about it, too. But he's ashamed of those thoughts because that's what we've been conditioned to feel. Well, I'm not ashamed of my love for girls. I'm normal, they're repressed. So, what do you say? Want to have some fun?"

"Get away from me! Stay away! Stay back! Just leave me alone, you monster!"

Carrie kicked at him, but she missed by a foot. Riley leaned back and laughed, amused by her reaction.

As he approached the door, he said, "I get it. Maybe next time. I guess I'll just have to play with someone else."

Carrie stopped screaming. She immediately thought about Allie. She was willing to sacrifice herself for her sister. She crawled forward.

She said, "Wait, wait. Okay, I'll do it. Let me see my sister and I'll do anything you say. Please, mister, don't leave me. Don't go!"

Riley exited the room. The door was locked from the other side again. Carrie lowered her head until her brow touched the ground. She punched the floorboard as she cried.

She whispered, "I'm sorry, Allie."

***

"Your special order arrived a few minutes ago," Dale said, voice muffled by his pig mask. He unlocked the basement door and said, "It's this way. The boss is waiting for you down here."

Riley raised his hand to Chuck, gesturing his directions: *wait here in the living room, I can handle this.* He followed Dale down the stairs and into the basement. A grin stretched across his face.

Over the drain at the center of the room, a nude man was tied to a heavy, rusty iron chair. The thin, frail man couldn't have been older than nineteen. He was malnourished and cadaverous. His brown skin faded into a gray tone, the whites of his eyes turned yellow, and he was bony. A few thin locks of black hair protruded from his poorly shaved scalp.

He trembled uncontrollably, rivers of tears flowing down his cheeks. He tried to say something to Riley, but his voice was muffled by the cloth in his mouth—a homemade gag.

Standing beside the prisoner, identity hidden by his own mask, Allen said, "This is what you asked for, right? A young, skinny, brown-skinned foreigner."

Riley said, "Well, those weren't my exact words, but it's close enough. I said I wanted a brown-skinned twink from Thailand."

"Do you want to know where he's from? Or do you

want to fuck him already?"

Riley chuckled, then he asked, "Do I look like a faggot to you?"

Yes, you look like a damn faggot—Allen heard the sentence uttered by his inner voice, but he bit his tongue and stopped himself from saying it out loud. He only cared about the money.

Riley approached the prisoner. His hands on his knees, he bent over, leaned in closer to him, and examined every inch of his body. The prisoner mumbled in an indistinct language, although it sounded like Spanish. But his eyes spoke in a universal language: fear, *desperation*. He found himself in a dungeon in an abandoned house in the middle of nowhere in a foreign country. His fear and confusion were justified.

His eyes on the prisoner, Riley said, "Let me tell you a story, 'Wolfman.' A few years ago, my father sent me to Thailand for a, um… 'rehabilitative experience.' That's what he called it. It's similar to my trip to this beautiful house of horrors of yours. I was supposed to let it *all* out for a few weeks—no rules, no laws—and come back to America as a more composed gentleman. It's like raping your wife before heading out with the boys so you don't rape anyone else. You know what I'm saying?"

Allen could only nod. He wasn't disgusted, but he was surprised. Riley was a twenty-six-year-old bachelor. He wondered if he learned about raping wives from his father.

"But the thing is: there *were* rules and there *were* laws," Riley continued. "I wanted to fuck a young hooker. The most beautiful girl I had ever seen. She was fourteen, maybe fifteen years old. But it turns out: she wasn't a hooker. She just hung out with a bunch of slutty cunts. So, I couldn't have her. I fought for her, but her brother—a little *bitch* like him!—fought back. And this little twink was part of a gang. He had these huge guys walking around with him, bigger than Chuck, bigger than *you.* I wanted to go to war with them, I wanted to fight for my Juliet, but my father wouldn't allow it. 'Too risky,' he said, 'we don't have the manpower out there.' So, for the first time in my life, I accepted defeat... and I went home. This man right here will act as a substitute, a... um... a surrogate. He will be punished for what that bastard did to me. Did you get the supplies I asked for?"

Allen responded, "I did. I don't think it'll be very effective, but I got everything on your shopping list."

"May I begin?"

"The floor is yours. Would you like me to record this for you?"

Riley smirked, tapped the side of his head, and said, "I have a photographic memory. I'm already recording."

Allen grabbed a duffel bag from the back of the room. He set it down beside the iron chair, then he walked backwards until he hit the wall behind him.

He said, "Since you don't follow the rules, I'll have to be present for this. Just a precautionary measure." He nodded at Dale and instructed, "Go upstairs and keep guard. I've got this."

As Dale exited the room, Riley said, "That's fine. That's perfectly fine. I work well with an audience."

***

The needle penetrated the prisoner's basilic vein.

Riley pressed down on the plunger, sending a clear liquid into his bloodstream.

Bouncing on the seat, the prisoner shouted, "Qué estás haciendo, gringo?! Qué pasa, güey?!"

What are you doing, white man? What's happening, man?

His voice was muffled, but the Spanish was clear. It didn't bother Riley, though. A Mexican sat before him, but he only saw the Thai man from his most humiliating memory.

Riley threw the syringe on the floor. He slipped his hands into a pair of latex gloves, then he looked through his supplies.

He said, "You probably don't understand me, but, in layman's terms, I just injected you with adrenaline. This is going to keep you awake and it's going to amplify the pain. It's going to make everything worse for you, basically."

The prisoner cried and jerked every which way, but to no avail. He couldn't break free from the chair. The tight rope around his wrists and ankles turned his hands and feet blue and purple.

Riley pulled a stainless-steel lighter out of the bag. With a flick of his wrist, the lighter swung open and the flame ignited. He held the lighter under the prisoner's fingertips. The man hissed in pain and clenched his fist. The flame danced around his knuckles, sliding between his fingers. The prisoner tried to pull his hand away, but he could only move it up-and-down and side-to-side.

Riley giggled, then he said, "Look at yourself. It hurts, doesn't it? The hands are very sensitive to pain. That's one of the reasons why a splinter under a fingernail hurts so damn much."

The prisoner growled and hissed and mumbled, moving his right hand in every direction. Riley kept his hand in the same position. He didn't have to move it, he only had to watch. The prisoner opened his hand, unable to withstand the pain across his knuckles. To his dismay, the flame immediately burned his palm and the bottom of his fingers.

His skin peeled, the white flaps hanging from his palm and fingers. It was as if he had a bad sunburn. The burning process began to accelerate. The flame tore through his second layer of skin, leaving bloody patches across his hand. Blood oozed out of the wounds, dripping down to the floor like water from a leaking faucet. His hand swelled up, too.

A minute passed. Then five. And then ten. Riley gazed into the prisoner's eyes throughout the entire burning process—never moving his hand. The prisoner screamed at the top of his lungs. He wheezed and he sobbed, he bounced and he squirmed, but he couldn't stop the torture. To him, ten minutes felt like ten hours.

Riley looked at his hand. The flame burned through his flesh, leaving bloody craters across his hand. His bones, muscles, and tendons were visible in the wounds. Through the blood—the *deep* red blood—he saw white, yellow, and brown. Charred bits of flesh crumbled from his hand and spiraled down to the small puddle of blood under the chair. Fortunately for the prisoner, parts of his hand became numb during the torching.

"Amazing," Riley whispered as he finally closed the lighter.

Allen stood in the back of the room with his arms crossed. He was impressed by Riley's patience. He was one of the most methodical torturers he had ever met.

Riley pulled a vegetable peeler out of the bag. He pressed it against the prisoner's forehead, then he grinded it down to his eyebrow. The skin peeled off with ease, falling to the man's lap with a moist *squelch.* Blood dripped into his eye socket and rained down onto his cheek. His skull was vulnerable, a slit of white surrounded by dark red patches of flesh.

"The forehead is just as sensitive to pain," Riley said. He pressed the vegetable peeler against his forehead again. He gritted his teeth and said, "I can't imagine what you're feeling right now. It hurts, doesn't it?"

He slid the vegetable peeler down to his glabella. The tool was jammed in his forehead, thick strands of skin tangled in the blade. He wiggled it, like a comb stuck in a girl's hair, causing blood to squirt out. The prisoner clenched his eyes shut and bawled. The pain was unbearable. He felt it across his entire body, surging across his brain and down his spine.

The second chunk of skin tore off, but it stayed connected to the vegetable peeler. Riley bit into it until it disconnected and fell to his feet. Blood smeared on his lips, he smiled at the man, as if to say: *yeah, I just did that, what do you think?* The man was horrified. He saw his fair share of violence, but Riley was a different type of beast.

His voice breaking, the prisoner stuttered, "Pl–Pl–Pl..."

Please—it was one of the only English words he

knew, but he couldn't say it. The sharp, tingling pain in his forehead smothered his voice.

Riley grinded the vegetable peeler against his brow until the blade scraped his skull—*screech!* Blood covered the prisoner's face, rolled down his neck and chest, and rained down on his crotch. He tried to peel the side of his head along his temple, but the vegetable peeler was covered in blood and skin. The blade slid off his face each time.

So, he pulled a skinner knife out of the bag. He sawed into his cheekbone, cutting a chunk off his face. He thrust the tip of the short, wide blade into the hole at an angle, then he sawed downward. The blade entered his mouth, nicking his upper gums. He shoved his fingers into the wound, grabbed a hold of his cheek, and then continued sawing into his face.

Blood flooded the prisoner's mouth. He retched and coughed, choking on his own blood. His head spun, he was dizzy and weak, but he couldn't faint. The adrenaline kept him awake through all of the pain.

Riley cut through the gag. He cut his cheek along the bottom of his gums, then he cut upward towards the crater on his cheekbone. It took him five minutes to cut off his cheek. But he did it, and he was proud. He threw the severed cheek at Allen. It hit the wall beside him with a *splat,* like a wet slice of bologna, then it fell to the floor. Allen was unperturbed by the gore. He didn't move an inch, as a matter of fact.

The left side of the prisoner's face was skinned from his hairline to his jawline. His skull, teeth, tongue, and gums were exposed. He gasped for air and whimpered. He tried to scream, but he could only unleash one hoarse breath after another. He looked up at the ceiling and whispered something to himself in Spanish.

'Dios mío.'
Oh my God.

Riley said, "You're weaker than I expected. I should have killed you in Thailand. It would have been so easy for me. I want you to know: when I return to your country, I'm going to fuck every girl I see. I'm going to kill your sister, but it's going to be much worse for her." He thrust the blade into his upper chest at an angle, then he sawed downward into his pectoral muscle. Through his gritted teeth, he asked, "*It hurts, doesn't it?*"

He cut a wide piece of muscle off his chest. He repeated the process—stab, saw, sever, *stab, saw, sever*. After stripping his chest of its skin and muscle, he thrust his blade at his exposed ribs. He cracked a few, he even snapped one, but he couldn't break through all of them. He had been torturing the prisoner for forty-seven minutes. He was tired.

He took a step back and caught his breath, swiping at the blood and sweat rolling down his face. He couldn't help but smile in admiration. Through the gore and pain, he saw art—his art, *his masterpiece*. The remaining bits of muscle on his chest resembled ground beef, red and fibrous. His organs pulsated behind his broken ribs and sternum—his heart, his lungs, everything moved.

The prisoner groaned, bloody drool dripping from his mouth. His eyes were distant, gazing into the afterlife. He was alive, living off foreign adrenaline, but his soul passed on. He was only waiting for his body to die with him. Any second, any minute, any hour now.

Riley glanced over at Allen and said, "I want you to keep him alive for as long as possible, but don't patch him up. Let him wallow in his pain. If he dies, try to revive him. I want him to stay between life and death for as long as possible. It's a special experience... or so I've been told. When he finally dies, when he can't be brought back anymore, call me. I need to see him." He grabbed a towel from the bag and started to wipe the blood off him. As he approached the stairs, he asked, "Where's your shower?"

"There's one outside," Allen responded. "Ask Dale. He'll show you."

"Thanks for this, but remember: I'm going to need more soon."

Allen took off his mask and stared at the prisoner, calm but curious. He wasn't scared of exposing his identity. The prisoner didn't stare back at him anyway.

"You were one unlucky bastard," he said. "I'm sure you won't be the last. Things are going to get a whole lot bloodier. Maybe you got off easy, huh? Yeah, maybe..."

Chapter Ten

A New Lead

Keith watched as Gerald tinkered with his cell phone—a Motorola StarTAC. He was impressed and saddened by the device. On one hand, it was a symbol of wealth, carrying a hefty price tag. It was mostly owned by doctors, lawyers, politicians, and drug dealers. On the other hand, it conjured sorrow and regret within him. It reminded him of his daughters. He wished he followed Lisa's advice and bought a cell phone for Carrie.

He grunted, then he said, "Looks like business is going well for you."

Gerald read a text message on the phone. He groaned in frustration. The phone couldn't send text messages, so he would have to wait to respond.

He sighed, then he said, "Business is great. People pay a lot of money to catch their cheating spouses. You should have joined me when I dropped out. We could have been partners."

Keith examined the three-story house across the street. Scorched by the previous summer's sunshine, tall, overgrown grass and dry, high weeds swallowed the front lawn. A tattered recliner, powdered with dust and stained in urine, sat on the front porch. The walls were decorated with graffiti and bird shit. The rain couldn't wipe it away. The windows were boarded up, blocking them from seeing any movement. The door was closed—*and locked.* The men checked as soon as they arrived.

"You know me," Keith said. "I don't really care about the money."

"You could have bought yourself a couple of cell phones if you had money," Gerald responded without taking his eyes off his phone. "We probably wouldn't be in this situation if you did, right?"

Keith didn't respond. He wasn't angry at Gerald. Instead, he glared at himself through the rearview mirror. Gerald stopped playing with his phone, eyes wide with fear as if he had just realized he poked a lion.

He said, "I'm sorry. That's not what I meant to say. I wanted–"

"This lead is a dud," Keith interrupted. "I need you to take me somewhere else."

"I'm guessing we're going to go talk to Carrie and Allie's closest friends?"

"Close, but no. The new 'Missing Persons Unit' is already interviewing them. And, besides, Brooke was Carrie's closest friend and she's gone now. We need to talk to a boy."

"A boy?" Gerald repeated, a quizzical look in his eyes.

"You know the Soto family? They live over on Hill Street? Carrie had a crush on their youngest, Eric, and I don't think most people knew about it. I need to talk to him before my colleagues get to him. Let's go."

They drove to a red two-story house on Hill Lane, unknowingly moving closer to the site of the abduction. At the front door, they met Michael Soto, Eric's father.

"Keith, brother, I'm sorry about the... I'm sorry, man," Michael said. He patted Keith's shoulder, a frown contorting his face. He said, "If there's anything I can do, I'm here for you."

If there's anything I can do—he had heard those words from dozens of people already. Some people said it out of habit, others were genuine. Michael's offer was sincere. He was a caring man and he respected Keith. Most people in Montaño loved that honest, hardworking cop.

Keith said, "I'll get straight to the point. I'd like to speak to Eric in private."

"Eric? Is he in trouble?"

"No, I don't think so. He's a good kid. I have some questions for him, though."

"Hmm... I've been asking him about this whole mess since I heard about it on the news. I saw him with Carrie one day when I was picking him up from school. I wish... I didn't see 'em, but I wish I could have given the girls a ride home yesterday. I'm sorry."

Keith could only nod. He wasn't interested in Michael's apologies. He wasn't responsible for the disappearances after all.

He asked, "Can I speak to him?"

Michael nodded and said, "Yeah, sure. Come in."

Gerald said, "I'll wait in the car."

Keith entered the house. He was led to the stairs and directed to the first door on the left on the second floor. Michael allowed him to speak to Eric unsupervised. He trusted his son and the cop.

Keith pushed the door open slowly. He found Eric sitting at his desk, his back to the door. The fourteen-year-old was quiet, calm and fragile. He would have been happy to see Carrie date a timid boy like Eric. *He's a good kid,* he told himself, *don't snap at him, don't scare him, just talk to him.* He stepped into the room.

Eric glanced over his shoulder as soon as he heard the floorboard creaking behind him. His mouth fell open and his eyes widened.

He stuttered, "Mis–Mister Klein..."

Keith sat down on the bed beside the desk, analyzing the boy as if he were a suspect in a violent crime. They sat in silence for a minute. Eric shuddered, Keith sat motionless.

"Eric, you're not in any trouble," Keith said, trying to speak as softly as possible. "I'm here to talk to you about my daughters. I know about your... 'friendship' with Carrie. Your father has already told me that he saw you with her a few times after school. He also told me that he already spoke to you about the... the news."

"Yeah," Eric squeaked out. "I told him everything, I swear."

"That's good, but I want you to go over it with me now. Tell me: did you ever meet Carrie anywhere unsupervised? Other than your school's campus?"

"No. We only talked before school, during lunch, and after school. We didn't, you know, go on any dates. We never ditched. We were too scared."

The sides of Eric's mouth twitched as he smiled.

Keith asked, "Did you have any plans with her this weekend? Or did she mention anything? A movie date? A party?"

"No, sir."

"Did anything happen at school recently? Any, um... Anything unusual? Like some bullying or maybe a fight between my daughter and someone else?"

"No, sir."

"Did you see any suspicious people or vehicles at school this week? Any ice cream trucks or homeless people?"

Eric stayed silent. He didn't know how to deliver the bad news. His answer, yet again, was: *no, sir.* It was a regular week at school for him.

Keith read the boy's eyes. He heard the answer in his silence. He clenched his jaw, closed his eyes, and swallowed loudly, fighting the urge to scream and cry. He hit a dead-end. He wasn't sure if the girls ran away together or if they were kidnapped. He didn't find any clues of abduction and he didn't have any suspects.

"Maybe they got lost in the woods," he said. He stood from the bed and patted Eric's head. He said, "Thanks for your cooperation, kid. Don't worry about them. They'll turn up soon."

Eric felt the doubt and sadness in Keith's voice. The cop didn't believe his own words. He was lying to protect Eric.

As Keith reached the door, Eric said, "Wait." Keith glanced over his shoulder. Eric said, "There's, um… I think there's something I have to tell you. Can you… Can you sit down?"

A blend of hope and horror flowed through Keith's veins—anxiety in its purest form. He sat down on the bed again. Eric didn't say a word. His eyes darted left-and-right while he slapped his bouncing thighs. The bulge on his neck was a secret, and it was choking him.

Keith asked, "What's wrong, son?"

"I… I saw something weird."

"About Carrie and Allie? Or Brooke?"

Eric shook his head.

Keith said, "Well, I'm here to talk about the girls, Eric. If you don't have anything for me, then I have to–"

"But maybe it's about them," Eric interrupted. "I don't know, I just don't want to get in trouble. I don't want my family to get in trouble, either."

Keith drew a deep breath through his nose and looked over at the door. He thought about Michael and the Soto family. He wondered if he misread him—if *Michael* was responsible for the disappearance of his daughters.

He said, "I'm listening, Eric. You won't get in any trouble. No one is getting arrested today. I'm a cop, you know that, but I'm not officially on-duty. Talk to me. What do you know?"

Eric leaned forward and, in a hushed voice, he said, "A few weeks ago, like in early October, I snuck into my brother's room. You know my brother, right? Oscar? I just wanted to see his stash."

"Stash of what?"

Eric grimaced and said, "Mags and tapes."

Porn—the boy was obviously talking about his older brother's stash of pornographic materials. Keith wasn't offended by it. He understood the common teenager's sexual curiosity.

He said, "There's nothing weird about that. It's normal. Do you know how many kids I've busted for stealing Playboys from Carl's store? I haven't arrested any of them, either. Just a quick scolding and that's it. You'll be fine, son. There's nothing to feel guilty about."

As Keith moved to get up, Eric said, "I watched

some of the tapes. I mean, I've seen them before, but this one was different." Keith sank into the bed again, eyes narrowed. Eric continued, "In the first one, there was a girl. Like, a *real* girl. I think she was younger than me. And she… she was crying, sir. She was crying so much."

He sniffled and wiped the tears from his cheeks. He turned his attention to the window over his desk, trying his best to keep his composure.

He said, "A guy had sex with her. He was wearing a–a mask. It was a… a wolf mask, like a werewolf. I don't know why, but then I watched another tape. It was worse than the first one, sir. There were these guys in the woods at night. They were wearing all black. And black pointy hoods, like the white KKK ones, you know? The–There was another girl, too, but I think she was a little older. They took her clothes off and then made her sit down on a tree stump. After that, they, um… They cut her with… What's it called? Um… They cut her with scythes. Like the Grim Reaper, you know? Her back, Mr. Klein… Shit, her back was so bloody. The video was blurry, but the cuts were so clear. It was so–"

Eric held his hand over his mouth and sobbed. He swallowed his saliva several times, stopping himself from vomiting. The videos haunted him, images of gruesome, tragic death carved into his retinas. Keith wanted to play it off: *maybe he saw some underground horror movie, maybe he has an overactive imagination.* But he recognized the fear in the boy's eyes and voice. He saw it in some of his unlucky peers, too. He saw it in the cops who arrived first at the scenes of grisly car accidents, who spoke to the victims of rape, who discovered the dead bodies of innocent kids, and who found babies in microwaves and ovens.

He said, "Eric, it's okay. You're going to be okay. I need you to tell me more."

Eric cried, "I can't. I don't want to think about it. I hate it. It's–"

"Okay, okay, okay. You don't have to tell me about the tapes. Forget about them. Really, just get them out of your head. Tell me about your brother. Where is Oscar? And where is his stash?"

"He's gone. My mom and dad sent him to Europe or Japan or something last week because he didn't want to go to college here. He wasn't working, he wasn't doing anything. He was just in his room, jacking off or something..."

"Shit. Did your parents know about the tapes?"

"I don't think so."

"So his stash is still there?"

Eric shook his head and said, "I checked again around Halloween. I was going to tell my mom and dad, but I couldn't tell them without proof or they'd think I was crazy. But when I went back, it was all gone."

Keith sighed, then he asked, "Do you have any idea where he might have purchased those tapes?"

Eric's eyes wandered to the ceiling. He thought about people and places. His brother was smart, introverted, and reclusive. He lost himself in a world of movies, video games, and pornography—all of which he acquired at a local video rental store.

He said, "Oscar always hung out at Jim's Video Shop over at the strip-mall. *Always.* Maybe he got them there?"

"Yeah, maybe," Keith responded. For the first time since the disappearance, he felt more hope than fear. He said, "If you remember anything else, call my house. Lisa, Mrs. Klein, she'll be there. I'm going to look into those tapes. And remember: you're not in any trouble. You did good today. Thank you, son. I owe you."

As Keith exited the room, Eric whispered, "I hope you find them."

Keith said his goodbyes to the family and then he headed out to Gerald's car. They drove back onto Hill Lane.

Gerald asked, "Where to?"

"You ever heard of a place called 'Jim's Video Shop?' It's at the strip-mall."

Gerald responded, "Yeah, sure. I haven't been there in a while, though." He chuckled, then he said, "The last thing I rented there was, um… Under Siege 2. They have a 'backroom,' too. Apparently, they sell a lot of porn. Hell, they even sell some foreign stuff. I caught a suspected cheater back there once. Guy just wanted to jerk it while his wife was at work."

Keith asked, "Are they still open?"

"Sun's going down. It's either closed or it's going to be closed before we get there."

"Alright. I need you to do me a favor tonight: find out *everything* you can about this place. I want to visit it tomorrow morning. We need to investigate some suspicious materials."

"Suspicious materials? Should we call your boss?"

Keith looked at him and asked, "What do you think?"

His eyes on the rain-bathed road, Gerald said, "I think it would be the right thing to do. They can help us, right? They're the good guys, aren't they?"

"There are a lot of cops on the force, but I'm not supposed to be involved and they're busy combing the woods and following other leads. They should focus on that while we focus on Montaño's underbelly. It's better that way."

"Yeah, whatever you say."

Keith looked out the window and said, "Just take me home. I need to think about this..."

Chapter Eleven

Dinner for Two

Boom!
The explosive, crashing, violent sound echoed through the abandoned house.

"No!" Carrie yelled as she sat up. "Oh my God, please!"

She crawled back to the corner while looking every which way. A slit of moonlight penetrated the boarded window, caressing her pale, sweaty skin. The old house spoke through creaks and groans, but she didn't hear any other *booms* and *bangs*. She didn't hear her sister or the other prisoners, either. At night, the home was quiet.

She stuttered, "It–It was a–a dream. It was a–another dream…"

She crossed her arms over her shins and shivered. Nightmares of Brooke's violent death plagued her sleep. She couldn't doze off without hearing those gunshots.

She gasped and hopped upon hearing a set of squealing door hinges. She heard Riley's sinister cackle. She swore she'd never forget it. She also heard a child's faint whimper. The cry was soft, so she couldn't tell if it belonged to her sister or another captive, but she knew it came from a child. Another kid was being tortured in the house.

She said, "Allie, I don't know how to help you. I don't know what to do. How do I stop them? Mom, dad, we need you."

She sobbed and mumbled incoherently, overwhelmed by her emotional pain. Her parents shielded her from the awful news on television and in the newspaper. Since her family wasn't connected to the internet, she didn't have the opportunity to desensitize herself to extreme violence. She had overheard her parents talking about some of the crimes in Montaño before, but she never understood it.

Navy spouse raped, murdered in her home.

Teen shoots and kills parents after argument over a video game.

Husband beats, stabs wife for allegedly cheating, charged with attempted murder.

She always asked herself: *why would anyone do such a thing?* She was young and sheltered. She faced her mortality for the first time in that house. She also encountered pure, emotionless evil for the first time in her life. She knew about child predators, but her mother never specifically told her about pedophiles, rapists, and serial killers—the real boogeymen of the world.

The whimpering stopped. A set of footsteps made their way down the hall, growing louder with each passing second. The person stopped on the other side of the door.

Carrie gasped as the locks rattled in the hallway. She squeezed herself into the corner and listened to the orchestra of *clanking* steel.

Riley strolled into the room, a soda can in each hand while balancing two plates on his forearms. He sashayed his way to Carrie, swinging his hips with each step. He placed a can and a plate in front of

Carrie, then he sat down on the floor and set down a plate and can in front of himself. Two pieces of cooked meat sat on each plate, swimming in puddles of red juices.

He took a bite of his meat. The meat was thick and tough, so he had to shake his head to tear a piece off. It was chewy, too, and he liked to chew with his mouth open. The moist sounds exploded out of his mouth and dominated the room, as if he were chewing through a loudspeaker. The juices rolled down his hands and dripped from his lips. It was delicious.

Carrie saw the sweat on his brow and neck. She noticed the specks of blood on his disheveled clothing. It looked as if he had participated in a fight.

She asked, "Is my sister okay?"

"Eat," Riley demanded.

"Did you hurt her?"

"Eat. I'll talk to you over dinner, but I won't talk if you don't eat."

Carrie was reluctant. She couldn't trust him, but she didn't have any other options. She was starved and parched. She grabbed a chunk of meat and examined it. It looked like beef fillet—*red meat.* She took a bite. As expected, it was durable. The juices caused her taste buds to tingle. *Pork,* she thought, *it's pork, isn't it?*

As she chewed on the meat, Carrie asked, "So, is my sister okay?"

"She's fine, sweetie."

"Really?"

Riley chuckled, then he said, "You really don't trust me, do you? Maybe you should get to know me better.

Go on, ask me something."

"O–Okay... Who are you?"

"I told you: my name is Steven Carter."

Carrie shook her head and said, "You're lying. That's not your name and you're not a cop. Show me your badge and your ID."

Riley gave her a slight smile. He was amused by her character. She was smart and spunky. She wasn't very strong, but she could act like a brave lion to protect her sister. He admired her ability to switch roles on a whim. He always wanted to be an actor, so he wished he could act like her. He opened his soda and took a swig.

Carrie asked, "So, what are you doing here? You're just here to... to hurt us?"

"I haven't hurt you, have I?"

"No, but there's blood on your shirt. You look like you killed someone. Are you the guy from the woods? Did you shoot Brooke?"

"Nope. You have the wrong man, sweetie. I don't play with guns."

"Okay, so... can you let us go then? I promise I won't tell anyone about you. I'll forget I ever saw you. I mean, I don't even know your real name or where you're from or anything like that. You're just a guy. That's all I can say, right? Can you please unlock these chains? Or can you... can you at least let my sister go?"

Riley puckered his lips and nodded, then he said, "My turn to ask you some questions. Do you have–"

"Hey, please let us go."

Speaking over her, Riley repeated, "*Do you have* a boyfriend?"

"No," Carrie cried.

"No? Okay. Have you ever had sex before? Or have you at least given a blowjob or a handjob to some kid at the back of the bus before? Anything like that?"

Carrie shook her head, tears welling in her eyes.

"Oh," Riley said, as if he were surprised. "So, has your father molested you before? You know what that means, don't you?"

Carrie's eyes said something along the lines of: *what the fuck?* She knew about molestation, and she knew her father never molested her or her sister. The question was bizarre and inappropriate.

Riley said, "Jeez, I'm not getting anything out of you. Should I talk about myself some more? You have any other questions or should I ramble? Hmm?" Carrie sneered at him. Riley smiled and said, "Let me tell you a story. It's about my mom. You have a mom, don't you? My mom probably isn't like yours. When I was a boy, around your sister's age, she started to teach me about sex. First, she started with lessons—*real* lessons. She told me about the human body—sex organs, you know?—and she told me about relationships and she told me about sex. It was very… professional, like something from a textbook."

Carrie closed her eyes and looked away. She wanted to cover her ears, but she didn't want to anger him for her sister's sake. Sex was taboo to her. She didn't discuss it with her parents or at school. She heard some references to it in music, but it was never as explicit as Riley's questions and speeches. *Incest*—she didn't know that word, but it disgusted her.

Riley shoved the rest of the meat into his mouth. Chunks of meat stuck between his teeth, the red juices squirted out with each bite. Carrie reluctantly ate some of her meal. The story was disturbing, but she was too hungry to ignore the food.

Riley continued, "After I passed those classes, I was given some 'hands-on' experience. She started with handjobs. One handjob every night. She told me it would help me sleep, and it did. Then she taught me about blowjobs. She was very good at that. I'd argue she was one of the best. Of course, after the blowjobs, we started having sex. By then, I was probably closer to your age, but it doesn't matter. It was fuckin' awesome. We kept going until the day she died..." He stared vacantly at the wall behind Carrie. Monotone, he said, "I was sixteen when she passed away. I guess a part of me died with her. And I guess it's her fault that I turned out this way. If she was still fucking me today, I wouldn't be fucking girls around the world. It's funny how things work out, huh?"

Carrie covered her mouth with her hands and whimpered. Tears dripped from her eyes, her teeth chattered, and her breathing intensified. She felt a knot in her stomach—anxiety, fear, *disgust.* The same question echoed through her head: *what the fuck? What the fuck? What the fuck?!*

Riley grabbed the plates and stood up. He said, "At least you almost finished the food. It was delicious, right? I cooked it myself." He made his way to the door, then he looked back at her. He said, "Don't worry too much about your sister, sweetheart. I'm taking good care of her. I've been teaching her a few lessons, just like my mom did for me. She's loving it. She still cries from time to time, but I *know* she's loving it. You'll love it, too. I promise. Good night and sweet dreams."

Carrie crawled forward and shouted, "No! Leave her alone! Take me, damn it!" The door closed behind Riley. She yelled, "Goddammit! Why are you doing this to us? We were good kids. We didn't do anything wrong…"

In the hallway, Riley handed the plates to Dale. He chugged the rest of his soda, then he unleashed a satisfying gasp—*ahh!*

He said, "That went well."

"Wait," Dale said, his brow furrowed. "Did she actually eat it?"

Riley smirked and nodded.

Dale asked, "Did you tell her it was human meat?"

"N-O. *No.*"

"Jesus, you're a real monster, man. I'm proud to have you on the team this week."

"I'm glad to hear it. I'm ready to have some more fun."

He cackled as he strolled down the hallway. Dale followed his lead, snickering and shaking his head in amusement.

Riley said, "Cook up some more of that meat for me, will ya? That bastard annoyed the hell out of me, but damn was he delicious. I love Thai food!"

Chapter Twelve

A Parent's Worst Nightmare

"Where were you?" Lisa asked, standing in the living room with her arms crossed. "You were gone all day, Keith. What happened?"

Keith removed his jacket and tossed it onto the coat rack near the front door. His face remained expressionless, despite the storm of emotions brewing in his mind. He didn't look at his wife, but he wasn't ignoring her. He searched for an optimistic response to her questions, but he only found the truth: *I failed again.*

Lisa approached him and asked, "Did you find anything? Did you hear anything? Did you..." She frowned, her bottom lip quivering. With a trembling voice, she stuttered, "Ta–Talk to me. I need to–to hear you. I was so... so lonely today. I kept hearing nothing, but I was waiting to hear... them. I've been having this 'bad' feeling. I think it's my, um... my mother's intuition."

Father's intuition wasn't a commonly discussed phenomenon, but Keith shared the same sensation as his wife. They were receiving distress signals from their daughters telepathically.

Lisa said, "I don't know what to think or what to feel. When I heard about the struggle in the woods, I thought it was over."

"Struggle in the woods?" Keith repeated, wide-eyed.

"You didn't hear? I heard it from Eddie first, then it

was all over the news. They said they found evidence of a fight in a wooded area near Hill Lane. They wouldn't say the exact location or if it was related to the girls, but... I know it's about them. I can feel it. I tried to call you. I called Gerald's office, I called some of our friends, but I couldn't find you. I couldn't ask Eddie to find you, either, because... I told him you were here with me so he wouldn't get suspicious. Did you find anything else? Do you think they're okay?"

Hill Lane, Keith thought. *I was just there. That's where Oscar Soto lives. Did they really send him away? Could he be responsible for this? Was I close to the girls?*

"Keith, talk to me," Lisa cried. She staggered forward until she fell into his arms. Face against his chest, she asked, "What's going on? Why won't you let me in? I'm alone out here. I'm so alone."

Keith patted the back of her head and said, "I'm sorry. We were looking for them today. We followed a few leads, but... we didn't find them. We didn't find any signs of foul play, either. So, I think they're okay. I'll follow-up on some more leads tomorrow. I'm doing my best, Lisa. I'm going to bring them back."

"I need them. I want to hold my babies again. I want to cook macaroni and cheese for Allie, I want to listen to music with Carrie. I want to tuck them into their beds and kiss them good night. I wonder if they're eating well. Are they drinking enough water? Are they getting enough exercise? Someone's taking care of them, right?"

"They're taking care of each other. They're good, smart girls. They're fine. I know it."

"I hope so. I really hope so..."

"Don't give up, honey. They need to feel you right now."

Keith's face tightened up as Lisa cried into his chest. He felt like he was lying to her—*to himself.* Pessimism turned his daughters' distress signals into funeral memorial cards. He held her closer to his chest before she could squirm away so she wouldn't see his tears. He was supposed to be the family's pillar. He couldn't allow himself to show any weakness. He needed a moment to recompose himself.

After a minute, Lisa pulled herself out of his hug. She gazed into her husband's eyes and said, "Let me help you, Keith. I'm wasting my time here."

As he walked away, Keith said, "You're not wasting your time. You're covering for me."

He went into the kitchen and opened the refrigerator. He acted as if it were a regular day. *What's for dinner?*—those words nearly escaped his mouth. Lisa followed him.

She said, "That's pointless. Let's face it: Eddie doesn't care if you're investigating on your own. He just told you that because it's his job. He wants us to find them."

Keith heard every word, but he didn't respond. He heated two slices of leftover pizza in the microwave.

Scowling, Lisa asked, "Why are you acting like this? They're my babies, Keith. I kept them here, in *my* body, for nine months *each*. They're a part of me. They're the *most* important part of me. Without them, I'm… I'm nothing. I'm dead. Let me help."

"No."

"No? Why?!"

"You're not ready."

"Not ready?" Lisa repeated, baffled. "What does that mean? Because I'm not a cop? Because I haven't investigated anything before? What? I'm not smart enough? I can help! I know my girls better than you! You bastard! You selfish–"

"Because you're not ready!" Keith barked. "You're not ready to see what's out there, Lisa. There are *bad* people out in the real world. Worse than the shit you see on TV. You want to know why? Because there's always someone worse out there. A kid shot his mom and dad last month over a video game, right? Tomorrow, a kid's going to cave his grandmother's skull in because she wouldn't give him five dollars. And then he's going to live in the house with her rotting corpse for a few weeks until someone finally notices. Yesterday, a dumb bastard shot his co-worker over some money. Tomorrow, a dumb bastard's going to shoot up his workplace because he didn't get a fucking promotion. It's getting worse out there, so I don't know what I'm going to find, but I know I'm strong enough to fight through the bullshit to find it. You're not ready for that. You understand me?"

Lisa was awed by Keith's speech. She teetered backward until she fell into a seat at the dining table, mouth agape. The microwave *beeped* three times. The pizza was ready.

Keith said, "I'm sorry." Lisa couldn't say a word. Keith took a knee in front of her, he held her hands, and he said, "It's a scary world, we're surrounded by real monsters these days, but I'm going to make sure I bring them back. Carrie, Allie, and Brooke. I need you to stay home. Call people, ask questions, get information. It's important. Someone needs to be here if they come back on their own, right? They can't come home to an empty house, can they?"

Lisa frowned, cheeks wet with tears. She raised one hand up to her shoulder and waved it, as if to say: *I don't know, okay?*

Keith said, "You should cook something tomorrow. Bake her favorite macaroni and cheese, make some fresh-squeezed lemonade. Who knows? The scent might even help them find their way home."

"Y–Yeah, okay."

"Come on, let's take you to bed."

He threw her arm over his shoulder and helped her walk to the bedroom. He laid her down on the bed and then he tossed a blanket over her shivering body. He placed Carrie's mixtape into a cassette player on the dresser. *Killing Me Softly with His Song* by the Fugees played through the speakers. He climbed into bed and spooned his wife.

They spent the night crying and reminiscing. They spoke about their daughters and their fondest memories—from their favorite foods to their favorite drinks, their favorite vacations to their most miserable trips, their cutest dreams to their silliest fears. They remembered every little detail about their precious girls. They even spoke about Brooke Page and her family.

Pillows soaked in tears, Keith sniffled and said, "I'm going to find them. Even if I lose my job, even if I have to break the law to get them, I'm going to bring them back. I promise, hun."

Chapter Thirteen

Boredom

Riley ate a stack of fluffy pancakes slathered in butter and soaked in syrup, a dollop of whipped cream on the side. The meal came from a popular café in town. To his disappointment, he wasn't allowed to visit the town with or without supervision. He ate breakfast in the old, dusty, grungy kitchen of the abandoned house. The colorful sprinkles on the whipped cream offered a stark contrast to the bleak room.

"Hey, Mr. Wolf," he said before shoving another forkful of pancakes into his mouth. "I appreciate the breakfast, it's delicious, but I'm bored. I need something to do. *Today,* not tomorrow. What's the next course?"

Allen sat across the table from Riley, reading the Sunday paper and sipping on some coffee from the same café. He lowered the paper and looked at Riley, like a strict father glaring at his insolent son. He sighed and folded the newspaper.

He said, "If you can be a patient boy, I can have another body out here in a few days. I can get one sooner, but then I wouldn't be able to guarantee a gender, an age, or an ethnicity. Either way, I'll need time."

"First of all, *stop* calling me 'boy.' Don't make me tell you again. Secondly, how much time?"

Allen leaned forward, elbows on the table. He asked, "Kidnapping without leaving a trail takes planning, skill, and time. The earliest? Maybe a day or two. The latest? Four or five days. Like I said before, I can also send you to another branch of the business. We have livestock in California and Texas. Sound good to ya, kid?"

Riley sneered and snickered upon hearing his last word—*kid.* Allen was being a smart-ass. He couldn't call him 'boy,' so he called him 'kid.' He got under his skin to show him who was boss.

"My father sent me *here* to play," Riley said as he stabbed the pancakes with his fork. "So I'm not going to California or Texas or Florida. He also gave you crystal clear instructions when he paid you. You're supposed to entertain me, but I'm bored. You see the issue, don't you? Should I bring Chuck in here for a chat? Maybe he can explain it to you."

Allen envisioned himself killing Riley. He could torture the young deviant while Dale handled Chuck. It seemed like a reasonable plan. Paul Watts was a powerful, connected man, though. He would have had them killed in an instant if they touched his son. The Wolves' Den needed the funds anyway. They couldn't afford to lose Paul's business.

Allen said, "Allison. Little Allie. Why don't you kill her?"

The chair groaned as Riley leaned back. He cocked his head to the side, like a curious pup listening to a squeaky toy for the first time. He didn't want to kill the girl—*not yet,* at least. He felt something magical with her. He couldn't admit it to the men in the abandoned house, but he thought it was love. He believed he was falling in love with an eight-year-old girl. He knew it was just a phase, though. He needed more time before he could commit to killing her.

He said, "I'm not ready for that yet. She's still fresh, you know? Maybe I'll kill her after the next session."

"Why don't you just fuck the other girl? She's older. She looks a little more like a woman. What? You're not into that?"

"It doesn't matter what I'm into," Riley snapped, slamming his fists on the table. "It's none of your damn business. I want to kill another person, but I want to take my time. Those girls can't handle the pain I want to inflict. Find me someone else. I don't care if he's old or young, man or woman, black or white. Just bring him to me before I lose my mind and burn this place to the ground."

Allen took another sip of his coffee. He said, "I can have someone here by noon, maybe. Considering the urgency of your request, you'll have to settle for a homeless man or woman. Maybe a crackhead. A drifter. Someone who won't be missed. Are you okay with that? Hmm? I don't want you complaining later, okay?"

He spoke to him as if he were speaking to a child at a toy store. *'Are you sure you want that toy? I won't buy you another one until your birthday.'*

Riley said, "As long as he's not already mangled or disfigured, I don't care. Make sure he's in 'decent' condition. I'd prefer a man, too. Men can handle more pain, and I'm going to make him suffer. Now go." Allen huffed and rolled his eyes. Before he could reach the archway, Riley said, "Wait."

Allen looked back at him, the folded newspaper clenched under his armpit.

Riley said, "Get some fresh strawberries and a can of whipped cream while you're in town. I want to eat it off those girls later, and I want them to eat it off me." Allen stared at him with a bored expression. As he turned to walk away again, Riley said, "*And,* bring me Belgian waffles next time. I hate pancakes."

Allen kept walking. Riley finished the rest of the pancakes. He opened his zipper and pulled his semi-erect penis out. He placed the dollop of whipped cream on his glans.

As he made his way upstairs, his dick swinging from side-to-side, he whispered, "Why wait until later?"

Chapter Fourteen

Jim's Video Shop

Virtual Insanity by Jamiroquai played through the speakers of Gerald's Cadillac. The song was part of Carrie's mixtape. Gerald sat in the driver's seat, bobbing his head while drumming his fingers against the steering wheel. Keith sat in the passenger seat, staring broodingly out the window. He spotted Dwight trudging down a sidewalk, blocking the sun with a wet newspaper from the previous month.

"I got a call this morning," Keith said, watching Dwight through the side view mirror.

"Yeah? So?"

"It was a call from our friendly neighborhood prostitute, Vanessa Arellano. She told me about a John who's staying at El Bonita Motel. He's a violent guy. 'Sadistic,' she said. Apparently, he beat the shit out of a friend of hers last night. I need you to take me to him after we speak to Jim."

"I don't know about that. If he's violent, then maybe we should call the cops. At the very least, you should call one of your partners to escort us. You've got friends on the force, don't you? I'm sure they wouldn't mind doing us a favor without telling anyone about it."

"It would take some time to convince anyone to take a risk like that on such a high-profile case. I don't have time to waste, Gerald. It's been three days since they vanished. You already know what that means when it comes to missing kids."

Gerald could only respond with a nod. He was aware of the statistics regarding missing children. Every minute, *every second*, mattered. He placed more pressure on the gas pedal and sped up. They arrived at Jim's Video Shop just as it was opening—11:00 AM. The shop, located at the end of a strip mall, appeared to be empty.

Keith said, "Let's go in."

The door chime danced down the aisles as the men entered the store. A middle-aged man stood behind the counter to the left of the entrance, organizing a collection of recently returned VHS tapes. His graying hair was thinning on top and his mustache sprouted over his upper lip. He didn't wear a uniform, but a name tag was clipped onto his white t-shirt. In sloppy handwriting, the name on the tag read: *Jim Phillips.*

Keith glanced at Gerald, then he nodded at one of the aisles, gesturing his directions: *take a look around.* He approached the counter while Gerald snooped around. He drummed his fingers on the countertop and glared at the back of Jim's head, as if he could see his eyes through his skull. Jim muttered to himself as he slid a few more tapes between the others on the shelf. He knew about the men—he heard the door chime and heard the footsteps—but customer service wasn't his forte. He wasn't eager to assist anyone.

After about two minutes, he turned around and said, "Welcome to Jim's Video Shop. I'm Jim, a film aficionado. You need new releases, you need recommendations, you come to me. Just please don't ask me for any kid stuff. If it's not on the shelves out there, then it's rented out. They're always rented out."

Keith looked at the man, then he examined the store. Jim wasn't the most hygienic person in town, but he looked like a normal guy. The store was normal, too. He didn't see an aisle labeled 'snuff.' He thought about Eric's story and considered all of the possibilities. *An overactive imagination? Or a real lead?*—he thought.

He said, "Nice to meet you, Jim. I think I've seen you around town before."

Jim responded, "Yeah, sure, it's possible. I live right here, upstairs on the second floor. Been in Montaño for a few years now, too." He chuckled and shrugged, then he asked, "Is that all you wanted to say, guy?"

"No. No, that's not all. I'm here to talk about movies. What kind of horror movies do you have in here?"

"A little of everything, I guess. Mainstream, classic, obscure. What are you looking for?"

"Definitely not mainstream or classic. I'm looking for something that might have been 'homemade' or imported. Very obscure and very, *very* realistic."

Jim smirked and said, "Oh, I see. Well, all my stock is out there. If there's a tape behind the placard, you can rent it. If not, you can reserve it and I'll call you when it's available. You know how it works. Right, guy?"

"I don't think this movie or *these* movies are going to be found out here in the open. It's darker than that. I'd assume you'd keep them in a special room here... or maybe at home. You catch my drift?"

Jim understood him, but he wasn't pleased by Keith's suggestion. His face twisted into a sneer of annoyance—or perhaps it was disgust.

He asked, "Who are you?"

"A customer."

"For who? For yourself?"

"What's that supposed to mean?"

Jim grinned, his chubby cheeks inflating like balloons. He said, "For yourself then. I guess you're out of luck: I don't know anything about 'those' movies. Try 'Butt-buster.' Those corporate bastards will sell you anything."

Gerald made his way through the shop. He found a library of movies organized in alphabetical order in sections separated by genre—action, comedy, horror, thriller, it was all there. He found a door at the back of the shop. A sign on the door read: *Private*. It was locked. Beside the door, a set of purple curtains covered a doorless doorway. Above the doorway, in red, a sign read: *18 & over only*.

"Wow," he whispered as he entered the room, doe-eyed.

Another small collection of VHS tapes filled the room. The movie covers depicted nude men and women as well as several different sexual acts—some of which involved bondage, feces, and urine. Some of the covers caused him to gag and cringe, but none of the material was illegal. The pornography was produced legally around the world, including the United States, Japan, and Mexico.

At the counter, Keith asked, "I'm not interested in 'Butt-buster' or their movies. I'm interested in *your* shop and *your* special collection."

"I don't know what you're talking about."

"Then do you mind if I look around?"

"Are you a cop?"

"Does it matter?"

Jim slapped his palms against the countertop and leaned forward. He kept his cocky smirk, but a fire burned in his eyes.

He said, "I know my rights. If you're a cop, then you need a warrant. You got one of those?"

Unperturbed by Jim's attempt at intimidation, Keith stood his ground and said, "I don't. Like I told you before: I'm just a customer who wants to talk about movies."

"In that case, you can do whatever you want."

Keith could see the curtained-off room and the locked door from over the freestanding shelves. He spotted Gerald returning to the entrance, unconcerned.

"Can I go back there?" Keith asked.

"Through the curtains? Sure, go for it. Just don't let your wife catch you back there. I'm not responsible for any second-degree murders that might occur while you're browsing."

While Jim chuckled, Keith clarified, "No, not the curtains. The door back there."

Jim stopped laughing. He asked, "Can you read? It says 'private,' guy. You can't go back there."

"Why?"

"Why?" Jim repeated in disbelief. "Are you five years old? Christ, what's wrong with you, asshole? That's my apartment, so it's private. Cops, customers, it doesn't matter. No one's allowed in my apartment, except me. Now if you're not going to rent anything, I'd like you to leave. I've got some dusting to do."

Keith clenched his jaw and nodded at Jim. He glanced over at Gerald, who stood beside him. Gerald gave him a shrug and a shake of his head—*I didn't find anything.* Keith exited the store and Gerald followed his lead. They hopped into Gerald's car.

"Park behind that tree, over there across the street," Keith instructed, eyes on the shop. Gerald followed his directions. Keith said, "This is good enough."

Gerald asked, "What's the plan?"

"I want to watch the place. He was, um... suspicious. Yeah, he wasn't acting right. My gut is telling me that the kid was right about him. Did you see anything in there?"

"A lot of movies and a lot of porn. It looked like a regular video shop, Keith."

"Then he's hiding something in his apartment."

"I agree with you, man: he was acting strange and hostile. But I'm not sure if he's hiding anything related to your case in his apartment. How are you going to convince him to let you in anyway? He hated your guts."

"I'll find a way. If my girls are in there, I'll do anything to get inside. I need to get to the bottom of those tapes, too. I need to find *something,* Gerald. Let's just watch him until his shop closes. Keep an eye out for any suspicious characters. Okay?"

Gerald saw his friend falling into a rabbit hole. His desperation was worrisome—desperate people did desperate things after all—but it was understandable. He sat there and watched the shop, thinking about Keith's limits.

How far is too far?

***

Bombastic by Shaggy from Carrie's mixtape played

through the car's speakers. The nearby shops began closing as nighttime arrived. Jim walked around his store, preparing to close along with the rest of the strip mall. Once again, his store was empty. The last customer left ten minutes earlier with a self-contained pan of stovetop popcorn and a copy of *Braveheart,* which came on two tapes.

Keith couldn't sit still, fidgeting and whining like an anxious dog at a veterinarian's office. He was convinced that his daughters were locked away in the apartment above the video shop.

"Wait here," he said as he put on a pair of gloves. "I'm going to have a word with him."

"What? Are you kidding me?"

"No. I'm out of time. One way or another, I'm getting into that apartment. I told you that already,"

"I know, but you can't just barge in there. It's his place of business. He can call the cops. If he does that, then they'll really put you under surveillance and you won't be able to look for your girls anymore. Call someone and get a–"

Keith opened the door and took a step out of the car. Gerald grabbed his arm and stopped him from exiting the vehicle. They glared at each other. Gerald was frustrated, but he wasn't angry. Keith, on the other hand, was furious. He was willing to hurt *anyone* who stood in his way, including Gerald. He was willing to go far beyond his limits—so very far.

Gerald said, "Don't do something you'll regret."

"If I don't go in there and if he knew even the *slightest* details about my girls, I'd be haunted by regret for the rest of my life. I'm out of time, man. I promised Lisa I'd bring them back. If I can't come home with them tonight, then I at least need to come home with something. I owe her that. You just wait here and keep a lookout. Honk and peel out if you see or hear anything suspicious. I'll be right back."

Gerald spoke with his wet, glimmering eyes: *please don't do this.* He knew Keith couldn't tame his anger, though. He saw the animal in his eyes—*the beast.* He reluctantly released Keith's arm.

"Ah, shit," Gerald muttered as he watched him leave.

Keith pushed the door open just as Jim reached for the lock. The door chime rang through the vacant store. Keith squeezed himself into the shop before Jim could shut the door.

Jim stepped back, smiled, and said, "Oh, you again. Sorry, guy, it's closing time. Come back tomorrow if you want to rent something. Hell, I might even have something for the kids."

"The kids? How did you know I was a father?"

"I didn't. You seem like the 'fatherly'-type, though. An uptight, stick-up-your-ass lookin' motherfucker."

"No, you're lying. You know about my daughters, don't you? You have those tapes–"

"Shut up," Jim interrupted, holding his finger up to Keith's face. "I don't have time for this shit. I tried to be the gentleman, but that clearly ain't working. So get the hell out of my store, you stupid sonuvabitch."

Keith breathed deeply through his nose, jaw and fists clenched. He was ready to fight his way into the apartment upstairs, but he didn't want to cause a scene. His investigation would end if he alerted the police. He needed to move away from the storefront windows. He bottled his anger, waiting for the perfect opportunity to strike.

Jim said, "Get out. *Now.*" Keith locked the door, then he walked past him. Jim scowled and asked, "What the hell was that? What are you doing? Get out of here!"

Keith strolled to the back of the store, leading Jim away from the door. He peeked into the backroom and found the library of porn—lots and lots of porn.

He said, "A little birdie told me about your shop, Jim. Do you know a 'Oscar Soto?' I heard he might have rented or purchased a tape from here. The videos depicted the murders of children. With the way it was described, I think the 'slaughter of children' is more appropriate. I'd like to see that tape or any tape like that. For *personal* reasons."

He stopped near the door labeled 'private' and turned around. Jim had followed him to the back of the store, his brow furrowed and his head tilted forward.

Jim said, "I don't know what you're talking about. Murder, slaughter, children… What the fuck is up with you, guy? Are you high? Get out of here already before I call the cops."

"I think you're lying and bluffing. You call the cops and I'll tell them about the tapes. They'll get a warrant before you can destroy them. I can guarantee that. So, tell me about Oscar and the tapes."

"Oscar? You want to know about Oscar Soto?" Jim asked, snickering. "I caught him jerking off to some of the tapes and magazines in the backroom a few times. Yeah, standing back there with his dick out like if he owned the place. I didn't do much about it 'cause it didn't seem like a big deal. He's a perv like the rest of us. So what? You gonna arrest me for that, officer?"

"Officer? You know I'm a cop... You do know about my daughters, don't you?"

Jim smirked, shrugged, and said, "Come on, man. You're all over the news. What do you think–"

Keith drew a handgun from the back of his waistband. He grabbed Jim's shirt at the chest, placed the muzzle of the gun against his jugular, and pushed him back until he hit the shelves behind him. Tapes fell to the floor, *clanking* against each other, while the shelves rattled.

He said, "Don't fuck with me."

"He–Hey, wha–what are you doing, guy?"

"Don't do anything stupid and I won't hurt you. Okay? We're going to go up to your apartment and we're going to have a little chat. Where are your keys?"

"I–I don't... What the fuck is this? You–You're going to get yourself–"

"*Where* are your *keys?*" Keith asked sternly.

Jim looked down at his pants without moving his head. Without moving the gun, Keith looked through the shop owner's pockets—lint, loose change, a wallet, *keys.* He pulled a key ring out.

He dragged Jim to the door and said, "If you move, I'll blow a hole in your neck and watch you choke on your own blood."

"Whatever, man," Jim said, hands up.

Keith checked each key until the door unlocked with a satisfying *click.* The door opened up to a staircase. Twelve steps led up to a landing, then another twelve steps led up to a door—*the apartment's entrance.*

Keith pushed Jim up the stairs and said, "Let's go. Come on, hurry up."

***

The apartment was small. The kitchen also served as a dining room. The living room windows overlooked the parking lot in front of the rental shop. To the left, a small hallway led to the bathroom, a closet with a washing machine, and a bedroom. It was perfect for a single person and comfortable for a young couple.

Keith dragged a chair from the kitchen into the living room. He pointed at it and said, "Sit."

Jim followed his directions. He was unarmed and weaker than Keith, so he waited for his own opportunity to strike. Keith checked the rest of the apartment. To his relief, the home was vacant.

He asked, "You live alone, right?"

"Yup."

"Any friends coming over tonight?"

"Nope."

"You're not lying to me, are you?"

Jim puckered his lips and shook his head. Keith dragged another chair into the living room and sat directly across from him.

He said, "I don't like you and you don't like me. I know that already. I need you to cooperate, though. It'll make things easier for the both of us. I don't want to hurt you, okay?" Jim sneered at him. Keith continued, "You know who I am and I've already told you why I'm here. Tell me about my daughters or the tapes. I know you know something."

"I only know one thing, guy: you're either going to end up dead or in jail. This… This is all illegal."

"Yeah, I know. But you're not causing a scene for a reason. You either know I'm not messing around or you're hiding something—or both. Tell me about the tapes, Jim."

"I've told you a million times: I'm a movie guy, not a snuff guy."

Keith snapped. He held the handgun by its barrel and swung it at him. The butt of the gun struck Jim's jaw, the force of the blow ejecting two of his molars, bruising his gums, and cracking his bone. Keith grabbed his shirt and stopped him from falling from the chair. Jim held his hands up to his jaw and mouth. He hurled slurred insults at him—*asshole*, *fucker*, *bastard*—as blood dripped from his mouth.

"Don't move, motherfucker!" Keith shouted as he marched into the kitchen.

He turned the faucet handle and left the water running. He grabbed a chef's knife, a pair of scissors, and a roll of duct tape from the drawers. He tried to place a strip of duct tape over Jim's mouth.

Jim yelled, "Wait! Stop! Help!"

Keith pushed him until the back of the chair hit the sofa behind them. He pressed the tape against Jim's mouth, muffling his cries. He kneed Jim's stomach, knocking the air out of him. While Jim attempted to breathe through his nose, weak and lightheaded, Keith taped his arms together at the wrists. He taped his thighs to the chair's seat and then he taped his stomach to the backrest. He used the entire roll of tape to restrain him.

As Jim reached for the tape over his mouth, Keith thrust the knife into his knee. The blade tore through his ligaments, cartilage, and arteries while scraping his bones. A column of blood shot out of his kneecap as he wiggled the blade inside of him. He released the handle, leaving the knife protruding from his knee. He held the scissors over his crotch and aimed the handgun at his stomach. He saw his fair share of violence on his beat, so he knew how to play rough.

He said, "No more talking. Show me the tapes. Where are they?" Jim snorted, sniffled, and moaned. Keith jabbed the scissors at his crotch and said, "If you don't cooperate *right now,* I'll cut your dick off."

Jim shook his head frantically and mumbled. His words were barely recognizable: *no, please, no.* Keith unzipped Jim's jeans, then pulled his penis out through his fly. He held the scissors around the shaft, the blades scraping his dick. He placed some pressure on the handles, causing the blades to squeeze his penis. He nicked him, too. A droplet of blood rolled down into his boxers, lost in his bush of pubic hair.

"I'm snipping it," Keith said, "In five, four, three..."

Jim lunged forward and shouted—*no!* He nodded at the corner of the room behind him—*over there, look over there!*

Keith said, "If you move, I *will* cut it off. Not an inch, Jim, not a damn inch."

He walked to the corner of the room. A trashcan was wedged between a desk and a wall. He opened the drawers on the desk—*nothing.* He dumped the trash on the desk, then he looked through the garbage and the bin—*nothing.*

He glanced back at Jim and asked, "Do you really think I'm playing?"

Again, Jim nodded at the corner and mumbled something at him. He said something along the lines of: *look again and let me go.* Keith illuminated the corner with a small flashlight. His eyes widened upon spotting a hole on one of the floorboards. Thanks to his light, he could see the shell of a videotape through the hole. He shoved his index and middle fingers through the opening, then he pulled the board up.

A cloud of dust hanging over the opening, covered in spider webs and insect droppings, a tattered shoebox sat on the floor under the floorboard. There was a stack of videotapes in the box.

Keith returned to the center of the living room with the shoebox. He placed it on the floor in front of Jim, then he squatted in front of him.

His head down, he grabbed one of the tapes and said, "I have a feeling I'm not going to like what's on this tape, but I think I know what's on it already. I have to be sure, though." He wagged the tape at Jim and asked, "Are my daughters in any of these tapes? My daughters or Brooke, the other girl who's missing right now?"

Jim shook his head. Sweat rolled down his forehead while blood stained the duct tape over his mouth as well as his chin. He couldn't stop his legs from shaking due to the pain emanating from the stab wound on his knee. He kept tapping the floor with his feet, like a student in urgent need of a bathroom pass.

"I have to be sure," Keith said, tears in his eyes.

He shoved the videotape into a VHS player on the entertainment center. The grainy, black-and-white video appeared to be shot from a tripod in the corner of a room. The small room—six-by-eight feet, to be exact—resembled a jail cell. A bed, a bucket, and a door were visible from that angle.

A young girl, no older than eight years old, sat on the bed, her feet dangling a few inches above the ground. She wore a princess dress—a Halloween costume. She whined and moped, though. She couldn't find any happiness in the gloomy room.

She was a princess in an evil king's dungeon.

The door swung open. A man in a mouse mask entered the room. He sat down beside the girl. She whimpered as he gently rubbed her thigh and whispered something into her ear. She leaned away from him as he caressed her neck, gliding his fingertips across her soft, sweaty skin. The video was unfocused at times, but her discomfort and fear were clear. The man tugged on the costume's shoulder straps, trying to pull the dress down to her chest in a seductive manner. The girl turned away from him. She looked at the camera and sobbed.

Keith stopped the video before the man could undress her. He stood there and stared at the television with a blank expression on his face, awed. He didn't have to watch the rest of the video to know its contents. It either led to sex or murder—*or both*. He couldn't watch the rest of the tape anyway. He didn't have the stomach for it. The young, innocent victim reminded him of Allison. *Eric was right,* he thought, *the tapes are real, and they might be connected to the girls.*

In a flat, toneless voice, he said, "Before I let you speak, I want you to know that I'm not bluffing. I don't want to start with lies. So, to make sure we start with the truth, I'm going to hurt you." He unplugged the VCR and returned to the center of the living room with the cord. He said, "These boxes are full of... of...

of *evil* shit. You deserve this, you sick bastard."

Keith folded the thick cord like a belt, then he swung it at the air beside the chair—*whoosh!* Jim flinched and cried and begged. Keith swung it at Jim's face, missing his nose by an inch, but Jim still felt the gust caused by the swing on his skin. He trembled uncontrollably, mucus pouring out of his nostrils as he begged incoherently. It was the reaction Keith had sought—*psychological torture.* But he knew time was of the essence.

He swung the cord with all of his might and struck Jim's face. The *whack* of the attack echoed through the building. The left side of Jim's face, from his cheek to his ear, turned red. Before Jim could respond, he swung the cord again and struck the right side of Jim's face. A cut, about an inch long and a centimeter thick, stretched across his cheekbone. He repeated the process fourteen times—left, right, left, right, left, *right.*

The cut on Jim's right cheekbone stretched and widened, reaching from his nose to his ear. Blood dripped from the wide gash and cascaded across his cheek, rolling over the wrinkled duct tape. A chunk of his other cheek was torn off his face during one of the swings, leaving a small hole on his face. The cord mostly landed across his cheeks, but it also struck his ears, forehead, and temples. His swollen face was red, white, and blue, like the American flag.

Keith wiggled the knife in Jim's knee, then he yanked it out. Jim bounced, lifting the seat up with him, but he couldn't escape the chair.

Keith swung the cord at his thighs—thud, thud, *thud!* Blood squirted out of the wound on his knee with each blow to his stabbed leg. It wasn't visible due to his jeans, but his thighs became red and purple. Petechiae—patches of bloody, red dots—developed across his thighs, too. After the fifteenth blow, Jim felt a tingly sensation in his legs. Parts of his thighs were numb, but the pain continued to surge across his legs.

Keith pulled the tape off Jim's mouth. Jim bellowed in pain, strings of slimy saliva and blood hanging from his mouth. Keith pushed Jim's chin up, closing his mouth and muffling his cries.

"Don't you cry, motherfucker," he hissed. "This is only the beginning if you don't cooperate. Tell me about the videos. Are my daughters in any of those tapes? Are they?!"

"No!" Jim shouted, barely able to open his mouth. "They–They're not the–there, I–I swear. Oh, fuck, you need to call... No, just take me to–to a fucking hospital! Pl–Please, guy!"

"I'll take you to a hospital as soon as we're done here. Where did you get these tapes? Did you make them?"

"N–No. I bought them for... for myself. I–I rent some of 'em out to–to make some extra cash on the side, but tha–that's it. I never fucked any kids, I swear! Take me to a hospital! It hurts!"

"Who made these movies? Where did you buy them?"

Gasping for air, Jim said, "It... hurts... so... fucking...

bad."

Keith held the knife up to Jim's exposed penis and said, "Answer me."

"Please don't." Jim cried, face scrunched up.

"Five, four, three, two..."

"Alvin! Al–Alvin Vaughn! I bought them from a guy named Alvin Vaughn!"

"Where can I find him?"

"I don't fuckin' know, man! I've never met him in-person before. We... We make our deals through 'couriers.' Tha–That's what he called 'em. The kids at the arcade—next to the theater—they deliver messages and tapes for him. I–I even pay those stupid kids and they give him the money. That's all I know. Come on, guy! Please believe me! Get me out of here! Take–"

Keith slapped his hand over Jim's mouth. He gazed into his eyes, searching for a hint of deceit. He struggled to accept the explanation: *teenage couriers selling snuff films and illegal porn for a guy named Alvin Vaughn.* It seemed absurd, but he couldn't ignore it. He looked at the shoebox, then at the television. He believed Jim. *They're not on those tapes,* he told himself. Truth be told, he didn't have the courage to watch another one anyway.

He said, "You don't know how many kids you've hurt by paying for this crap. You're just as bad as the people who made these movies. You're a monster. And I know—*I know*—you're connected to my girls. You knew about me before I even walked into this store. You might not have them on these tapes, but you've heard something, haven't you? I can tell I won't be able to get it out of you, but... but I can still avenge everyone you've hurt. This is for the victims, you miserable bastard."

Keith sawed Jim's dick off with the knife. It took less than five seconds to sever it. His flaccid, shriveled penis landed on the floor beside the chair. Eyes bulging from his skull, Jim jerked and squirmed and screamed. He stared down at his lap in disbelief, watching as warm blood squirted out of his crotch and landed on his face. He felt like his penis was set ablaze, he felt the shaft *burning,* but it wasn't even attached to his body anymore. Phantom pain was a terrifying phenomenon.

Keith dragged the chair towards the entertainment center. He kicked Jim's chest, sending him plummeting to the floor.

Jim kept squirming and screaming. He covered his crotch with his restrained hands. He slowed the bleeding, but he couldn't stop the pain. He heard the sound of creaking wood. He looked up and he saw his heavy tube television falling from the entertainment center. He managed to yell for a split-second—*nnn!* He tried to shout 'no,' it was the first word that popped into his head, but he didn't have time to finish it.

The television landed on his head with an explosive sound. It slid off his head, leaning against one side of his face and revealing some of his injuries. His forehead was pushed *into* his skull, leaving a massive indentation on his brow, while shards of glass entered his scalp and face. Blood leaked out of his mouth, nostrils, eyes, and ears. His legs and arms shook for twenty seconds, then he stopped moving.

Keith staggered back, his hand over his mouth. He watched Jim's body for several minutes, as if he were expecting him to awaken—but he didn't. The man was dead, and he murdered him in a fit of rage. He had aimed his firearm at suspects before, but he never pulled the trigger. Murder was a jarring experience. He kept telling himself: *he was a pedophile, most people would have done the same, he deserved it.*

He went to the sink and washed the blood off his gloved hands, but it wasn't enough. He took off the gloves and washed his hands again, scrubbing his fingertips, knuckles, palms, and wrists with a bar of soap and a scouring pad. He scrubbed until his skin turned blood-red. Then he drank some water and splashed some more on his face. His hands shook as he put his gloves on again.

"I was right. He would have hurt someone else if I didn't stop him," he muttered as he walked around the living room.

He searched for any obvious evidence of his crime. He couldn't find any fingerprints or strands of hair. He looked at the shoebox. He considered burning the tapes, but he figured the police needed them to identify the victims and find the criminals. He took one final glance at Jim's dead body. The rancid stench of the dead body would surely lead to his discovery. There was nothing he could do about it.

Dead body disposal wasn't his specialty.

He took the keys and ran out of the apartment. He exited the store and locked the door behind him, then he dropped the keys in a sewage drain. He jogged across the street. He was relieved to find Gerald waiting for him in the same parking spot.

He climbed into the car, knocked on the dashboard, and said, "Go to the arcade on Main Street. We need to talk to some kids."

"Kids? Which kids? What happened over there, Keith? You look pale, man."

"I don't want to talk about it right now. Just drive to the arcade. Please, Gerald."

Gerald glanced over at the strip mall. The light from the apartment shone through the windows above the storefront. He didn't see any movement, though. Something was wrong, he felt it in his gut, but he wasn't eager to find the truth. He followed Keith's directions and headed to the arcade.

Chapter Fifteen

Round Three

Dwight's eyes flung open to the darkness of a black plastic bag. He looked to his left and then to his right. He saw some patches of sunshine through the plastic, but most of his vision was black. A cool breeze caressed his skin. He heard groaning tree branches and swishing bushes. He felt stiff, crackling leaves falling on him and spiraling to the ground around him. He tried to stand up, but he found himself strapped to a heavy chair. The bag rustled as his breathing intensified.

It didn't take him long to piece it together: he was naked, tied to a chair, and forced to sit under some trees in a wooded area.

"What the fuck?" he muttered. "Hey, what is this? What are y'all doing to me? Get me outta here, goddammit! I ain't play–"

A sinister cackle interrupted him—*ha-ha-ha.* Then he heard footsteps around him, leaves *crunching* under a set of boots.

"Who's there?" he asked, looking in every direction—left, right, up, down. "Hey, stop fuckin' with me! Come on, damn it! What... I don't... I didn't do anything to deserve this. That money, that money in the cup, I... I just took it. I didn't know it belonged to anyone. It was just there! Who–Who leaves money in a cup under a truck like that? Who?!"

Dwight referenced the day he stole money from a local drug dealer. Considering the circumstances—kidnapped, restrained, and deprived of sight—he figured he had messed with the wrong cartel. He read about cartel violence in discarded newspapers and heard about it from fellow transients who often worked as drug mules. He wasn't willing to die for less than a grand.

He stuttered, "I–I stashed the money. O–Okay? I didn't spend it. Not a dime, okay? If–If you let me go, I'll give it back. How's that sound? Huh? Can you hear me?"

He heard the footsteps again. Someone walked to his left, then behind him, and then to his right. The person stopped in front of him and leaned forward, hands on his knees. He could see his outline through the plastic.

"My name is Steven Carter," Riley Watts said. "I'm going to get straight to the point. I'm going to hurt you. It's not about money or drugs or anything like that. It's just for fun."

"What the fuck?"

"And, unfortunately for you, I've been told that I won't have another plaything out here for a few days, so I have to make you last. You're going to suffer for a very, *very* long time. It'll feel like... like a day in Hell, like you're falling into the inferno, like you're dying over and over. Trust me: within a few minutes, you're going to be begging me to kill you."

"I–I don't get it. Wha–What is this? Why are you doing this to me, brother?"

"Don't call me 'brother.' Call me 'executioner.' Let's begin."

"No! No! No!"

Riley giggled as he removed the bag from his prisoner's head. Wide-eyed, Dwight glanced around. He was surprised by Riley's appearance—a handsome yuppie. He saw an abandoned two-story house behind him. They were surrounded by leafless trees and shrubs. He couldn't identify his location, though. He could have been outside of Montaño, he could have been in a different state. He thought about the kidnapping, but he drew a blank. *How the hell did I get here?*—he thought.

Riley said, "Take it easy. At least you're getting some fresh air. The last guy was stuck in a stuffy, disgusting basement. You should be thankful."

"Fuck! Fuck, somebody help me! Help!"

"Don't bother. No one can hear you out here. Just accept it."

"Fuck you!"

Riley pulled a toothpick out of a duffel bag beside the chair. He picked a chunk of human flesh out from between his central incisors. He dropped the toothpick in a pile of mud near the seat. He picked it up and wiped it clean with his gloved fingers. Then he grabbed Dwight's penis in his left hand and stroked him—a good ol' fashioned handjob.

Dwight stammered, "Wha–Wha–What are you doing?"

Once Dwight was semi-erect, Riley forced the dirty toothpick into his urethra. Dwight howled as he felt a stinging pain *inside* of his penis. Riley jiggled the toothpick inside of his dick, like a key inside of an old lock. He shoved it into his urethra until only a millimeter of the birch wood protruded from his penis.

While Dwight screamed, Riley went back to the duffel bag and said, "You know, a lot of people do this for pleasure. I've never tried it before, but it always sounded painful to me. How does it feel? Good?"

"Get it out of me, you little prick!"

"Looks like you're the little prick to me."

Dwight gasped as Riley masturbated him again. He felt the toothpick gliding inside of his urethra with each stroke. His eyes widened as he spotted the sewing needle in Riley's other hand. He shrieked. In his mind, he was begging for mercy in an articulate manner—*please, mister, don't do this.* He couldn't say a word, though. He only screamed.

Riley pushed the point of the sewing needle into his urethra above the toothpick. It took more pressure, but he managed to jam it in. One inch, two inches, two-and-a-half inches—the sewing needle came to a stop halfway through his penis. The toothpick snapped inside of his dick, the splinters stabbing the walls of his urethra.

Riley grinned as he shook the needle inside of his penis. He saw the point pushing up against the shaft, forming a temporary lump on his dick. His glans turned red—*blood-red.* A droplet of blood oozed out of his urethra. He shook the needle again. Blood jetted out of his urethra in short bursts, like cum.

Some of it landed on his thighs, some rolled down to his scrotum.

To Dwight, it felt like his penis was being split in half from the inside. The pain was excruciating—surreal, otherworldly.

Riley slapped his soft penis and said, "I wouldn't worry too much about it. You're going to be dead soon, so at least you won't have to feel your urethra being swallowed by genital warts. I heard that can happen if your 'sound' is dirty. That's what this is called: *sounding.* Did you know that? Weird name, huh?"

Saliva spurting from his mouth, Dwight barked, "Fucker!"

"Yeah, yeah. I've heard it all before. 'You bastard, you motherfucker, you monster, you little rascal.' Sticks and stones, man, sticks and stones."

Riley emerged from the duffel bag with a hammer and a box of nails. He placed the tip of the nail against his shoulder. He swung down at it, but he stopped before he could make contact with the nail. Crying, Dwight swayed from side-to-side and tried to knock the chair over. His frantic movements decreased Riley's accuracy.

"Stop moving," Riley said. "If you don't..."

He stopped mid-swing again. Dwight screamed and wiggled, hysterical.

Riley shouted, "Then let's start somewhere else!"

He pressed the tip of the nail against Dwight's right temple, then he struck the head of the nail. The nail penetrated his forehead and scraped his skull. He hit the nail again, driving it deeper into his brow. From the wound, blood streamed across Dwight's forehead and dripped from his eyebrow. Some of the blood entered his eye.

Dwight cried, "Why are you doing this to me?"

"I told you already: for fun."

"You're crazy. You–"

Riley hammered another nail into his forehead. He repeated the process until five nails protruded from the homeless man's brow and two from his cheekbone. He returned to Dwight's shoulder. Since Dwight was only concerned with the pain pulsating from his forehead and penis, he stopped paying attention to Riley. He didn't move from side-to-side. He could only groan, whimper, and pant.

Riley hammered a nail into his right shoulder. Each *thud* echoed through the woods, along with Dwight's bellows. The first nail ruptured his bursa—a gelatinous sac between his bones and soft tissues. Dwight felt it burst inside of his shoulder. Before he could react, another nail tore into his shoulder. The nail cracked his bone. A third nail entered his shoulder and broke his clavicle.

Dwight looked away, closed his eyes, and gritted his teeth. He didn't want to see the torture. He counted each nail driven into his shoulder, though. One nail. Two nails. Three nails. Four nails. Five nails. *Ten nails.* He counted each bead of blood rolling down his torso, too. To his dismay, his captor wasn't finished with him yet.

Riley hammered six nails into his right pectoral

muscle, eight nails into his right kneecap, and five nails into his right foot. He tore through his muscles, ligaments, tendons, and bones without any trouble, as if he were working on a do-it-yourself home improvement project. By the end, thirty-four nails stuck out of Dwight's old, frail, wrinkly body.

The right side of his body—from his forehead to his foot—was covered in blood. The loss of blood and the unbearable pain rendered him lethargic.

Riley threw the hammer into the duffel bag and said, "It's time to put the big toys away. No more sewing needles, no more hammers. I don't want you to die so soon, remember? I have something else planned anyway. It might take me a while to finish, so I better get started now."

"K–Klein, he–help me," Dwight said weakly.

He was an old, lonely homeless man. He couldn't cry for his mother or his father. They had been dead and forgotten for years. At that moment, during his worst suffering, he cried for the only person he trusted in Montaño—*Officer Keith Klein.*

Riley emerged from behind a tree with a bucket. It was filled to the brim with hundreds of thumbtacks. He sat the bucket down at Dwight's feet. He grabbed a thumbtack, examined it for a few seconds, and then he stabbed Dwight's left hand between his knuckles. He pushed it in until only the cap protruded from his flesh.

He said, "You will be my masterpiece."

He stabbed him repeatedly, covering his hand in thumbtacks. He moved up to his wrist and then his forearm. He planned on covering the entire left side of his body in thumbtacks, one by one.

Chapter Sixteen

Couriers

"Don't move!" Keith shouted as he marched into the arcade. "Stay where you are!"

The chaotic clacking of buttons and clicking of joysticks joined the cacophony of video game music, clinking quarters, and chattering kids. Young teenagers played an assortment of arcade games: *Area 51, Mortal Kombat 3, X-Men, Metal Slug, Killer Instinct,* and *Street Fighter 3: Third Strike.* The arcade was a teenager's paradise. For many of them, it was a home away from home.

Keith and Gerald approached a group of six high school students at the back of the arcade. The teenagers sucked on Slurpees and ate Cheetos while hanging around an arcade cabinet of *The Simpsons*, stacks of quarters sitting on the control panel. They bickered and laughed, unaware of Keith's rage.

Keith stopped in front of them and asked, "Which one of you paid for all of this?"

"What's it to ya?" a blonde-haired teenager responded, a childish smirk on his face.

"Don't make me repeat myself, you little punks."

"Punks? Jeez, man, what crawled up your ass?"

"Probably one of his batons," another teen said, snickering. He nodded at Keith and said, "You need to chill out, dude. We didn't do shit."

Keith didn't care about their disrespectful

behavior. He recognized one of the teenagers: *Alejandro 'Alex' Diaz*. He jostled past the students and cornered Alex between a wall and the arcade cabinet. He glared down at him, huffing and puffing. Alex smiled nervously and glanced around, searching for a way out and asking his friends for help without saying a word.

A bald teenager tapped Keith's arm and said, "Hey, are you fuckin' high? Back off, homie."

"That's Officer Klein," a girl whispered at her friend from a different arcade cabinet.

Gerald listened to all of the gossip: *what's Officer Klein doing here? Why is he arguing with them? Is he even working now? Wasn't he on the news? His daughters are missing, aren't they?* It made him anxious. In Montaño, whispers sounded like shrieks—there were no secrets. The attention jeopardized their investigation.

Yet, Keith didn't hear a word from the other customers. He thought about Alex—and *only* Alex.

He said, "Alex... Alejandro Diaz, Montaño High School, eleventh grade, Stern Lane, you live with your older brother, younger sister, and your parents. You were at Marty's Auto Sales two weeks ago, trying to buy a new Impala in cash, but you ran out when they got suspicious. I took the report. I remember. And I saw you hanging out with Carrie after school once. Am I wrong?"

"N–No," Alex stuttered. He chuckled, then he said, "You know me, Mr. Klein. Wha–What's up? What are you doing here? Did I, um... Did I do something wrong or something?"

Keith read Alex's eyes. They said something along the lines of: *I'm guilty and I'm sorry.* A head full of secrets, the kid had something to say, but he was reluctant. Keith guessed he knew something about Carrie, but he didn't want to be labeled a 'snitch.' He was one of the good ones.

The bald teenager said, "You don't have to talk to this pig, Alex. Fuck him." He stepped in front of Keith and asked, "Did you hear me? *Fuck. You.* If you wanna talk to someone, talk to me. What's up? What do you wanna know about? Come on, pig, don't pussy out now. I can help you out. I scratch your back, you scratch mine. Something like that, right? Just ask me and I'll–"

He threw the Slurpee at his face, he shoved him, and then he ran off. His friends, as well as some of the bystanders, followed his lead. They yelled and giggled, excited by their bad behavior.

As he hopped onto his bike outside of the arcade, the bald teenager said, "Don't say shit to him! Let's dip!"

"Dude, that's fucked up," another teenager said as he casually hopped onto his bike. "His daughter's probably dead."

"So? I didn't kill her, so I don't give a fuck."

The other teenager laughed and said, "You're wild, man. Psycho!"

Keith lost his balance on a pile of flavored slush, but he stayed on his feet. He chased the teenagers out of the arcade and followed them into the dark, filthy alley beside the building. Four of them rode bikes while two of them ran as fast as possible. Alex lagged behind the group on a bike, swerving as he adjusted his backpack. It was all on purpose. He *wanted* Keith to stop him.

Keith grabbed Alex's backpack and pulled him off the bike. He slammed him against the wall beside a dumpster, his forearm against his chest.

"Hey!" Gerald yelled as he jogged to them. "Keith! Calm down!"

Ignoring his partner, Keith asked, "Talk to me, Alex. Don't make me arrest you. I can drag your whole family into this. Your kid sister, your parents, your granny, everyone. You don't want to disappoint them, do you? Your sister, that angel, she looks up to you. You don't want her looking at you through the bars of a jail cell, right?"

Gerald grabbed Keith's arms and tried to pull him back, but to no avail. He said, "Keith, brother, don't do anything you'll regret."

"You hear that, Alex. What do you think? Huh? Should I do something I'll regret?"

"*Keith*, relax. What the hell is wrong with you?"

Without taking his eyes off the teenager, Keith said, "I have to play rough to speed up this investigation. Go wait in the car if you can't handle it."

"Play rough? He's a kid!"

"And my kids aren't here right now! They're out there somewhere, waiting for me to find them! And I think this 'kid' knows something about it!" Keith yelled. He pressed his forearm against Alex's neck, choking him slightly. He shouted, "I know you know something, Alex! What did you do, you little punk? Where's Carrie?"

"I don't know!" Alex cried out, grimacing. "I don't know shit about Carrie or Allie or Brooke, I swear! I just... I would... I did... Oh, fuck, I don't want to go to jail, Mr. Klein! Please!"

Keith slammed him against the wall again and said, "You won't go to jail if you cooperate. Now, *talk*. What happened? Hmm? Is it true? Have you been working for someone? Have you been distributing some tapes for Jim? Jim Phillips?"

"You... You know about that?"

"I don't know enough."

"M–Me neither."

"Oh, come on. Don't play stupid with me now, punk. I'll beat the shit out of you if you don't talk."

Gerald's eyes and mouth widened. He could hardly believe what he was hearing: *I'll beat the shit out of you.* He felt the sheer ferocity and sincerity in Keith's voice. The man was willing to attack a teenager to retrieve information from him. He crossed the line and hurled himself into a world of corruption. There were no more limits.

The private detective stepped forward. He placed one hand on Keith's stomach and a leg behind Keith's legs. He was ready to drop him to the ground if things got out of hand.

Keith said, "Right now, I don't care about your crimes, Alex. In fact, if I find my girls unharmed, you'll get off scot-free. I can guarantee that. But I need your help to find them. I think the tapes are connected to their disappearance. So, who have you been working for?"

Teary-eyed, Alex said, "Okay, okay. I, uh... I don't know everything, alright? We just started delivering tapes for this older guy. This, uh... George-Clooney-lookin' motherfucker. He gave us some tapes and a note with addresses and drop-off spots. Sometimes it was at houses or apartments, sometimes we left 'em in trash cans or park benches. We delivered them and then we got paid. We did some work for Jim, too. Pick-ups and drop-offs. That's it, Mr. Klein."

"I know all about Jim. Now I need to know who made those tapes. Who was the other guy? Give me a name, goddammit."

"I don't know. I really don't know. We called him... 'The Ice Cream Man.' He drives around in an ice cream truck selling ice cream to kids. He never gave us a name and we only did business outside of his truck, so I don't know where he lives."

"Where did you meet him?"

Alex looked down, disappointed.

Keith shook him and said, "Come on, kid, where did you meet him?"

"*Everywhere.* Here, outside of the arcade or the movie theater. Near the schools—high, middle, and elementary. Over on Hill Lane and Green Street and Rosario Park and... and outside the Montaño Police Station. His truck was usually white, but sometimes it was blue. He had a different license plate each time we met him. He always changed the, uh... the menu stickers outside of his truck, too. Mr. Klein… it's been a few days since we've last seen him. Actually, we haven't seen him since the day after Carrie, Allie, and Brooke disappeared."

"When the investigation started…"

Keith released his grip on Alex. He stared down at the ground as he adjusted Alex's hoodie. The information overloaded his mind. He thought about Jim, the tapes, and the elusive 'Ice Cream Man.' He knew of at least six ice cream truck drivers in Montaño—two full-time, four part-time. None of them seemed capable of the alleged crimes.

He asked, "Did you watch any of the tapes?"

Alex frowned and said, "No, but… but Nolan, my friend, he said he watched one of them. He told us that… that… that it showed some kid being tortured with fire irons. We thought he was just joking because he was smiling when he told us about it. Then… I don't know how to explain it. I started getting this feeling that he was telling the truth and I was doing something wrong."

"I know what you mean. Listen, Alex, I'm sorry for getting rough. Thank you for your cooperation. Do me a favor? Call my house if you remember anything else. Lisa is there and she's trying to connect all of the pieces. *And,* stay away from the 'Ice Cream Man' and that Nolan kid, okay? I have a feeling they're nothing but bad news."

Alex said, "Yeah, okay." As Keith walked away, Alex said, "Mr. Klein."

Keith stopped and glanced over his shoulder. A

soft drizzle befell the area, the rain glistening on his leather coat.

Alex said, "I really hope you find them. Carrie... she's a great girl. So cool, you know? It's just sad. It's real fucked up. I'm sorry."

Keith nodded at him. It seemed like the most appropriate response. The men returned to the Cadillac parked in front of the arcade. They sat in silence for a minute, surrounded only by the soothing sound of rain.

Gerald said, "I'm doing this as a favor. I'm doing this because I believe it's the right thing to do. I still believe in right and wrong, Keith. So, I will not betray my character for you. If you lay a finger on another kid, I will quit this investigation and I'll report you to the police. Do we understand each other?"

"Yes. I'm sorry about my behavior. It won't happen again," Keith said, staring down at his lap with a pair of glum eyes. "Fortunately for us, I don't think we'll have to deal with anymore kids. We got what we needed."

"Yeah, good. We should start looking into the local ice cream truck drivers tomorrow. It's too late to find them on the streets now. You ready to head home?"

"No. You're right about the ice cream truck drivers, but there's one more lead I have to follow-up on tonight. Take me to El Bonita Hotel. I have to speak to one of the guests. A John who's been on my mind since this all started..."

Chapter Seventeen

Round Four

"Wait! Give me a damn second! It... It hurts!" Dwight cried as he hobbled down a hallway.

From his scalp to his toes, hundreds of colorful thumbtacks covered the left side of his body. Five thumbtacks cut into his areola, surrounding his erect nipple like the petals on a flower. He tasted blood due to the pins tearing through his cheek. A terrifying tingling sensation emanated from his mutilated armpit, spreading across his body in waves. Although the sewing needle and broken toothpick stayed in his urethra, the shaft of his flaccid penis was stabbed with a dozen thumbtacks. The glans was spared. A few thumbtacks were dislodged with each step, falling to the floor like colorful, bloody raindrops.

Riley and Chuck led him to the last door on the right. Dale followed them, supervising the torture under Allen's strict instructions.

"Pl–Please, guys," Dwight said, his voice shaking. "I–I need a hospital. I feel woozy and cold and sick. Christ, why are you doing this to me?"

Grinning with pleasure, Riley said, "Ah, don't worry, old friend. I had them prepare a bedroom for you. You'll have a comfortable bed, some delicious food, plenty of water, and painkillers and bandages so you can recover. We want you to have a pleasant stay here in the *Wolves' Den*. Come on, let's get you inside."

He pushed the door open, revealing another homemade prison cell resembling the other bedrooms. The floor, however, was flooded with thumbtacks—*thousands.*

Dwight's diet consisted of garbage scraps, donated leftovers, and cheap beer, so he was a skinny, fragile homeless man. Chuck and Riley, on the other hand, were strong and healthy. They lifted Dwight from the floor, holding him by his bony arms and legs. More thumbtacks fell from his body, hitting the floorboards with rhythmic *taps.* He screamed, he wiggled, but he couldn't stop the inevitable. The men tossed him into the room.

One yard, two yards, three yards, *four yards.*

He landed near the wall at the other end of the room. The landing knocked the wind out of him. Thumbtacks fell out of him just as new pins stabbed him. He wheezed as he crawled to the nearest corner, the nails protruding from his right kneecap scraping the floorboards. He made the mistake of standing up. Three thumbtacks stabbed the sole of his right foot. He leaned against the wall, standing on his only good foot—gasping and whining.

Jolts of pain surged from every part of his body. His heartbeat slowed, accelerated, and then slowed again. His head bobbed as he struggled to stay conscious. Then his eyes widened as a loud *crashing* sound roared through the room. A wine bottle exploded at the center of the room. Another bottle shattered as it struck the wall beside Dwight. Three more bottles hit the floor, shards of glass blending with the thumbtacks.

Riley cackled as he lobbed a sixth bottle into the room. The bottle cracked, but it didn't shatter. It rolled to the opposite corner of the room. To Dwight, it felt like an ocean of sharp objects separated him from a useful weapon.

"Listen up," Riley said. "If you can make it out of this room on your own, I won't kill you in this house. I won't take you to a hospital, but I'll let you walk—*or crawl*—out of this awful place. You can find your own way home if you can make it. Maybe I'll give you a water bottle if I'm feeling nice. If you decide to stay, then you'll suffer for the next two or three days."

Dwight didn't believe him. He was aware of the evil lurking in the world. He saw the Devil in Riley's eyes. But he was out of options. He thought about breaking through the boarded window, but his hand was injured and he was weak. He used the side of his foot to swipe at the shards of glass and thumbtacks in front of him, sweeping them away.

He took his first step, planting his foot firmly on the empty space. Some of the smaller shards and glass particles stabbed his sole, but the pain was minuscule compared to the rest of his suffering. He repeated the process for each step: sweep with his foot, take a step, sweep, step, sweep, *step.* It took him nearly ten minutes to reach the doorway. He was two lunges away from exiting the room.

He saw the deceit glimmering in Riley's wicked eyes. He couldn't trust the man who tortured him. He bent over, legs wobbling under him, and he grabbed a shard of glass. The glass sliced into his palm, but he didn't feel any pain. A numbness was setting in, starting at his extremities. He gasped as he fell to his knees. The nails were driven deeper into his right kneecap, causing blood to burst out of the wounds like water from a broken pipe.

Yet, he was determined to escape the chamber of torture. He held his breath, gritted his teeth, and shimmied up to the doorway on his knees, the nails *screeching* against the wood. He aimed the shard at the men like a knife. Riley kept grinning as he stepped back, his hands up. Chuck's face remained steady and emotionless. The bodyguard stepped aside with his arms crossed—bored, impatient.

Dwight leaned against the doorway and slid up to his feet. He aimed the shard at Chuck, then at Riley. He spotted Dale from his peripheral vision. He was startled by the pig mask. He questioned his sanity: *is that a real pig-man or am I dreaming?* He swung the shard at him, too. Dale slunk into a neighboring room, unwilling to involve himself in the torture.

"Sta–Stay back," Dwight stuttered. "I–I got outta there fair and square. You stay away from me unless you want me to shank ya."

Riley responded, "A deal is a deal, friend. Go on, get out of here. I'm sure someone is waiting for you back home. Let's just hope they can recognize you."

Dwight trudged out of the room. He ignored Dale. As far as he knew, Uncle Oinks was a pain-induced hallucination. He leaned against the wall and hopped backwards, aiming the shard at Riley and Chuck while warm blood dripped from a cut on his palm. His captors didn't follow him.

Riley smiled fondly at him and wiggled his fingers while waving at him—too-da-loo, *à tout à l'heure.*

Dwight muttered, "What the fuck?"

The homeless man made it to the stairs. To his utter surprise, the men stayed in their positions. He hobbled down the stairs, one hand on the handrail while aiming the shard behind him. He swayed from side to side, he lost his footing a couple of times, but he managed to avoid a nasty tumble. He reached the bottom of the stairs after a five-minute struggle.

He looked up—*silence.* He couldn't help but smile as he limped out of the house. He drew a deep breath as the cool nighttime breeze caressed his sweaty, bloody skin. He limped across the rickety porch, but he lost his balance as he reached the top of the steps. He unleashed a bloodcurdling scream as he fell to the ground face-first. The thumbtacks sank deeper into his flesh—especially on his face, shoulder, chest, and stomach.

"Goddammit!" he shouted. He hissed and moaned and sniveled as the pain re-emerged. He struck the mud with the bottom of his fist and muttered, "I'm so close, damn it. Gimme a break..."

He dug his fingers into the mud, then he dragged himself forward. He stopped two yards away from the porch upon hearing a set of footsteps behind him.

"Oh God, no," he said as he glanced over his shoulder.

Riley strolled across the porch, taking his sweet

time. He walked ahead of Dwight, then he stopped and turned around. He knelt in front of him and blocked his path.

He slapped him and said, "You didn't really think you were going to get away, did you? I tried to keep a steady face up there when I saw that stupid look in your eyes. You know, the relief, the gratitude, *the hope.* It was so embarrassing. But I wanted to drag it out as long as possible because I didn't want to kill you yet. Well, you want to know something else? I'm ready to kill you now." Without taking his eyes off Dwight, clearly speaking to someone else, he said, "Start the car."

Dwight stuttered, "I–I never hurt nobody. I–I was only trying to–to surv–"

He yelped as Riley grabbed a fistful of his hair and tugged on his head. He was dragged to the driveway where a black 1996 Lincoln Town Car was suspended on a floor jack. Chuck sat in the driver's seat, revving the engine. The rear wheels spun so fast that the grooves of the tires were imperceptible to the human eye.

Riley held Dwight's face close to one of the rear tires. He shouted, "Look at it! This is death! This is how you die! Any last words?!"

"Please! Please, kid, don't–"

"Kid? Did you just call me 'kid,' motherfucker?"

"Don't do this! I'm a good per–"

Riley pressed Dwight's face against the tire. Dwight convulsed violently underneath him. He screamed until his vocal cords ruptured. His crying changed from loud and shrill to weak and raspy. His skin peeled and burned as soon as he touched the tire. Blood splattered on the rear bumper and Riley's face. Riley felt the vibrations of Dwight's skull across his hands and arms. He tightened his grip on his head and placed more pressure on it. The stench of burning skin meandered into his nostrils, causing him to lick his lips in delight.

After three minutes, he yelled, "Enough! It's over!"

The engine stopped purring. The tire slowed, squeaking as it glided on Dwight's exposed skull, then it stopped after fifteen seconds. Riley stared down at Dwight's body. The homeless man wasn't breathing. He pulled his face away from the tire and examined the damage.

The right side of Dwight's face was torn off, leaving only some patches of skin. A skid mark stained part of his exposed skull while blood covered the rest of the bone. His right eye popped out of its socket and dangled over his cheek. Half of the eye appeared gooey, dripping a bloody gel-like fluid as if it had melted due to the heat from the friction. Only the upper half of his ear was attached to his head. Locks of his bloody hair—from his scalp and beard—spiraled down to the driveway. Plumes of steam rose from his face and the tire. Bloody chunks of his flesh were stuck in the tire's grooves, like meat between a person's teeth.

Riley said, "Take him to the basement. I need him for a game."

He released him, allowing Dwight to fall face-first

under the wheel. He wiped his face with a handkerchief while Chuck carried Dwight's body into the house. Riley stopped on the porch. Dale stood beside him, hands stuffed in his pockets. He looked out into the woods, unbothered by the violence.

"Did you get the barrels I asked for?" Riley asked. Dale nodded. Riley said, "Good. I need you to do me another favor. Give me the keys to the girl's room. The older one, not sweet lil' Allie's. I'd like to pay her an unsupervised visit."

Dale stared at him, but his eyes were barely visible because of the pig mask. His expression was blank anyway. Allen was locked away in his office, dealing with the business side of the Wolves' Den, so Dale was responsible for their guests—*all* of them.

Riley said, "Come on. It'll only take a minute." He leaned closer to him and whispered, "I need to 'relieve' myself, Mr. Pig-man. My dick got so hard while tearing that man's face off... I might actually finish in less than a minute. If you do this for me, I'll let you play with Allie next time. We can tag-team her. What do you say?"

Dale didn't have to think about it. Riley was powerful thanks to his father, so he could make things happen. *Finally,* he thought, *I can fuck an angel.*

He handed him a key-ring and said, "I cum first."

"We'll talk about it later."

"Deal."

Riley returned to the second story of the house. He looked at the door at the end of the hall—*Allen's office.* He snickered as he hunched down and tiptoed to Carrie's room, like a child sneaking out to see Santa Claus. He unlocked the padlock slowly, trying to stop the keys from jingling. He crept into the room and closed the door behind him.

"Hey, sweetheart," he said. "I bet you weren't expecting me tonight. Don't be scared. That screaming out there, it doesn't involve you. Really, I swear."

Carrie sat in the corner of the room, shivering. Her eyes and nose were red due to her endless weeping. Her dried, flaky lips were cracking. She wore a large white t-shirt—one of Allen's—because she pissed herself before one of her regularly-scheduled bathroom breaks. (She was allowed to urinate and defecate in a bucket three times a day.) She hid her hands under her thighs.

Riley knelt down in front of her and said, "We've known each other for a few days now. I usually don't wait this long to make the first move, but... you're a special girl." He squeezed her bare foot gently, then he ran his fingertips across her shin. He said, "Do I love you? No, no. I wouldn't say it's love. Maybe it's respect, maybe it's curiosity, maybe... Hell, maybe it *is* love. I wouldn't know. What do you think? Do you love me?"

He leaned forward and caressed her kneecap. He ran his fingertips up her thigh. He licked his lips as he reached her shirt. The outline of his erect penis was visible against his white pants. Breathing through her nose, Carrie shivered and sniveled. Goosebumps spread across her arms and legs. His gentle touch and his inappropriate words were eerie.

Riley slid his fingers under her shirt and said, "You sure are quiet tonight. Don't worry. I'll make you moan and cry... and scream. Have you ever been fingered before? It feels like–"

"Die!" Carrie yelled.

She pulled her right hand out from underneath her. She held a makeshift knife made from a crushed soda can folded into a triangle. She thrust it at Riley. She aimed for his throat, but she stabbed his face instead. She sliced into his upper lip, leaving a large gash to the right of his philtrum—*a cleft lip*. The can even grazed his gums.

Riley fell back, bug-eyed. He crab-walked backwards as Carrie lunged at him again, swinging and thrusting the can with murder in her eyes. He crashed into the wall beside the door, his hands over his mouth. The chains stopped Carrie near the center of the room. She stretched out as far as possible and tried to stab him again, grunting and groaning.

Riley's lips and chin were covered in blood. He tasted it in his mouth. In fact, the blood painted his teeth red. He spat a blob of saliva and blood at the floor. His wrists on his knees, he sat and stared at Carrie, analyzing her feral behavior. Although he was injured, his perfect face tarnished by a grisly wound, he smiled and chuckled at the girl. And his chuckle quickly evolved into his signature cackle.

He wagged his bloody finger at her and said, "You shouldn't have done that." He stood up and adjusted his clothes. He said, "Your precious sister will pay for that."

Carrie swung the soda can at his leg again and said, "You... You... You fucker!"

"Oh, I'm fucking something tonight. I'm going to have a lot of fun."

"Shut up! I'll kill you!"

As he exited the room, Riley said, "Sweet dreams, darling. I'll see you again soon."

Carrie screamed at the top of her lungs. Riley closed and locked the door, but she didn't stop swinging the can. After a minute, her anger turned into sadness and regret. She curled up and cried as she thought about Allie.

"What did I do?" she whispered.

Chapter Eighteen

Motel Hell

"I said no room service!" a man yelled from the other side of the door.

The number above the peephole read: *12.* Keith stood there with his thumb over the peephole. Gerald stood beside him. A downpour flooded the vacant parking lot behind them, causing low visibility and providing a natural soundtrack of noise. The door swung open. A strong, middle-aged man stood before them, wearing a wife beater and striped boxers, muttering about the disturbance.

Upon spotting his visitors, the man raised his brow and asked, "Who are you? What do you want?"

Keith responded, "My name is Keith Klein. I work with the Montaño Police Department. We've received several noise complaints over the last couple of nights. I was wondering if I could come in and ask you a couple of questions."

The guest ran his eyes over the men. They weren't dressed like cops, but they could have been plainclothes officers.

He said, "The Montaño Police Department, huh? Interesting. So, what's your partner's name?"

Gerald stuttered, "G–G–Gerald, um…" He hesitated. He didn't want to give him his real name. He said, "Gerald Wilson."

"Gerald Wilson," the man repeated, grinning and

nodding. "You wouldn't happen to have badges, would you?"

Keith responded, "Sir, I'm asking for your cooperation. If it was nothing, then great. We can all go on with our nights. What's the problem?"

"The problem is: I'm not stupid. I know my rights. If you are cops—and that's a big *if*—then you need to present me with identification and probable cause or a warrant. If you're granny-mugging thugs looking for a quick and easy robbery, I suggest you look for another mark. I won't make it quick and it won't be easy for you. Now get the hell out of here."

Keith put his boot in the doorway as the man tried to slam the door. He pushed his elbow up against the door, but he didn't tackle it. He wasn't ready to commit—not yet.

The man asked, "What the hell are you doing? Huh? You really want to play this game with me?"

The sound of a lamp tipping over on a table emerged from behind the door. Keith was a cop. He knew exactly what was happening behind the door. The man was reaching for a weapon.

"I'll be back with a warrant," Keith said.

He pulled his foot out from between the door and the doorway. The door slammed shut, but the loud *thud* was masked by the rain. None of the neighbors heard it. He leaned back against the wall beside the door.

Gerald said, "Hey, let's call the cops. This guy he's, um... He's a psychopath, man. He's dangerous and I don't think we should be messing with him."

"Do you have your gun?"

"My gun? No, no, no. I know what you're thinking, but don't–"

Keith grabbed his arm and pulled him away from the door. He drew his handgun, took it off safety, and then he held his index finger over his lips and shushed his partner. Gerald looked at him with wide eyes, then at the door, and then back at him. He saw it all in his head before it happened—a vision, a premonition, a memory of the future. His lips flapped, but he didn't say a word. He reached for his holster.

In one swift move, Keith turned and kicked the door open. As expected, the guest stood behind the door, one eye closed as he peeked through the peephole. The door struck his forehead, launching him backwards. Dazed, he leaned against the dresser and looked through the top drawer. He grabbed a revolver.

Before he could pull the gun out, Keith grabbed his forearm and aimed his pistol at his head. His eyes told tales of bloody murder—*Jim's murder.*

The man asked, "Who the hell are you?"

"I told you my name. Now it's time for you to tell me yours."

"I'm not giving you shit, asshole."

Gerald entered the room and closed the door behind him. He drew his handgun, but he didn't touch the safety engagement notch. He aimed the gun at the floor, too. He cared about the Klein family, but, with doubt lingering in his mind, he wasn't ready to shoot someone over the investigation. He stood near the bathroom and watched as Keith forced the man to sit on the foot of the bed.

"Lock the door," Keith demanded. Gerald didn't move an inch. Keith repeated, "*Lock the door.*"

Gerald snapped out of his contemplation. In his mind, he told himself: *walk out, this is bad, you'll lose everything if you're wrong, walk out!* Like a zombie, he shambled to the door. The doorknob was broken, but the chain lock was functional. He secured it, then he walked to the bathroom door, unable to stop himself from shaking.

Keith said, "I know you're scared, but I need you to be strong and smart. Remember: it doesn't matter if this man is connected to our investigation. He is suspected of several other *violent* crimes against the women of Montaño. That's the truth and you know it."

Rubbing his rosy forehead, the man said, "I don't know what he's talking about. Open the door and let me out. Don't follow this guy 'cause he's only going to lead you to trouble."

"He isn't innocent," Keith continued, gun pointed at his head. "Keep your eyes on him while I search the rest of the room. Make sure he doesn't die."

Gerald repeated, "Doesn't die? What do–"

Keith shot at the man's legs—*bang, bang!* The first bullet went through his right thigh, stopping in the mattress underneath him. The second bullet became lodged in the torn tendons and broken bones of his right kneecap. Blood from his thigh soaked the white bed sheets while blood spouted out of the wound on his kneecap, like an uninterrupted flow of tea from a teapot.

The man covered the wounds with his hands and rolled onto the bed, bawling. Gerald gasped and staggered back. He glanced over his shoulder. *Did they hear it? Is anyone in the rooms next door? Are we safe?*–he thought. While Keith looked through the drawers, Gerald bolted into action. He tore the pillowcases and tied them about two inches above the gunshot wounds to create two homemade tourniquets. The bleeding slowed, but it couldn't be stopped.

"You shot me!" the man yelled.

Hands drenched in blood, Gerald shouted, "You shot him! A–Are you insane?!" He placed his palms against his brow, inadvertently smearing the blood on his face. He said, "We're in trouble. I shouldn't have followed you. As soon as you asked me about my gun, I should have walked away and called the cops. Keith, do you know what's going to happen to you? After we find the girls, you're going to jail. *We're* going to jail."

Keith blocked out the ranting and crying. He pulled a wallet out of the drawer. The picture on the California driver's license resembled the guest. The name on the ID read: *Alvin Vaughn.* In the wallet, he found one-thousand dollars—ten one-hundred-dollar bills—two condoms, and four credit cards. One of the cards belonged to a Melissa Ortiz.

He unloaded the revolver, then he placed it on the dresser beside the tube television. He found an eightball of cocaine and an ounce of marijuana.

Gerald said, "Keith, stop it. None of that matters anymore. It's... It's inadmissible. We have to take him to a hospital before he bleeds out."

Keith opened a door beside the dresser. A suit, a jacket, some t-shirts, and a pair of jeans hung in the closet. There was a briefcase and a black plastic bag on the floor. In the bag, he found a pocketknife, brass knuckles, and a garotte made of wire. Old blood was smeared on all of the tools. He opened the briefcase.

Tapes.

Three videotapes.

The world around him was muted. His eyes welled with tears as he examined the tapes. Images of the innocent princess and the man in the mouse mask flashed in his mind. He thought about Jim's Video Shop, which led his mind to the couriers. He glanced over at Alvin. His eyes were drawn to the man's salt-and-pepper Caesar haircut. Then it all came together—*it clicked.*

He turned around and showed the tapes to Gerald. Gerald stopped speaking, awed by the revelation, while Alvin continued screaming.

Gerald grunted, then he said, "It's, uh... Shit, I don't know what to say. I can't... Keith, we don't know what's on those tapes."

"I know what's on them," Keith said as he tossed the briefcase on the dresser. "You can watch them yourself if you want. Go ahead, there's a VCR right there."

He approached the foot of the bed, a sneer of disgust contorting his face. He stepped on Alvin's kneecap. A *crunching* sound emerged from his leg as blood bubbled out of the wound. Alvin sat up and gasped, then he fell back, hitting the mattress with a loud *thump.* He breathed in short, strained gasps.

Keith muttered, "A George-Clooney-lookin' motherfucker..." He kicked the bed and said, "If you don't want me to step on your other leg, you'll answer my questions. What are you driving?"

"Wait... Wait..." Alvin cried weakly.

"I won't repeat myself."

As Keith stepped on his thigh, Alvin shouted, "A van! A–A van!"

Keith and Gerald locked eyes. Keith lurched out of the motel room. Rain pouring down on him, he scanned the parking lot. His eyes stopped on a white high-top van to his left. He didn't notice it when they first arrived. He walked around to the other side of the vehicle. There was a large rectangular concession window beside the passenger door. Around the window, sticker residue clung to the van. The menu decals were recently removed.

His theory was confirmed: Alvin Vaughn, Jim's connection, was the Ice Cream Man. He had known about him since the night of the disappearance when Vanessa warned him about the psychopath. Regret and shame twisted his stomach into itself, sending jolts of pain through his torso. He returned to the motel room and locked the door behind him, head hanging down in disappointment. He disconnected the VCR and television cables, then he tossed them on the bed.

He aimed his gun at Alvin and said, "Tie his wrists to the bedposts. He's the guy Jim and Alex told me about. He's Alvin Vaughn, *the Ice Cream Man*."

Gerald was an experienced private investigator. *A van!*—he identified Alvin as soon as he heard those words. The man on the bed was now suspected of beating and raping several prostitutes, producing and distributing illegal pornography, and kidnapping three girls. He was a vile person, a beast from the deepest depths of hell, but he was still afraid of harming him. He was an investigator, not a vigilante.

"Don't worry, he won't try anything funny," Keith said. He aimed the pistol at Alvin's genitals and said, "If he does, I'll blow his balls to bits. Go on, tie him up."

Gerald reluctantly followed his orders. It gave him a reason to holster his handgun. One after the other, he tied Alvin's wrists to the bedposts with the cords. The knots cut off the circulation to his hands. His legs trembled violently. His face turned pale, brow and cheeks wet with a cold sweat. He panted, drawing just enough breath to fill his chest.

Gerald retreated to the corner of the room, tears in his eyes. He interviewed hundreds of people throughout his career. The situation in the motel room was different. He was witnessing Keith's 'enhanced interrogation techniques.'

Keith said, "Alvin, I want you to tell me about the tapes. Did you make them?"

"You... You're fucking... with... with the... wrong people."

"Answer the question. If you don't, I'll be forced to hurt you."

"You… You're dead."

Keith approached the nightstand and said, "I've learned some things about pain and violence since I joined the force. I've seen it all: men stabbed in their guts, intestines popping out of their wounds; necks slit with broken beer bottles; children beaten black and blue by flip flops, belts, tire irons, golf clubs, and anything their parents could grab; prostitutes beaten with brass knuckles and burned with cigarettes before being raped or strangled—*or both*. I learned more through other cases, too. Through the news, even. Do you know how hot a light bulb gets when it's lit up like this?"

Alvin was baffled by the question. The pain in his legs hindered his concentration. He heard the words, but he didn't understand him. He tried to reach for his legs, but he couldn't move his arms. His survival instincts told him to cover the wounds.

As he unscrewed the light bulb, his hand protected by a glove, Keith said, "About 300 degrees depending on the watts of the bulb. Sometimes 400, maybe even 500. It's even hotter inside. The light is just heat after all. So, if you won't answer my first question, why don't you answer this for me: where should I shove this bulb? In your mouth or up your ass?"

Alvin understood those words. He said, "Wait… Give me a–a second."

"If I wait too long, the bulb will cool down. You have five seconds, then I'll choose for you. Five, four, three..."

"I–I didn't make the tapes. I'm the distributor and the money-man. O–Okay?"

"Where can I find your employer?"

Alvin laughed nervously, then he stuttered, "I–I can't tell you that. He–He–He'd kill me. Whatever you do to me, he–he'll do something worse."

"Give me something to work with."

"Ta–Take me to a hospital."

Keith sighed, then he whispered, "Up your ass."

He pulled Alvin's boxers down to his bloody knees. He knelt on Alvin's stomach, pushing the rest of the air out of him. Face as red as blood, Alvin couldn't scream or sob. He could barely draw a satisfying breath. He tried to kick, but his legs were weakened by the gunshot wounds.

"What are you doing?" Gerald squeaked, like a rat in a wall. "This is bad. It's so bad, Keith. We have to stop. Someone's going to hear us."

Keith ignored him. He flipped Alvin onto his side, he spread his ass open, and then he slid the light bulb towards his anus. Glass first, he screwed the bulb into his rectum until only the metal cap stuck out of him. A sizzling sound came out of his anus as the hot glass burned his rectum. A cracking sound immediately followed. The bulb was breaking in the tight space.

Alvin clenched his fists and gasped. The blazing pain reverberated across his crotch. A sensation of pins-and-needles spread to his scrotum. Then his penis became semi-erect. He stayed on his side due to fear and shock. He was afraid of laying down on his back because of the hot light bulb in his ass, and he was shocked because *there was a hot light bulb in his ass.*

Gerald held his hands over his mouth. He turned around and faced the wall, sickened by the violence.

Keith said, "Breathe, Alvin. You'll faint if you don't breathe. If you faint, you'll lose control of your body. You don't want that right now. Now, you should focus on relaxing your sphincter. If you don't, that bulb is going to explode in your rectum. It's going to get a lot hotter and a lot bloodier in there. I know you hear it cracking."

Alvin whimpered as he breathed through his nose. He looked down at himself and thought: *how the hell do I relax my sphincter?*

Keith said, "Answer my questions and I'll take it out. I have all night, but remember: the clock is ticking. It'll burst any second now."

Alvin's eyes wandered in every direction. He looked at himself, Keith, the bed, the ceiling, and the headrest. Tears rolled down his face and soaked his pillow. *Crack*—the noise came from his anus again. The bulb was close to breaking under the pressure.

He stammered, "I–I–I can't tell you. If–If I do, they–they'll skin me and that... that... that damn pig will eat me alive. Go to the–the crack house. The one on... on Green Street. It's a... a... like a warehouse and a distribution center ran by a bunch of crackheads. They–They'll tell you anything. They're sellouts. I know it. I–I never trusted them."

"And you're not a sellout?"

"Fuck you. I–I can't give you anything else. My boss, my coworkers... They're real psychos. If they found out–"

"They'd stick more than a hot light bulb up your ass, right?"

Alvin nodded.

Keith said, "Unfortunately for you, I can't let you go. If you're even partly responsible for the kidnapping of my daughters, then I have to punish you. I need vengeance, Alvin. That's as simple as I can put it."

Gerald placed his hands on his head and asked, "What are you saying, Keith? What the hell is going on? You can't–"

The bulb cracked again.

Alvin said, "Take it out. Pl–Please take it out. Hurry up."

"No," Keith said, shaking his head.

"Please! It's going–"

The light bulb exploded in his ass with another loud *crack* and a *pop*. A wave of heat flowed through his rectum while the hot shards stabbed his rectal walls. Some of the smaller shards rode a wave of blood out of his anus. The pain caused his anus to twitch, which caused the shards of glass to shatter into smaller fragments.

Writhing in pain while holding his breath, Alvin said, "Bas–tard..."

Keith nodded at Gerald and said, "Get out. Check on the clerk. Make sure he's distracted. I'll meet you in the car in fifteen, maybe twenty minutes."

Gerald asked, "Are you going to kill him?"

"You already know the answer to that question. You don't have to watch this, you don't have to get your hands bloody. You've done enough tonight. Please, get out and wait for me."

Gerald covered his face and cried. He exited the room. He walked in the rain, hoping the water would wash away his sins and the blood. He was complicit in an act of torture. He saw murder in Keith's eyes. *He's going to kill him,* he thought, *and I'm doing nothing to stop him, so I'm killing him, too.* He took a deep breath, then he walked into the front office and inquired about renting a room.

Keith secured the latch lock on the door. He took the brass knuckles out of the bag in the closet and slid them over his fingers. He bent over Alvin and gazed into his eyes.

He said, "I'm going to make your boss suffer, too. He'll join you in hell soon."

Alvin couldn't beg for mercy. The words wouldn't come out. Keith swung down at Alvin's ribcage, cracking a bone with each blow—*thud, thud, thud!* Alvin bounced on the bed with each hit. He felt and heard one of his ribs *snapping* in half. Each short, panicked breath set his chest ablaze. He coughed up a mist of blood. It drizzled back down to his mouth and cheeks.

Keith swung down at Alvin's face, but he stopped himself before he could hit him. He figured Alvin wouldn't be able to experience the torture—*the suffering*—if he were knocked unconscious.

He slapped him and said, "Stay awake. I'm almost done."

"Bas... Bas... Let... Hmm..." Alvin babbled in a daze.

Keith returned to the bed with the pocketknife. During his career as a police officer, he responded to multiple calls of stabbings—jealous lovers, bitter friends, morons with knives. From the victims and paramedics, he learned that being stabbed in the stomach caused the most pain while stab wounds in the neck and thigh often led to a quick death.

So, while staring into his dull eyes, he stabbed Alvin in the stomach. He twisted the blade inside of him. Alvin grimaced and whimpered as his body stiffened. Thick veins bulged from his forehead and neck. Keith stabbed him through his belly button, then below his sternum. He watched the color fade away from his eyes—from bright blue to dim gray. His pupils dilated as he stared absently at the ceiling. A stream of piss shot out of his penis, blending with the blood on the bed sheets.

Keith thrust the blade deeper into him. He leaned closer to Alvin's ear. Alvin's short, rasping breath touched his face, barely perceptible.

"You're dying," Keith whispered. "What does it feel like? Does it hurt? Are you scared? You know nothing's waiting for you on the other side, right? It'll all go black soon. Soon... God, I wish I could have kept you alive longer. You deserved more pain for what you did to those innocent kids. I should have... I should have... I don't know what I should have done exactly, but I should have done more. Fuck it. Die already, so I can go kill your friends next."

His eyes half-shut, Alvin stopped breathing. His hands swung from side to side for fifteen seconds afterward, causing the bedposts to groan. He stopped moving.

Keith pulled the blade out. He took one step away from the bed, but then he stopped. He glared at Alvin, as if the corpse had insulted him. He couldn't leave the room without absolute certainty. He slit Alvin's throat, sawing into his neck with a pocketknife. He severed his jugulars and cut through his Adam's apple. The blood shot out of his neck, soaking the pillows and even landing on the nightstands.

Alvin was already dead. No one could revive him.

Keith exited the motel room, leaving behind an assortment of evidence—a dead body, a pocketknife, brass knuckles, tapes, and bullets from his gun. The rain washed the blood away from his face and neck, but the water couldn't scrub the blood stains off his clothes. He sat down in the passenger seat of the Cadillac.

Gerald was already buckled into the driver's seat. The sound of rain pattering on the vehicle and the mechanical rhythm of the windshield wipers brought a sense of comfort to him. It was familiar. He remembered driving through storms on road trips with his family as a child. He was brought back to a world of deceit and violence with Keith's return from the motel room.

The men avoided eye contact, staring forward at the windshield.

Keith asked, "Did you speak to the clerk?"

"Yeah," Gerald said.

"How did it go?"

"I asked about their rates and the area. Acted like an out-of-towner. He didn't hear a thing. No one heard anything."

"Good. He didn't ask for room service, so they won't visit his room until dawn at the earliest. We have time to make a move. Take me to the house on Green Street."

"No."

Keith looked at Gerald, but Gerald didn't look at him. Gerald wasn't comfortable around him anymore. He understood his situation—he cared about the missing girls, too—but he didn't agree with his methods. Some people weren't capable of murder, no matter the circumstances.

Keith said, "Gerald, I need a ride. I have to check that house."

"I'm not taking you there."

"Why?"

"Because… Because I'm not a killer, Keith. And I'm not trained to raid a house like that. You aren't either. I'm calling the cops."

Keith sighed, then he said, "Don't do that. You heard him in there, you've seen all of the evidence, but they haven't. They won't believe a thing we say. Yes, we can prove it eventually, but *eventually* is too late. The people at that house, the crackheads, they can lead me to my girls."

"That's *if* they're even connected to all of this. They

could be lost in the woods, Keith. You might be out here ki... ki..."

"*Killing,*" Keith said. "Killing people. That's what you want to say, right?"

Gerald sniffled, then he said, "Yeah. Yeah, Keith, you might be out here killing people for nothing."

The men took a breather from the tense conversation, listening to the peaceful sound of rain while vortexes of conflicting emotions swirled in their minds.

Keith said, "The tapes. I saw the tapes at Jim's Video Shop. I even watched the first few minutes of one of 'em. You heard about them yourself from that kid, Alex, at the arcade. Now you've seen them here with the 'Ice Cream Man.' You're right, I haven't found evidence directly linking this business to my girls, but you have to trust my intuition here, Gerald. I *know* this is going to take me to them. I won't ask you to get your hands dirty, but I will ask you to let me finish this. If they're not at that house, you can walk away. I'll take the blame for everything. Please. For Carrie, for Allie, for Brooke."

Gerald drew a deep, shaky breath. The evidence was circumstantial, but the theory made sense to him. While searching for a runaway during one of his investigations, he stumbled upon a group of gangbangers attempting to smuggle a teenage girl into Mexico. She had befriended one of them before the attempted kidnapping. If it weren't for Gerald, she would have been sold as a child prostitute or a drug mule—or both.

He didn't want Carrie, Allison, or Brooke to become statistics in a tragic case of human trafficking. He didn't want to hurt anyone, either.

He said, "I'll take you to the house tomorrow. I can't—"

"Now, Gerald. We're running out of—"

"I know! We're running out of time, I know that already! But I need a break. You need a break, too. If everything he said is true, then we need to be prepared for them. I'm not going out to that house at night during a storm like this. The visibility is shit and we wouldn't be able to hear anything. We'd be walking into a death trap. Tomorrow morning, okay? I'll call you before I'm ready to pick you up."

Keith pictured himself hopping out of the car and marching to the other side of Montaño to raid the crack house. He imagined himself finding the missing girls in a dusty attic, injured but alive. Then, he saw a homeless drug addict shooting him from behind because he couldn't hear him during the storm. *He's right,* he thought, *it's too risky now.*

He said, "Tomorrow morning."

"Tomorrow morning," Gerald repeated. "We'll bring those girls home if they're there. I promise."

Chapter Nineteen

Three Barrels and a Pea

Carrie walked down the hallway, cuffed at the wrists and ankles. Riley walked beside her, his arm over her shoulder. His sliced lip was cleaned, sutured, and secured with surgical tape. He smiled as he led her down the stairs, as if he had forgotten about her vicious attack. Chuck followed behind them, guaranteeing Riley's safety. Dale led them to the basement door. He opened the door, stepped aside, and beckoned to Carrie—*ladies first.*

The chains between her feet rattled as Carrie stopped in her tracks. Riley gave her a gentle shove, like a father pushing his shy child to meet new kids.

"Go on," he said. "Don't worry, we're not going to hurt you, sweetie. I have a surprise for you down there. Come on, I'll go with you."

Riley held her hand and led her down the stairs. At the bottom of the steps, a draft struck the back of Carrie's neck—a quick, chilly breeze. But there were no windows in the basement. There was a table with a vise, a black garbage bag filled to its capacity, and three large barrels in the room. The black barrels were lined up in front of the drain.

"*Surprise!*" Riley shouted with his arms stretched away from his body. He strolled to the center of the room. He pointed at the barrels and asked, "Do you know what this is? Hmm? Do you? No? Come here, I'll tell you about it."

Carrie looked at the exit. Dale and Chuck stood at the top of the stairs, blocking the doorway with their bodies. She couldn't overpower the men without a weapon. The handcuffs and legcuffs didn't help, either. Escape was impossible. She glanced over at Riley, who continued to grin at her. She reluctantly shambled towards him.

Riley placed his hands on her shoulders, then he spun her around until she faced the barrels. Carrie's nose wrinkled as she caught a whiff of a rancid stench—feces and boiled eggs and burnt hair and cooked meat, all of it mixed together in a blender, consumed, and vomited on a sweltering road during a hot summer.

Riley said, "This game is called 'three-shells-and-a-pea.' Maybe you know it as the 'shell game' or something like that. You've seen it before, but on a smaller scale. I know it. Gamblers in alleys, kids behind the cafeteria, or people playing with their dogs and cats. Something 'special,' like a treat, is placed under one of the shells or cups or whatever you want to use. The shells are moved—fast, fast, *faster*—and then the player has to guess which shell is hiding the treat. In this case, we're playing with heavy barrels, so we can't move them, but the goal is the same. You have to find the treat."

"Wha–What's the treat?"

"I'm glad you asked."

He walked to the other side of the barrels. He tapped each one as he walked past them. He stopped behind the barrel at the center.

He said, "Your sweet, precious baby sister is in one of these barrels. If you find her on your first try, I will let both of you go. *Guaranteed.* If you find her on the second try, I'll let *one* of you go. You can discuss it afterward. If you fail to find her by that second turn, then you'll both stay with me in this house until I'm bored of you. You have nothing to lose and everything to gain, sweetheart. So, which barrel would you like to open first?"

The house was quiet. Rain didn't batter the house, wind didn't sing through the woods, men didn't scream in agony. The barrels were quiet and motionless, too. She approached the barrel to the left. She reached for the lid, but she stopped as she caught another whiff of the rotten odor. She glanced at Riley, who snickered and shrugged.

She approached the barrel to the far right. The stench grew stronger. She bent over, her ear hovering a foot above the barrel. She didn't hear anything—a whimper, a whisper, a breath, *nothing.* She had smelt stink bombs before. A group of eighth graders once set off dozens of stink bombs in the cafeteria before graduating from junior high. The stench in the room was different. It was as strong as it was tragic.

She pointed at the barrel: *this one.*

Riley nodded at her and said, "Go on, pop it open. Give it a good tug, sweetie."

Carrie choked down the lump in her throat. She tugged on the lid until it *popped* open. She caught a glimpse of Dwight's dead body in the barrel. The bony homeless man was curled into a ball and jammed into the tight space. His face was torn off and one of his eyes was missing. A large, wet rat ran across his chest, scurrying towards his bare crotch. Two more rats chewed on his feet at the bottom of the barrel.

Human physiology was fascinating. Shock told her brain to protect her. So, less than two seconds after spotting the body, her vision went black. A tingly sensation spread across her entire body. She felt as light as a sheet of paper, capable of floating away with the breeze of a weak fan. When she opened her eyes, she found she had taken three steps back without realizing it. She couldn't see Dwight anymore.

Riley held his hands over his stomach and guffawed. He tasted her fear, he *savored* it. The men upstairs stayed quiet.

Carrie breathed heavily and shook her head. She was speechless. She witnessed the death of her best friend in the woods, but the tragic memory couldn't compete with the mutilated body in the barrel. Those two seconds scarred her mind.

She closed her eyes and stuttered, "Clo–Close it."

"You still have a chance to save your sister... or yourself," Riley responded. "Open another one."

"I won't open another one until you close that one. I... I don't want to see him again."

"Excuse me? Are you making the rules now?"

"Pl–Please... I can't see him like that. I'll play, but I don't... I can't do it if I can see him. I just can't."

Riley pushed his tongue against the side of his

mouth. He sighed and smiled, then he closed the barrel.

He pointed at the other barrels and asked, "Happy? Good. Now which one will it be? I'll open it for you, sweetheart. That'll make it easier for you."

Carrie took a step to her left. She analyzed the barrel, searching for the slightest sign of life. *Give me a hint, Allie,* she thought, *cry or whisper or do something!* To her dismay, she didn't hear a peep from the barrels. She looked back at the stairs and thought about running.

Riley said, "I thought you'd be more excited about this. You can save yourself or your sister right now. Worst case scenario: you're stuck with me for a few more days. I mean, we don't have to play if you don't want to. Do you give up? Hmm?"

"N–No. I pick... I pick that one," Carrie said as she pointed at the barrel to the left.

"This one? Are you sure?" Riley asked as he grabbed the lid. "No take-backsies."

"She's in that one. I know it."

"I like that. I *love* your confidence. Let's see what's behind Barrel Number One."

He gripped the lid and waited for fifteen seconds, purposely attempting to build the suspense. He winked at Carrie, then he popped the lid open.

Empty.

The barrel was empty.

Her lips shaking and tears falling from her jaw, Carrie looked at the barrel at the center and said, "I'm... I don't... I'm sorry."

"There's no need to apologize to me, sweetie-pie. You lost. Or... are you apologizing to your sister?"

"Can–Can I... Can I see her? Pl–Please?"

Riley slunk over to the closed barrel. He said, "You've been pretty mean to me. Why should I do something nice for you?"

"Please let me see her. I'll do anything. I promise."

"Anything?"

Carrie shouted, "Anything! Please let me see her! Please!" She turned her attention to the barrel and yelled, "Allie! Allie, I'm here! Wake up and come out!"

Riley said, "You heard her, Allie. Come on out."

Riley opened the lid. Allison's tiny body, covered in a blanket, was squeezed into the barrel. Her bare shoulders—sooty, bruised, bloody—could be seen over the blanket. She was naked. Her soft brown hair, grimy and disheveled, covered her forehead and eyes. Her cheeks were bruised, black and blue. The bruises replaced her freckles. The freckles were beaten off her face. Her lips were pale, dry, and lacerated, flaky blood around her mouth. She didn't move.

Carrie couldn't handle the shock. Before she could say a word, her eyes rolled back and she collapsed. On her way down, right before she fainted, she saw Riley's sinister grin. His face melted into the ceiling, stretching out like a stroke of paint. In the darkness of slumber, she saw and felt nothing. An hour passed in what felt like the blink of an eye. She awoke on the floor of her prison in the abandoned house, her vision blurred. The room was dark, but she spotted the other person in the room.

"Allie," she cried.

Her sister's corpse lay in the opposite corner of the room, a blanket draped over her body. Her eyelids had been propped open since she passed away, causing horizontal, reddish-brown stripes to form across her eyes. The French called it: *tache noir de la sclerotique*. Death extinguished the bright, hopeful glimmer from her eyes.

Carrie knew about life and death, she witnessed a murder after all, but she didn't really *know* about it until that moment in the room. Her sister—once a vibrant, funny, and intelligent girl—was reduced to a slab of cold meat. Their relationship ended without any goodbyes. She wondered if her death was scary or painful.

Whimpering, she repeated, "Allie…"

Chapter Twenty

Good Morning

Keith stood in the doorway leading to the attached garage, drying his wet hair with a towel. His skin was rosy from his scalding shower. Lisa stood in front of the washing machine, holding his bloody coat in her steady hands. She formed a vague but accurate idea concerning the previous night's events.

"Did you find anything?" she asked.

Keith said, "I'm going to follow a few more leads. I think I know where they are."

"Where?"

In a crack house operated by part-time human traffickers, part-time drug addicts, he told himself. *What else can I say? They're being molested and raped for some perverted bastard's video collection? They're being sent to Mexico to work as prostitutes? It's all awful, honey, and I hate myself for taking so long to get to this point.*

Coat in hand, Lisa approached him and repeated, "Where?"

"I'll... I'll let you know later."

"You're keeping me in the dark again," Lisa said. Her voice had changed from smooth to hoarse due to all of her recent sobbing. She asked, "Can you give me something, Keith? Can you help me feel like I'm... like I'm actually important to you and this family? I want to help for Christ's sake. Tell me: are my babies okay?

Is this–this–this *blood* something I should worry about?"

Keith marched into the garage, his bare feet slapping the concrete. Early morning sunshine poured into the room through the garage door windows and warmed his back. He filled a duffel bag with a coil of rope, a hammer, and a box cutter. He grabbed his service pistol from a locker—a Glock 17—along with two extra seventeen-round magazines. A small self-defense revolver, a riot shotgun, and a bulletproof vest followed. He loaded the weapons with the appropriate ammunition, ensuring he was ready to shoot to kill.

To Lisa, it looked like her husband was preparing for war. But the streets of Montaño had been quiet since the girls vanished a week ago. The police discovered Jim's body in his apartment, but they kept the brutal details under wraps so they could get ahead in the investigation. Dwight's disappearance went unnoticed by most people in the city. Dozens of questions ran through her mind, but, at the end of the day, she trusted her husband and she only cared about her daughters.

Knocking echoed through the home. Keith looked at the garage door, Lisa stared into the house through the doorway. They looked as if they had expected a raid. Someone knocked again—*tap, tap, tap*. Lisa hid the bloody coat in the washing machine. She washed her hands, then she rushed to the front door. Keith zipped up the duffel bag. He hid it under his bed, put on a t-shirt, and then he headed to the door.

In the living room, he found his wife standing on her tiptoes and peeking through the peephole. Upon feeling his presence in the room, she glanced over at him and mouthed: *Eddie.*

"I'll handle it," Keith said as he beckoned to her.

He opened the door. As expected, Captain Eduardo 'Eddie' Martinez stood on his porch. He removed his cowboy hat and shook Keith's hand.

"How you holdin' up?" he asked.

"We're, um... We're holding up, I guess. What's going on? What are you doing here?"

"I have some news and I figured you'd want to hear this from me in person."

Lisa asked, "Did you find them? Are they safe?"

Keith furrowed his brow and shook his head. He wondered if the police had already raided the crack house.

Trying to keep his composure, he said, "Okay. Do you want to come in for some coffee?"

"No, no," Eddie responded. "I unfortunately don't have time to sit today. It's going to be a busy one for me. I still have some men combing the woods. Plenty of volunteers, too. I came to tell you about Sullivan and Garcia."

"Yeah? How's their investigation going?"

"Well, they've informed me that they suspect foul play, but–"

Lisa covered her mouth and gasped.

"*But,*" Eddie repeated. "They haven't found a reason to believe that they've been injured. I'm sure you've heard about the suspected 'struggle' in the woods. We have reason to believe your girls, as well as a young Brooke Page, we're abducted at that site."

Eyes unblinking, Lisa stepped forward and asked, "Who? Who took them? Did you find out? Are you getting them out now?"

"Well, ma'am, the bad news is: I can't promise you we'll find them today. The good news is: we have three possible suspects and we will be conducting three simultaneous raids this evening. There's a chance, Mrs. Klein. Yeah, there's a chance we can find them today."

Lisa was overwhelmed by relief and fear. Although she experienced one disappointment after another, she couldn't stop herself from hoping for the best. She imagined herself hugging her daughters and welcoming them home with a homecooked meal. At the same time, the worst possibilities crept into her mind and stabbed at her brain: *they were kidnapped, they were injured, they're dead.*

"Who are you raiding?" Keith asked. Eddie hesitated. Keith said, "You've kept us in the dark long enough, Captain. We're getting updates from Tracy Farnsworth instead of you. Give us something."

Eddie sighed, then he said, "We'll be raiding the home of Saul Castro, a convicted sex offender who cut his bracelet a few months ago. We've also got a lead on a thug, Jaime Pulido, who was arrested for the attempted kidnapping of a child about a decade ago. He's suspected of possessing and distributing some 'obscene material' now. And then we have Jared Wilder. Sure, he's mentally-impaired, but he was spotted on Hill Lane on the day of the disappearance and he has been caught harassing kids outside of schools before."

"A sex offender, a child kidnapper, and a 'mentally impaired' man harassing kids at schools?" Lisa said, face wrinkled in disgust. "Why are these people out on the streets? They should be arrested. No, they… Why aren't these bastards castrated?"

While Eddie and Lisa discussed the suspects, Keith's mind wandered off. He thought about Saul Castro, Jaime Pulido, and Jared Wilder. Saul and Jaime were capable of kidnapping and harming children, but he wasn't sure about Jared. Fortunately, he trusted the police to raid their homes and interrogate the men without remorse.

Instead, he focused on Jim Phillips, Alvin Vaughn, and the crack house. His investigation led him to an underworld of Montaño that even the police didn't know about. His thoughts were interrupted as his boss patted his shoulder.

Eddie said, "There's one more thing. If we don't find those girls tonight, if we don't find a new lead, I will be calling the Feds for help. You see…" He smacked his lips, grunted, then said, "Our resources will be spread thin soon. Sullivan and Garcia can't work this case forever because, well, we've discovered a homicide. As a matter of fact, just before I got here, I got called about *another* body at the Bonita Motel. That's two in one week, Klein. That's a record for us out here. Something's not right. I don't like the smell of it, you get me?"

"I get you, Captain," Keith responded. "Find my girls and maybe it'll put an end to the crime and violence. If you need any help, you're welcome to reinstate me."

"Yeah, yeah... Keep your nose clean, kid. Don't meddle."

Lisa stepped between the men. She jabbed her finger at Eddie's chest and said, "Find. My. Girls. If they turn up de... de... if they're hurt, it will be on *you*. I think our girls are more important than whatever the hell you're trying to get at right now. Stop wasting time. Please, Eddie."

Eddie nodded and said, "Okay, alright. I'll be back to give you an update as soon as possible. Stay safe and stay strong."

Lisa slammed the door. She leaned back against it, closed her eyes, and sniveled. She fought for her husband, but she was weakened by the news. The kidnapping was confirmed. Kidnappings were either peaceful or violent—there was no middle ground. She taught her daughters to run at the first sign of trouble. She feared her daughters could have been injured if they followed her advice.

She opened her eyes upon hearing a set of footsteps in front of her. Keith approached the door, dressed with the duffel bag slung over his shoulder.

He said, "I'm going to drive out to Gerald's office. Then we're going to follow-up on our lead."

"Aren't you worried about Eddie?" Lisa asked as Keith exited the house. "What if he knows about this?"

"I'm not and he doesn't. Truth is: he doesn't want to know. Just wait for me, keep a lookout, and be ready for anything."

As her husband exited the house, Lisa said, "Be careful. I... I lo..." Keith walked down to his vehicle in the driveway without saying another word. As she watched him drive off, Lisa whispered, "I love you."

Chapter Twenty-One

Sex Ed

"Why are you sitting all the way over there, sweetie?" Riley asked.

He squatted near the center of the room. He played it safe, keeping his distance so she wouldn't surprise him with another attack. Dale stood in the doorway behind him, breathing noisily under his pig mask. He tapped his foot, too. He was excited about something.

Carrie didn't move from her corner. She watched the single slit of sunshine seeping past the boarded window. To protect herself, she emptied her mind and thought about nothing. She loved her sister, but she couldn't handle the pain. She had reached the fourth stage of grief: *depression.* Yet, she continued to sniffle and shudder. Her sister's corpse lay in the opposite corner, eyes still open.

Riley said, "I'm sorry. I didn't want it to end this way. I liked her. Your sister was very sweet and gentle during our time together." He chuckled and said, "She didn't cut me like you did."

Carrie heard all of Riley's words, although she tried to block the world out. She sneered at him, disgusted by his laughter. *Fuck you!*—she caught the shout in her throat. Her chest and throat hurt due to her excessive crying. If she had screamed at him, her voice would have cracked. She didn't want Riley to laugh at her frailty, too.

Riley continued, "You know, it's kind of your fault. I didn't do anything to you, but you attacked me. Look at what you did to my face. My soft, beautiful face... It's nothing compared to what I did to your sister. That's what you're thinking, right? But I'm a model. I'm a *celebrity*. I was supposed to star in movies. You've made that much more difficult for me. You... You might have destroyed my career. So, in a sense, you killed me. A life for a life. That's fair, isn't it?"

"Leave me alone," Carrie said softly.

"Ah, *there* you are. You feel guilty, don't you? That's why you're so silent. It's okay to feel guilty about killing your sister. It's normal, really."

"I didn't kill my sister. You did it. You and that pig and that wolf. She was probably... dead before I cut you. You're just lying because you–you're crazy."

"That's not true. I'm telling the truth. If it weren't for you, I would have let her live. Lil' Allie was my favorite girl. I will never forget the time we spent together. Gone too soon, huh?"

For a moment, Carrie believed him. His voice was tender, so he sounded honest and caring. His eyes revealed his true deviance, though. She huffed at him and rolled her eyes.

She said, "I don't believe you. Even if you're telling the truth, you still... you... you killed her. I didn't touch her. You didn't even let me see her. You... You... You bitch."

Riley frowned and lowered his head. He flicked his finger at the splinters protruding from a floorboard. He appeared sad and remorseful. Then he smiled.

The smile led to a snicker, and then his signature cackle followed. He was proud of himself. His performance was convincing. His career in acting was still promising.

He said, "Okay, you were right. I killed her just a *short* while before you stabbed me. The game, the bruises, *the show*, that was all because of you. I wouldn't have done that if you didn't attack me." He stood up and began pacing. He said, "I taught your sister a few things about sex while she was alive. She was inexperienced—*obviously*—and I'm sure you're not anything different. So, how about I teach you a thing or two?"

"No. Don't. Do whatever you want, just stop talking."

"No, no, no. That's one thing I can't do. I love talking. I love the sound of my voice. It's sexy, or so I've been told. And I need to teach you about sex so you understand what I'm going to do to you."

"I won't listen," Carrie said as she placed her hands over her ears.

Speaking louder but not shouting, Riley said, "There's normal sex. That's the penis going into the vagina. There are your typical handjobs, blowjobs, rim jobs... Well, maybe you don't know much about that last one. A rim job is when one of the participants licks the other's anus." He flicked his tongue at her and giggled. He continued, "There's more, though. In layman's terms, bondage is when a participant is made into a slave. It's kinda like your position now: chained up. There's, uh... sadomasochism, too. It's not exactly sex, but it's… How do I explain it? It's when you feel sexual pleasure from giving or receiving pain. I'm a sadomasochist. You probably know that already. I don't know why, I just love seeing people squirm. Tears are like water to me. I need it for survival. Anyway, let's move on to something a little more interesting. Did you know that there are people out there who *fuck* animals? Yes, they *fuck* animals. Someone, somewhere, is sticking his dick in a cow or a dog right now. Maybe in some barn in rural America or some shithole country. But it's *really* happening. Think about that. Fucking crazy, but… I can't really judge until I've tried it myself, I guess."

"Why won't you shut up?" Carrie cried.

With all of her strength, she pressed her palms against her ears and tried to block out the noise. She felt as if she had placed her head in a vise. Riley spoke louder with each sentence, forcing her to hear every nasty, awful word.

He knelt down in front of her and said, "You don't hear a lot about it on the news. Animals are innocent just like children, but you never see a protest against animal-fuckers, right? I think that's wrong. The relationship between adults and children is 'taboo.' Do you know what that means? It means it's frowned upon by society. It's illegal, too. You know what I'm talking about, don't you? It's all that other stuff—fucking, blowjobs, handjobs, etcetera—but between an adult and a kid. I think things can always get worse, though. Have you ever heard of necrophilia?"

Nothing, nothing, nothing—Carrie repeated the

word in her head, trying to drown out the noise with her inner-voice. It didn't work very well.

Riley said, "It's when you fuck a corpse—*a dead body*. I fucked Allie, then I killed her, and then I fucked her again."

"Shut up! Get out! Leave me alone!"

"No, I'm here to teach you a lesson. I want you to be ready 'cause you're next, and your time is coming."

"I'll kill you!" Carrie shouted as she slapped him. She struck him again with her other hand. She cried, "My dad is going to kill you! We'll never forgive you! You monster!"

Riley stepped back. He rubbed his pink cheeks. A droplet of blood hung from his upper lip. Her slaps aggravated the cut, causing him to bleed. He licked the blood off his lip and smiled.

He said, "Pig-man, you can start now."

Dale rushed into the room, tripping over himself. He had been waiting for those words. He fell to his knees beside Allie's body. The outline of his erection was visible against his coveralls. He unzipped his clothes as quickly as possible, shaking so bad that he looked like he was dancing.

Carrie closed her eyes and covered her ears. Riley sat beside her. He grabbed her, pulled her over his lap, and pried her eyelids open with his fingers. Carrie shrieked for five seconds, then a coughing spell interrupted her. She watched as Dale removed all of his clothes, revealing his soft, sweaty, and hairy body. He didn't take off the pig mask, though. He threw the blanket aside, then he trembled with excitement, like a child who just unwrapped a wonderful present on Christmas Day.

Carrie jerked and wiggled, she coughed and wheezed, but she couldn't escape from Riley's grip. She tried to close her eyes, but Riley dug his long fingernails under her eyelids and forced them open. A surge of adrenaline stopped her from fainting. She could only watch in horror as Dale defiled her sister's corpse.

The pig's actions in that room were indescribable.

Chapter Twenty-Two

The Raid

Keith leaned against the wall beside the front door, a pistol in his right hand and a flashlight in the other. He wore a bulletproof vest over his flannel. Gerald stood across from him, back against the wall. Sweat rolled down his face while his stiff limbs shuddered. He was armed with a handgun, but his torso wasn't protected by a bulletproof vest. He was vulnerable.

"I'll go first," Keith whispered. "Count to fifteen, then follow. Are you ready?"

Barely moving his head, Gerald nodded. The raid was dangerous and illegal. It was lunchtime, the neighborhood was abandoned, but the risks remained high. A pedestrian could have walked by, heard the commotion, and informed the police. Or, even worse, a police officer could have wandered into the neighborhood out of curiosity. But he couldn't turn back.

Keith kicked the door. His steel-toe boot cracked the wood. He stepped back, then he kicked it again. The door burst open. The sound of the wood snapping and popping echoed through the street.

He shouted, "Police! Police! Let me see your hands!"

He walked into the kitchen. A table at the center stood on two legs, slanted like a ramp. The cabinet doors were either broken off or swinging on one hinge. The refrigerator door was missing. The shelves stored stacks of paper as well as some dirty dishes with rotten food. Drug paraphernalia—glass pipes, plastic bottles, burnt spoons, lighters, aluminum foil—littered the counters. There was no one in sight.

Gerald counted slowly: *one-Mississippi, two-Mississippi, three-Mississippi, four-Mississippi, five-Mississippi.*

Keith made his way through the archway and entered the dining table. Some rolls of cash, held together by rubber bands, sat on a dusty dining table on top of some stacks of paper. From a quick glance, he made out some addresses crudely-written on the paper—*delivery addresses? Drop-off points?* There was no one in the room.

Six-Mississippi, seven-Mississippi, eight-Mississippi, nine-Mississippi, ten-Mississippi.

Keith went through another archway. Through a doorless doorway on his right, he could see the staircase and the front door.

He entered the living room instead. The tube television was broken. Someone had kicked it with a heavy boot. Bookcases hugged the walls, but the trash and drug paraphernalia replaced any books that once sat on those shelves. The sofa and recliners were covered in dust, urine, feces, and blood. The coffee table was dusted with leftover cocaine and stained with blood. Again, there was no one in sight.

He rushed through another archway and found himself near the front door. He marched up the stairs, his finger on the trigger.

Eleven-Mississippi, twelve-Mississippi, thirteen-Mississippi, fourteen-Mississippi, fifteen-Mississippi.

By the time Gerald entered the house, Keith was already clearing the bedrooms on the second floor. Gerald retraced his steps on the first floor.

Keith kicked a door open and shouted, "Police! Po–"

Mid-sentence, a bullet struck him in the abdomen. The bullet became lodged in the bulletproof vest, but it felt like someone had hit him with a sledgehammer to the gut. The flash from the muzzle temporarily blinded him, too. It gave him a vague idea of the shooter's location, though. He staggered back as two more gunshots rang out. The bullets whizzed past him. He took cover behind a wall.

The shooter shouted, "Don't you fuck with–"

Keith connected the flash of the muzzle and the voice to locate the shooter—*kneeling behind the dresser.* He jumped out from around the corner and let off four rounds. The shooter shot back once before a bullet struck his collarbone and exited through his shoulder. A second bullet entered his jaw and exited out the opposite cheek, tearing through his gums, tongue, and teeth. A severed piece of his tongue slid out of his mouth. He dropped the gun and fell to his side, moaning.

"Don't move!" Keith barked.

He barreled into the room, grimacing in pain. He kicked the gun away from the shooter, then he scanned the rest of the bedroom with his flashlight. A dilapidated bed frame sat to his left. The mattress was missing. There was a single nightstand nearby. The closet was open, revealing the mountain of garbage bags inside.

The man on the ground wore a pair of soiled, oversized briefs. His long, graying hair was painted black by soot and grime. There were track marks across his arms as well as bruises between his toes and fingers. The blood from his wounds spread from his jaw to his neck and his shoulder to his hand. Fragments of his teeth fell out of his mouth like crumbs from a graham cracker.

"You–You... You ain't... no cop," the man mumbled, his hand on his jaw.

Gerald heard the shooting from the kitchen. He thought about running out of the house to call for backup, but he could only think about Keith's safety. He muttered to himself—*what the hell am I thinking?*—as he ran up the stairs. He looked down the hall to his right, then to his left. He heard the sound above him in the kitchen, so he concluded the shooting occurred in one of the rooms on the left.

As he crept down the hall, he shouted, "Keith! Keith, are you–"

He gasped as a nude woman wielding a box cutter stumbled out of the last room to his right. The woman screeched as she lunged at Keith from the hallway. Keith glanced over his shoulder and caught a glimpse of her just as she pounced. He wasn't some trained gunslinger in a Western movie. He couldn't draw, aim, and fire with pinpoint accuracy in less than a second, even at close range. He froze up, his life flashing before his eyes. The woman swung the box cutter at his neck.

Five gunshots echoed through the house.

The woman missed his neck by a meter. The box cutter fell out of her hand. She teetered until she hit the wall, then she fell onto the garbage bags in the closet. There were five gunshot wounds on her left side—one in her shoulder, two in her ribs, one in her abdomen, and the last in her hip. Gerald shot her, and he didn't miss a single shot.

Keith kicked the man and hissed, "Don't do anything stupid, motherfucker."

He grabbed the man's handgun, then he went into the hall. He stopped in his tracks. Gerald continued to aim the gun at the doorway, his eyes blank like a kid addicted to Saturday morning cartoons. He had no intentions of shooting Keith. He had never shot anyone before. It was a shocking experience.

Keith pushed his arms down and forced him to lower his gun. He said, "It's okay, it's alright. You saved me, brother. Thank you." Gerald didn't say a word. Keith said, "Gerald, I know what it feels like, but you did the right thing. You know that, don't you?"

A single tear clinging to his left eye, Gerald asked, "Is she dead? Did I kill her?"

"I don't know. She would have killed me if you didn't shoot, though. I know that, at least."

"Am I a murderer?"

"Gerald..."

Keith couldn't answer the question. He didn't want to call himself a murderer for killing Jim and Alvin, so he didn't feel right pinning the title on Gerald. But, at the end of the day, there was no gray area. Premeditated, an act of passion, or accidental, you were either a murderer or you weren't.

The sound of footsteps emerged from the third floor.

Keith said, "There's a perp at the end of the hall. I think he's drugged out and he's already been shot. Keep an eye on him. I'll clear the rest of the house." He shook Gerald's shoulder and said, "Hey. Gerald, can you do that for me? Gerald, can you hear me?"

"Y–Yeah, I–I can do that."

"I'll be right back, okay? *Okay?*"

"O–Okay."

Keith went up the stairs. He shouted, "Police! Show me your hands!"

Gerald entered the bedroom, his weapon down. He found the shooter on the floor under the boarded window. The man rolled from side to side, twitching and moaning in pain. He could barely move his left arm due to his shattered shoulder. He used his good hand to keep his mouth shut. He thought his jaw would fall from his skull if he didn't hold it up. Blood kept oozing out of his sealed lips, staining his mouth, cheeks, chin, and neck.

Gerald sniffled as he looked at the woman. She passed away in a crack house, face-down in a pile of garbage. Her arm was tied off and a needle protruded from the crook of her elbow. She was shooting up heroin during the raid. She was unaware of their intentions. She probably thought it was a robbery.

Guilt burdened him, haunting his mind with endless 'maybes.'

Maybe she was innocent. Maybe she was a product of her environment. Maybe she had a family. Maybe she didn't deserve to die.

Keith entered a room on the third floor. The blue walls, decorated with fluffy clouds, were stained with a dark liquid—*feces? Blood? Coca-Cola?* Behind the broken baby crib at the center of the room, a young man in tattered, disheveled clothing attempted to reload a double-barrel shotgun. He squeezed the barrels of the firearm between his shaking knees. Shotgun shells fell out of his hands, bouncing on the floorboards like Mexican jumping beans.

"Drop it!" Keith demanded. "Put your hands up! Now!"

The man stopped fiddling with the gun as the second shell entered the chamber. He stared at Keith, but he couldn't identify him because of the flashlight. He closed the shotgun and raised it.

Keith shot him in the chest three times. The bullets broke his ribs and punctured his lungs. He cleared the room—*empty*. He grabbed the shotgun, then he checked the man's pulse. It was weak, but he clung to life. His nostrils flared as he struggled to breathe.

Keith said, "Damn it. I didn't want to shoot you, but you left me no choice. Stupid kid… If I'm wrong about this and if you can hang in there, I'll take you to a hospital. Don't move."

He exited the room, aiming the double-barrel shotgun down the hall. He checked the nearby bedrooms. The rooms were empty. One of the rooms was devoid of furniture. Blood stained the floorboards, though. He didn't know it, but it resembled the rooms at the abandoned house in the woods. Snuff films were shot there on more than one occasion.

He approached the last door at the other end of the hall.

"Freeze!" he shouted.

He found a young woman standing in what appeared to be a home office. The woman wore a white camisole and matching panties. There were track marks on her arms and groin—another heroin addict. She couldn't have been older than twenty-one. She was dumping gasoline on a pile of cardboard boxes in the corner of the room.

Keith entered the room and said, "Step away from the boxes. Go on, move."

The woman raised her hands over her head and stepped back. Tears dripped from her eyes, mucus rolled over her lips.

She stuttered, "My–My–My name is Ver–Veronica. Veronica Walton. I–I go to Montaño Community College. I went there, I mean. Pl–Please don't kill me. You can have the cash and the stash. It–It's yours, okay?"

Keith said, "These are tapes... What's on them?"

"I–I–I don't know."

Keith aimed the shotgun at her. He said, "I know what's on the tapes. You worked for Alvin Vaughn, the Ice Cream Man. Do you know more about his operation?"

"N–No," Veronica said, blatantly reluctant.

"Is that your final answer?"

"I don't know shit, I swear."

"That's not what I wanted to hear."

"Wha–"

Keith pulled the first trigger. The shotgun blast was louder than the gunfire from his pistol. The weapon roared like a wild beast. Veronica was launched back against the wall behind her, her chest riddled with pellets. She stared at Keith with wide eyes, then she slid down to the floor. She drew short, raspy breaths for twenty seconds. She whispered something—*a last plea for mercy? Her final goodbyes?* She died with her eyes stuck on Keith.

He exited the room and returned to the nursery. The young man was alive, panting and weeping. He mumbled to himself about death and drugs. He wanted one more hit before passing away.

Keith crouched beside him and said, "You won't tell me about the makers of those tapes, either, will you?" The young man stared at the ceiling, his eyes distant as if he were staring into the heavens above. Keith said, "Maybe you can't. I shot you up pretty good. But, as it turns out, you're guilty. I was right, so the offer's off the table. Any last words?"

"One… One last… hit," the man croaked out.

"Sorry, kid. I don't have any dope for you. Just close your eyes. I'll put you out of your misery."

The young man swallowed loudly, then he closed his eyes. Tears ran down the sides of his face, falling from his ears to the floor. Keith aimed the shotgun at his head. He took a deep breath, then he pulled the second trigger. The close-range shotgun blast blew a chunk off his forehead. Bits of his brain, pieces of his scalp, and shards of his skull splattered on the floor. His mutilated brain, chunky and bloody, was visible through the massive crater on his head. His left eye was detached from its socket, too, hanging *into* his skull and touching his brain.

Keith walked back to the bedroom with Gerald, the shooter, and the dead woman. Gerald sat on the bed frame, rattled by his actions. The shooter stayed on the floor with a puddle of blood forming under him.

Keith said, "Let's make this quick. I know about Alvin Vaughn, 'the Ice Cream Man.' I know about the tapes. The murder, the pornography, the distribution network... I know all about that. Right now, I need to find the creator of these tapes. I need the source. You understand me?"

"Fu–Fuck you. You a–ain't no cop," the shooter said, mouth half-closed.

"You're wrong about that, but it doesn't matter. Your friends are dead. All of them. If you don't want to end up like them—*or worse*—you'll tell me about the source. Who gave the Ice Cream Man those tapes?"

"You–You're crazy. I don't know shit."

Keith placed the muzzle of the handgun against the man's right bicep. He said, "I can shoot you a dozen times across your body and still keep you alive for thirty minutes. Maybe even an hour. It'll be the

Into the Wolves' Den 219

worst pain you've ever experienced. I won't give you another 'hit,' either. I'll melt that heroin and shoot it up into that corpse. What a waste, huh?"

"Fu–Fuck..."

"You know something. Tell me and I'll let you walk out of this house. You can keep all of the drugs and money, too. This isn't a robbery, buddy. I just want information. Who made those tapes?"

"Okay, o–okay. There's a house... a house in the woods. It's far, far, *far* from this damn shithole. You, um... You get on Hill Lane and drive out of town, you see? Before you... Before you hit the interstate, there–there's a dirt road. It's got two big fuckin' rocks on each side. Drive through there... you–you'll stop at a tree, you know? Like a–a trunk or whatever you wanna call it. It's layin' there on the road. Then you just go on-foot until you find an old house. It's like one of them haunted houses. A... An abandoned house. That's it. That's where they make 'em. I think..."

"You think?" Keith responded. "And what makes you think that?"

"I followed that damn ice cream truck once. I–I was going to blackmail 'em, you see? But Veronica, that scared cunt, she told everyone it was a bad idea. Fuck, look where we are now, huh? You killed her, didn't ya? The young cunt upstairs? I don't smell a fire, so I know she could–couldn't do her damn job right. And you–you're going to kill me next, a–ain't ya?"

Keith memorized all of the information—*down*

Hill Lane, dirt road surrounded by rocks, fallen tree, walk to a house. He was daring, but he wasn't stupid. He understood the risks of the raid. Someone could have heard the gunshots and called the police. He was out of time.

He said, "At least you're right about that last part."

Gerald said, "Keith, wait. Let's–"

At point-blank range, Keith shot the man in the head, right between his eyes. Gerald sighed in disappointment.

As he walked out, Keith said, "Let's go before more of them show up. I don't want to bump heads with the cops, either."

Gerald sat in the room for another thirty seconds, listening to the sound of Keith's footsteps. He entered the house as an honest, honorable, and kind private investigator. He left the house as a deceitful, cowardly, and violent killer. He drove off, unable to look at himself in the reflections of his mirrors. They drove around town, trying to place the vehicle everywhere except the crack house. Keith didn't want the police to suspect them when he was so close to the finish line.

At dusk, Gerald stopped the car in Keith's driveway. They sat in silence. They didn't discuss the raid after it occurred.

Breaking the silence, Keith said, "I'm sorry about what you saw in there, about what you had to do to save me. I don't want you to help me anymore. You'll still get all of the credit for finding the girls, but... you were never here. Go home, sleep it off, and move on with your life. I'll take care of everything else." He exited the car. Before closing the door, he said, "I can never thank you enough for everything you've done for me. I'm really sorry."

Gerald drove off without saying another word. Less than a quarter mile away from the Klein house, he pulled over on the side of the road. He struck the steering wheel and screamed, devastated by the massacre.

Chapter Twenty-Three

Round Five

"You were paid handsomely," Riley said as he paced back-and-forth in the hall. "We paid in cash. I even tipped you! Now you're saying I can't play with my toys?"

Allen leaned against the door to Carrie's room with his arms crossed and his face steady with a dull expression. Dale stood behind him while Chuck stood behind Riley.

Allen said, "We had an agreement, and we've fulfilled our end of said agreement. As a matter of fact, *kid,* we've done more than what you paid for. Your fee covered two bodies: a kid and an adult. You played with the younger one for days and you slaughtered your 'special order' in the basement. Then we got you that homeless fella. We didn't complain because that was an easy job and we aim to satisfy our customers, but this kid is far more valuable than some bum. I have clients across the country... No, around the *world,* who would pay a premium price to play with a girl like this. I can sell her to some millionaire in the Middle East looking for a child bride, to a cartel looking for a foreign prostitute or a drug mule, or to the Chinese so they can harvest her organs. That girl is money. She. Is. *Money.*"

"So what are you saying? Hmm? You want me to

pay for her? Is that it?"

Allen chuckled, then he said, "Well, that's obvious, isn't it?"

"How much?"

"One hundred twenty-five."

Riley stopped pacing. He glanced over at his bodyguard, then he huffed at Allen.

He said, "I'm guessing we're not talking about one hundred and twenty-five dollars."

"*Obviously.*"

"One hundred twenty-five thousand. That's more than my last fee."

Allen smirked and said, "I know. Oh, I know. You see, we're talking about supply-and-demand. I have one girl left and you *really* want her. Therefore, the price has gone up. Like I said before, if you can't afford her, we have plenty of other clients who will happily take her. Some of them might pay double after they see her. Nasty men love innocent things."

The side of Riley's mouth twitched as he smiled. He was irritated and infuriated, but he tried to hide his rage from Allen. He didn't want to give him another reason to act so smug. He nodded at him. Keith beckoned to Dale. Dale handed Riley a cell phone.

Riley dialed a number, then he held the phone up to his ear. He tapped his foot as he waited for the call to connect.

He said, "Donate one hundred twenty-five thousand to the 'special' account." He paused for a minute and nodded, listening to the other person. He said, "It won't bother my dad. It's part of my allowance anyway. Get it done by tonight."

He disconnected the call and handed the phone to Allen.

Still smiling, Allen said, "I'm going to call your dad to confirm the deal. If you're trying to pull a fast one, I guarantee you and your little bodyguard will both be dead by midnight."

Riley responded, "You can call him or one of his assistants whenever you want. You have the numbers. I did my part, now it's time for you to do yours." He marched up to Allen, leaving a foot of space between them. He said, "Let me play."

The smile was wiped off Allen's face. Riley pushed him to his boiling point with his disrespectful behavior, but Allen didn't move a muscle. He wanted Riley to make the first move so he could have an excuse to hurt him. Instead, the men glared at each other.

Riley said, "I can see the *stupidity* in your eyes. You speak like a smart one, like an 'intellectual,' but you're controlled by your emotions. And emotional people are stupid people. I'm under your skin. I can see that. You want to kill me. I can see that, too. But, if you touched me, you know my father would mow this place down with a thousand bullets. Hell, he'd knock it down with machine guns. That's not something you want, especially with one hundred twenty-five thousand *fucking* dollars coming your way. So drop the tough-guy act and let me play with my toy."

Allen tossed the phone at Dale and said, "Call our

source. I want to speak to him." He unlocked the door and said, "Don't get injured this time. We're responsible for your safety, but not when you break our rules. And don't forget to have fun."

He opened the door and beckoned to him—*get your ass in there*. Riley sneered at him as he entered the room. Then, Allen closed the door behind him.

"Keep your eyes on him this time," Allen instructed. He took the phone from Dale and said, "I'll be in my office. Call me if anything goes wrong... *again.*"

Riley muttered, "I'm going to kill that asshole." He sighed, then he grinned at Carrie. He asked, "Did you miss me?"

Carrie sat in the corner, facing the wall. She was alive, but she appeared motionless. Her breathing was slow, calm and composed. The room had been silent since his last visit. She didn't scream or whimper or talk to herself. The noxious stench hanging over the room didn't bother her anymore, either. She was physically and mentally defeated by the abuse.

Her sister's corpse lay on the floor on the other side of the room, face-down. The blanket covered most of her torso. Her legs were snapped at the kneecaps, causing the back of her knees to point up at the ceiling. A bone poked through an open fracture on her left leg. Her left arm was broken at the forearm, the other was snapped at the elbow. The men destroyed her body during their acts of deviant sex.

Riley stepped on the back of Allie's head. He twirled his foot, as if he were trying to get gum off his boot.

He said, "Too bad about your sister. But I hope you took notes, my precious princess, because I just paid a *whole* lot of money to play with you. It's time for Round Five."

He grabbed a fistful of her hair and dragged her away from the corner. He slapped her twice—palm first, backhand second—then he pushed her to the floor beside her sister. Carrie didn't yelp or sob, although her cheeks reddened due to the powerful force behind the slaps. She stared up at Riley, unfazed by his attack.

"You toughened up," Riley said. "That's great. It's fabulous. I love durable toys, sweetheart. Now I can get my money's worth."

He mounted Carrie's waist. He swung down at her, pummeling her face with a barrage of jabs and hooks—left, right, left, right, left, left, right, *right*. She lost her hearing in her right ear for a few seconds. Her cheeks swelled up, changing from red to redder to a slight tone of blue. Blood spurted from her mouth as her teeth were pushed into her gums.

Riley grabbed her throat and squeezed it softly. She coughed and wheezed, but she didn't fight back. She starved his sadomasochism by bottling her pain and refusing to give him a reaction. He lifted her head from the floor, then he slammed the back of her head against the floorboard. He repeated the process five times. He smashed his elbow against her head, dropping all of his weight behind each blow. She was knocked unconscious after the first hit to the temple.

Between each blow, he barked, "Scream! You... bitch! Why... won't... you... scream?!"

Carrie awoke during the beating. She coughed again, but she didn't scream. She refused to let him win. The deaths of her sister and best friend simultaneously weakened and strengthened her. She lost everything already, so she couldn't lose again. She was broken until there was nothing left to break. She was unbreakable.

"Goddamn you!" Riley shouted as he beat her.

Chapter Twenty-Four

Goodbye

Keith entered his bedroom. Lisa lay on the bed, her back to the door. There was a bottle of whiskey, a shot glass, and a sealed bottle of sleeping pills on her nightstand. Like leaves littered on a lawn, Polaroid photographs covered the bed around her. Some of the photographs landed on the floor, others were stacked on the nightstand near the booze. She took a drunken trip down memory lane.

He sat on the bed and checked her pulse. To his utter relief, she was alive. His wife always kept a bottle of sleeping pills on her nightstand. But suicide had crossed his mind several times since the disappearance of their daughters. He believed Lisa considered it on more than one occasion as well. Carrie and Allie stopped them from killing themselves, though.

Without looking back at him, Lisa said, "I was alone today. I'm alone every day, actually. I call people. Lynn comes over sometimes. So does Janice. I see you almost every night and every morning. But it doesn't change the fact that I'm alone every day. You're not really here, even when you're *here*. You know what I mean? My girls aren't here, even when I'm looking at their pictures. I don't feel them anymore."

They're not dead—Keith wanted to say those

words, but he didn't know the truth. He believed his daughters were kidnapped by dangerous, deviant people. He rubbed her shoulder, trying to comfort her with his gentle touch.

Lisa continued, "I thought about what Eddie said. Saul, Jaime, and Jared. He didn't repeat those names, but I couldn't forget them. What could a sex offender do to our babies for over a week? What could a thug—a child kidnapper—do to our kids? What could a–a 'mentally-impaired' kid do to our girls? I've read and seen all of the awful things on the news. What if that's happening to Carrie and Allie? What if… what if…"

Keith sniffled and looked away. Warm tears spilled from his eyes and his throat tightened up. He wanted to tell his wife about the tapes and the murders, but he didn't want to overwhelm her. He couldn't tell her about the danger their daughters faced *and* the crimes he committed to discover the truth.

He said, "I know where the girls are. Eddie was right about Hill Lane and the struggle in the woods, but he was wrong about the suspects. That's why he hasn't called. But I'll be honest with you: I think they're still in trouble. It might be worse than some random sex offender or some thug. I don't know if they're injured, I haven't seen any proof of that, but I think they're with some bad people. I'm going to get them back. If I have to kill someone to do it… then I'll do that. I promise you: I *will* bring them home."

Lisa turned over on the bed, wide-eyed. She asked, "Where are they?"

"They're not in Montaño, but they're close. I'll drive out there tomorrow morning."

"Out where?"

"I'm not going to tell you, Lisa, and you can't come with me."

Lisa shouted, "Why?! Why are you always like this?! Why… Why are you pushing me away?"

"It's for your own safety," Keith responded calmly. "It's not because you're useless or because I don't trust you. It's because these are some real dangerous people. I may have to do things that… that you won't want to see. And I don't want you to see what I've become. I–I'm a bad man, honey. I'm a very bad man."

Lisa saw the demons in his eyes. She felt the sincerity in his shaking voice. Yet, she couldn't help but feel proud of him. He was the man she married, the man who vowed to protect his family by any means necessary.

She said, "I'm willing to… to get my hands dirty, too. Okay?"

"I know you are, but I don't think you're ready for it. If you get involved, if you did half the things I did, you'd be haunted forever. You…" He laughed nervously, then he said, "You wouldn't be able to look our girls in their eyes. Stay home tomorrow. Or, if you want to help, go to Lynn's or Janice's at sunrise. Get the police to focus on you, then I'll head out to settle things."

"Are you sure about this? You're talking like… like I'm never going to see you again."

"I'm going to bring them home. That's the only

thing I'm sure about."

Keith exited the room. He went to the garage. He reloaded the magazine, placed a few more in his bag, and loaded an ammunition belt with shotgun shells. He tossed a baton, a taser, and a ski mask into the duffel bag, too. He remembered their family trip to the snowy mountains a few years prior as he stared at the ski mask.

Lisa watched him from the doorway, sad but appreciative. Keith's sacrifice broke her heart and rekindled her hope at the same time.

Keith said, "I'm going to leave you a note with all of the information you need. I don't plan on dying or disappearing, but... just in case, you know? Gerald knows everything, too. I'll head out after you leave tomorrow. If you don't hear from me in twenty-four hours, take Gerald to Eddie. Tell Gerald to tell him everything about me, my actions, and our investigation. As long as our girls come home safely, I'm okay with whatever they say about me."

Lisa wiped the tears from her eyes and said, "I understand."

Keith approached her. He placed his hands on her hips, he kissed her forehead, and then he hugged her.

He said, "I'm sorry for everything. This is... This is our goodbye for now. I'll do my best, but I can't promise much. I'm just going to save the girls. I have to. God, I'm sorry. I'm fucking sorry, Lisa."

Lisa dug her fingernails into his back and sobbed into his chest. She wanted to say the same: *I'm fucking sorry.*

Chapter Twenty-Five

Search and Rescue

A squirrel scampered across the gnarled surface of the fallen tree trunk. Birds chirped and bounced on the branches of the surrounding trees. A gust of wind carried the autumn leaves across the woodland. There were no people, vehicles, or houses in sight. The main road wasn't visible through the rearview mirror, either. The area was abandoned.

Keith climbed out of his police cruiser. He slid the ski mask over his head and put on his bulletproof vest. He placed the small revolver in an ankle holster and his pistol in the back of his waistband. He threw the duffel bag over his shoulder, then he grabbed the riot shotgun from the backseat. He was ready for war.

He whispered, "So far, so good."

He vaulted over the tree trunk and followed the path on foot. After a mile of walking, he spotted tire marks in the woods a few meters away from the road. After another quarter-mile, he found footprints and a single tire mark on the road. He didn't see or hear anyone, though.

He theorized that the suspects avoided the dirt path and instead drove through the woods while driving to and from the main road. The footprints and the single tire mark told him that someone used a wheelbarrow to move a person or object from a truck. The footprints also said: *you're getting close.*

He crouched and moved away from the dirt road. He walked through the woods while following the path, hiding behind trees and bushes. He moved stealthily, close to the ground with his head down. Time was of the essence, but he couldn't save his daughters if he died before finding them. He had to survive long enough to free them.

He traveled another mile—and then he saw it. A two-story house in the middle of nowhere. Moss and vines spread across the exterior of the building. The windows were boarded, allowing only thin slits of the sunrise sunshine to enter the home. The porch was dilapidated, planks of the wood railing falling apart. It was the abandoned house from the junkie's description.

Yet, there was an expensive Lincoln Town Car parked in the driveway.

Breathing heavily, Keith placed his finger on the shotgun's trigger and said, "He was right. It was all true. Carrie, Allie, I know you're in there. Daddy's coming."

He jogged up a hill. He slid into cover behind the Lincoln Town Car. He noticed the blood on the ground behind the vehicle and he heard *creaking* wood inside of the house. He didn't hear his daughters, though. Their silence was worrisome. He thought about the princess in Jim's tape. *Are they waiting to be molested in some dungeon? Are they gagged right now? Are they dead?*—he thought.

He couldn't wait any longer. He ran onto the porch, the wood howling under his boots. He hugged the wall beside the door. He heard a muffled voice inside of the house.

A man asked, "You hear something?"

Someone responded, but he was farther away, so his voice was barely audible.

Now or never, Keith told himself.

The old, rickety door burst open after a powerful kick. Screws fell to the floor while the doorknob spun in place.

Chuck sat on the sofa in front of the boarded fireplace. A lantern near the fireplace illuminated the room. His hands were full with a paperboard cup of coffee and an Egg McMuffin from McDonald's. It was time for his breakfast break. He barely caught a glimpse of the intruder before Keith shot him from the doorway. The pellets ripped into his right shoulder, causing him to flinch and clench his fists. He crushed the paperboard cup in his hand, drenching his hand in hot coffee. His burned hand shook uncontrollably, his skin changing from white to a rosy pink. The Egg McMuffin crumbled in his fist.

Keith pumped the shotgun, took a step into the house, then shot at him again as Chuck stood up. The second blast hit the small of his back. He felt the pellets puncturing his intestines, burning his organs from within. Despite the unbearable pain, he jumped over the neighboring sofa and hit the floor with a loud *bang*. The landing amplified the pain. He dodged a third shot from Keith. The shotgun blast tore a hole through the wall beside him. Splinters of wood spiraled down to him.

Curtis Cox—the man who tortured Jeremiah Ellison, slicing his face with a box cutter and forcing him to chew on his own testicles—was a regular star in the company's snuff films. He stood in the kitchen, a cup filled with coffee from McDonald's in his right hand. He was killing time, waiting for another body to arrive so he could produce another film. He certainly wasn't expecting a raid. *Police*—it was the first word that popped into his mind.

He grabbed his pistol from the counter and slunk to the archway to his left, his sneakers gliding across the grimy linoleum tiles in the kitchen. He peeked around the corner.

Keith and Curtis spotted each other at the same time, but Keith was quicker on the draw. He fired at the archway, missing Curtis by a few inches. The pellets destroyed a cupboard on the wall.

He pumped the shotgun again and shouted, "Police! Drop your weapons!"

Allen and Dale heard the ruckus from the office on the second floor. Stacks of cardboard boxes sat in every corner of the room. The boxes were filled with videotapes and sheets of paper. The videotapes stored footage of violent murder and deviant, illegal sex while the sheets of paper identified clients, bank accounts, and addresses. Two cell phones, four pagers, and a binder full of client information sat on his desk. There were dozens of burner cell phones and pagers in the desk drawers, too. The men were sitting on a mountain of evidence.

And a man just announced himself as a police

officer downstairs.

Allen cleaned the desktop, pushing everything into a trash can. He grabbed a bottle of charcoal lighter fluid from a drawer. His contingency plan was simple: *burn it all to the ground.*

"Hold 'em off," he said as he squirted the fluid into the trash can. "I just need a few minutes."

Dale hesitated.

"What are you waiting for?!" Allen shouted. "Get out there! Kill them! Kill them all, you stupid son of a bitch!"

Dale stomped and muttered to himself. He drew his revolver and exited the room. Allen peeked through the slit of a boarded window. The *Wolves' Den* was a controversial business. If the authorities knew about it, he expected an army of law enforcement members to surround the house. There were no police cruisers, SWAT trucks, or firetrucks in sight, though. He didn't hear any helicopters, either.

He whispered, "What the hell is going on down there?"

Riley and Carrie heard the gunfire from the bedroom. Carrie was barely conscious. Her eyes were swallowed by her swollen cheeks and forehead, as if she were suffering from a severe allergic reaction. Her cheeks and forehead were painted with tints of blue and purple—dark, painful bruises. Her mouth and chin were covered in blood. Her hearing faded in and out, but she recognized the voice downstairs.

Weak, she said, "Dad–Daddy. I'm–"

Riley slapped his hand over her mouth. He leaned

closer to her face and hissed, "Shut your filthy mouth. Daddy isn't here. He isn't coming." He felt her lips moving on his palm. He cackled, then he said, "You really think it's your dad, don't you? Well, I'll tell you what. I hope it *is* your dad. I want him to see your dead sister, then I want you to watch him die, and then I'll kill *you*. No witnesses, right?"

Carrie fought back, reinvigorated by her father's voice. She scratched at Riley's cheek with one hand and at his neck with the other. She kicked at his legs and wiggled under him, trying her best to squeeze out from under him. Riley wrestled with her, slipping and sliding on top of her.

Keith stepped forward, cycling his aim between Chuck and Curtis. He found a trail of blood leading to the side of the sofa. He spotted Chuck's shaking leg. The man was bleeding out. The unwounded gunman posed a greater threat, though, so he turned his attention to the kitchen.

As Keith took his first step through the archway, Curtis fired at him from behind the kitchen island, emptying his magazine. One bullet hit Keith's torso and knocked the wind out of him, but it didn't penetrate the bulletproof vest. The rest of the bullets struck the walls around him, some missing him by mere centimeters.

Keith shot back, but he missed Curtis by a meter. The pellets hit the boarded window above the sink. Curtis screamed as he leapt out from behind his cover. He grabbed the shotgun and pushed Keith up against the wall. He hit Keith with a headbutt. His forehead hit Keith's jaw, causing it to crack. He injured his own neck in the process. He tried to headbutt him again, but he missed. The side of his brow caressed Keith's ear.

Keith pushed him back towards the island at the center of the kitchen while tugging on the shotgun. He kneed Curtis in the stomach. Curtis staggered, legs wobbling like a drunk's, but his grip didn't loosen. In fact, he nearly yanked the shotgun out of Keith's hands. Keith kneed him again, but Curtis raised his leg and blocked the attack with his own knee. They bounced from the island to the counters and then to the sink.

More gunfire disturbed the house. The men flinched as the bullets struck the walls around them. A bag of McDonald's food on the counter exploded as a bullet struck it. Chuck shot at them with a pistol from the living room floor.

Curtis shouted, "Stop, you fucking idiot! You're going to–"

He stopped as he felt the muzzle of the shotgun on his thigh. He looked Keith in the eye, begging for mercy without saying a word.

Keith pulled the trigger. At point-blank range, the pellets blew a crater into his thigh. Blood splattered on the cupboards under the sink. His jeans were torn to shreds, bloody flaps swaying like flags in the wind. Chunks of his flesh and skin hit the floor—*splat!* Geysers of blood squirted out from the obliterated femoral artery. He screamed and fell to his knees, which boosted the pain in his leg.

Keith pumped the shotgun, placed the muzzle against his head, and pulled the trigger—*nothing.* He was out of shells. Scared of losing his advantage, he tossed the shotgun aside and pulled the baton out of his duffel bag. He held the baton over his head. He hesitated for a second. He saw fear in Curtis' eyes. He was human, not beast.

Curtis cried, "Wait! I have money! I can–"

Keith swung the baton at his head. The vibration of the blow reverberated across the baton and up his arm. Curtis screamed again, but Keith couldn't hear him. A surge of adrenaline caused his ears to ring. He swung at him again. The baton hit Curtis' temple, knocking him unconscious in an instant. He fell to his side, snoring and groaning.

The sound of each blow echoed through the house as the beating continued. *Three thuds, four thuds*—the side of Curtis' head was split open. Blood flowed across his buzz cut hair. *Five thuds, six thuds*—the gash widened and the top half of his ear turned crimson-red. *Seven thuds, eight thuds*—an audible *crack* emerged from his head as his skull was fractured. The blood ran down his forehead and cheeks. *Nine thuds, ten thuds*—Curtis convulsed, saliva frothing on his lips. His eyes moved under his closed eyelids.

Keith stepped back and caught his breath. The baton was bent slightly, blood dripping from the tip. He threw it into the sink. He watched Curtis, analyzing every twitch and moan. The man's limbs locked up as he trembled violently. Blood joined the foaming saliva on his lips. He severed his own tongue during his seizure. He lost complete control of his body.

"You... You bastard," Chuck said weakly from the living room. He shot into the kitchen again as he dragged himself back to the other side of the sofa. He muttered, "Damn it... Goddammit... Shit, I'm dead. I'm dying. I'm... I'm dead."

Keith reloaded the shotgun while keeping his eyes on the archway. Dale stood at the top of the stairs, holding the barrel of his revolver up to his lips, as if he were shushing someone. Allen went from drawer-to-drawer in his office, soaking every file, tape, and device with lighter fluid. Riley and Carrie continued to wrestle. Riley wasn't fully committed to murdering her yet. He paid a pretty penny for her, so he wanted her to survive for as long as possible.

"If you drop the gun and put your hands up, I'll let you limp out of here," Keith announced as he inched towards the archway.

"Go... fuck... yourself," Chuck said as he coughed up blood between every word.

"This is your last warning."

"I'm... I'm ready for you, you cunt."

Keith shot at the front door through the archway—*a distraction.* Chuck grabbed the sofa's armrest and lifted himself up, then he shot at the kitchen. But there was no one there. As soon as the shooting stopped, Keith sidestepped through the archway. He shot at Chuck while moving. The first pellets hit his shoulder and ear. The second blast wiped his face off his skull. The pellets tore pieces of his upper lip and nose off while puncturing his eyeballs and penetrating his cheeks.

Keith shot at him again, but he missed the third blast. Chuck fell back, dead. Keith stopped at the bottom of the stairs, aiming the shotgun at the sofa—unaware of Dale's presence above him. Dale narrowed his eyes as he aimed at the intruder. He wanted to kill him with one shot to the head, but doubt wouldn't allow him to keep his arm steady. He pulled the trigger.

The bullet went through his trapezius. Keith grimaced in pain and stumbled forward. He turned around and shot into the staircase. Splinters of wood and a cloud of sawdust burst into the air, obscuring Dale's vision. Keith tackled the basement door near the staircase. He couldn't stop his momentum. He tumbled down the stairs, bones popping against the edges of the steps. He rolled to a stop at the bottom of the stairs, blood shooting out of his shoulder. His shotgun landed beside him while his supplies fell out of his bag.

Dale crept down the stairs to the first floor. He clenched his jaw upon spotting Chuck's dead body in the living room. He looked at the basement door. He heard the crashing sound, so he knew his prey was down in the basement. He went to the front door and peeked outside. Except for the Lincoln in the driveway, there were no vehicles in the area. He thought: *a one-man raid?*

As he approached the basement door, he said, "You

ain't no cop. You came to rob us. That's why you're wearing that ski mask, huh? That's why you're shooting to kill. Well, little man, I've got to break it to ya: you fucked up. You picked the wrong house. You're dealing with some *real* killers in here, you hear me? And there'll be more of us here soon. You're not getting out of here alive. No way, no how."

He jumped in front of the door and shot down into the basement, emptying the cylinder. From the floor, on his back, Keith shot up at the door. Keith was hit in the leg and chest. The bullet in his leg stopped in his muscle, missing his bones and arteries. Once again, his bulletproof vest saved him from a potentially fatal gunshot, stopping the other bullet before it could penetrate his rib cage. Dale, on the other hand, was hit in the chest. The pellets stopped in his fat and his thick pectoral muscle, unable to puncture any of his vital organs.

Dale lurched down the stairs, holding his revolver from its barrel, like a hammer. Keith tried to shoot at him again, but he was out of ammunition. Dale pounced on him. He dropped his body on top of his and swung the butt of the revolver at his head. Keith's vision faded for a moment. He felt his brain rattling in his skull. He covered his head with his arm and blocked the second blow.

Keith reached for the closest weapon—*a box cutter.* The blade shot out with a rapid succession of *clicks.* He swung it at Dale and sliced his forearm open. An unstoppable flow of blood leaked out of the long wound. Within seconds, the sleeve of his coveralls was heavy with blood. He stabbed him in the chest. He tried to stab him again, but the flimsy blade was bent.

Dale hit him with hooks. His fists—rough, dry, calloused—were like rocks. Every punch was a haymaker. During the beating, he inadvertently aggravated the cut on his forearm. It widened, exposing the white dermis, the yellow fat, and the fibrous muscle underneath to the dirty air. Blood sprinkled from the sleeve of his coveralls, raining down on Keith's mask.

Keith reached for another weapon—*the taser.* He shot it at Dale's stomach. The prong penetrated his abdomen, sending jolts of electricity through his body. He stiffened up and fell to his side. Keith struggled to his feet, teetering in every direction. He bumped into the barrels at the center of the room. One of the barrels fell over. It was empty, but it once stored Allie's body. Another barrel fell over, the lid popping off as it hit the floor. He saw the dead body, but he didn't recognize his old acquaintance—*Dwight Rodgers.*

He drew the handgun from the back of his waistband. Before he could aim, Dale tackled him. He gripped his neck in one hand and pushed his arm up with the other. Keith shot at the ceiling three times. Dale slammed him against the wall and tightened his grip on his neck.

He shouted, "Who the hell are you?!"

Keith felt his life fading away. *He'll snap my neck before he suffocates me,* he thought, *I can't die now, I'm so close.* He was willing to fight dirty to save his daughters. He pulled his leg back, then he thrust it forward. He kneed Dale's crotch with all of his might. Dale crossed his legs and held his breath. Yet, Keith hit his genitals with his knee again. He swore he heard one of his testicles *pop*, like a jaw after a powerful hook.

He rubbed his neck and caught his breath while Dale staggered about with his hands over his crotch. Dale picked up his revolver and headed to the stairs. *Bullets*—it was the only word in his head. Keith grabbed the coil of rope and the bent box cutter. As Dale took his second step up the stairs, Keith wrapped the rope around his neck from behind and pulled him back. The men fell to the floor.

Keith wheezed under Dale's heavy weight, but he wasn't ready to quit. Lightheaded, he wrapped his legs around his body and tugged on the rope, tightening the noose around his neck while restricting his movement.

Dale scratched at his throat, but to no avail. His thick, crusty fingers couldn't fit under the rope. His face and neck reddened, then a wave of sweat splashed his skin. His eyes, as red as his blood, bulged from his skull. Thick veins stuck out from everywhere. After a two-minute struggle, his eyes fell shut and his arms dangled down to his sides.

Keith was a beat cop, but he discovered several murder victims and he stopped a few attempted murders throughout his career. He studied past cases and learned some basic first-aid during his time in the academy, too. He knew it wasn't *that* easy to strangle someone to death. He held the ends of the rope in one hand, keeping the pressure on his neck. He stabbed Dale in the neck with the box cutter, directly through his jugular.

Dale flinched, but his eyes remained closed. Keith dragged the bent blade across his neck. He pulled the box cutter out of him after severing his other jugular. The gash widened as he pulled on the rope. It looked as if he were about to decapitate him. Dark blood cascaded across his neck and soaked the chest of his coveralls. He saw some whites and blues in the cut—*muscle? Veins?*

Keith crawled out from under him, allowing the back of Dale's head to hit the concrete floor. He watched as Dale twitched for another minute. A gurgling sound came out of his mouth—or maybe through the massive hole on his neck—but he didn't appear to be breathing.

Keith leaned against the wall and sneered at the man. He didn't know him, he never saw him before, but he had a certain look to him that said: *'I'm a fat, dirty pedophile.'* He screamed as he stomped on his head. The wound on his neck continued to stretch, widen, and deepen. His blood pooled under him, then flowed towards the drain at the center of the room. His head was barely attached to his body, swinging in every direction with the slightest touch like a bobble-head toy—blood sprinkling out of his neck. His cervical vertebrae cracked under the pressure.

"You sick bastards," Keith said as he limped up the

basement stairs, pistol in hand. "You're all guilty. I see it in your eyes."

He caught a whiff of smoke as he headed up the stairs to the second floor. He stopped upon hearing a soft cry. He thought of Allie first. He hobbled into the hallway. Plumes of smoke danced out of the room at the end of the hall. The orange glow of a fire flickered out of the room through the open door. It looked like a gate to Hell. He approached the room.

Carrie coughed up a drizzle of blood. She stared at the ceiling, but she couldn't see a thing through her damaged vision. The old wood looked like a brown blot of ink. Riley's bloody hands trembled as he yanked the boards off the window. He heard the gunfire, he smelled the smoke. The jig was up, and he was ready for his great escape.

Keith leaned against the doorway. He aimed his handgun at Allen's back. Unaware of his presence, Allen threw a lit match into a file cabinet. Flames shot out of the drawer.

"Don't move," Keith said. "Put your hands up and turn around. Slowly, motherfucker."

Allen followed his instructions. He raised his hands over his head and turned around. He narrowed his eyes and tilted his head. He expected the FBI or the state police to kick his door down. He stared at a man dressed in casual clothing with a head covered in a sweaty ski mask.

He said, "You're not here to arrest anyone."

"That's right."

"You're here to kill, aren't you? You're a masked

killer. A real ruthless son of a bitch. Oh, I'm not complaining or anything. I won't beg for mercy. I accepted the fact that this day would come sooner rather than later a *long* time ago. I just... I need to know. Why? Why are you doing this? Who the hell are you?"

Keith removed his ski mask.

Allen smiled, shrugged, and asked, "Am I supposed to know you? Have we met before? Are you famous?"

"I guess you haven't been paying attention to the news, hiding out here in the middle of nowhere. I'm a lot of things, mister. I'm a cop. I'm a husband. I'm a father. I'm an *angry* father. My daughters went missing about two weeks ago, you see?"

Allen stopped smiling. He murdered a girl and kidnapped two young siblings about two weeks ago. Considering Keith was shooting up the place, he assumed the intruder knew about the business. Keith examined the room. He saw the cardboard boxes filled with videotapes in the corner to his right. Considering Allen was burning everything in the room, he assumed he was in the correct place.

The men locked eyes again. Chips of steel and ashes began to fall from the burning file cabinets.

Allen said, "I expected to leave this business in a casket, but not like this. I've been doing this for decades and I've never had a man or woman search for us like you did. If the cops caught wind of us, we'd pay 'em and move to a different town. But you caught us before we could leave. Incredible. Fuckin' incredible. How'd you do it?"

"I know people. A lot of people. And now I'm done talking. Where are my daughters?"

"Don't you want to know about the other girl?"

"Where are they?!"

"The girl—the one you ain't related to—I killed her."

Keith's face twitched—lips, nose, eyes. His finger slid on the trigger. He heard Allen's next confession before he even opened his mouth: *then I killed your daughters.*

Allen said, "There's a young man in the other room. It's going to be the second door to your left after you exit this one. He killed your youngest. He's about to–"

Keith pulled the trigger. The bullet struck Allen's lower abdomen. Allen stumbled back. He crashed into the file cabinet behind him. The file cabinets beside it fell like dominos. Burning pieces of paper spiraled out of the drawers. The flames spread across the room, igniting the lighter fluid on the other furniture and boxes.

Allen leaned over his desk, his hand over the gunshot wound. He coughed and laughed, unafraid of death.

He said, "I deserved that, but killing me won't solve anything. I'm... I'm the producer and the supplier, but I ain't the only one. Others will step in to fill my shoes. You think... You think this is the only Wolves' Den in the country? In this state? You'll have to kill the buyers if you want to stop this, if you want true vengeance. There ain't no suppliers without buyers.

That's... That's business."

Tears rolling down his cheeks, Keith said, "Carrie. Where's Carrie?"

"I... I told you. She's in the... the room... *with him*..."

Keith looked back into the hallway. He stared at the second door to his left. He had walked past his daughter's prison, unaware of her suffering.

Allen said, "That asshole in there... Kill him for me, will ya?"

Keith shot at Allen again. One bullet entered his throat, rupturing his windpipe and exiting through the back of his neck. The second bullet went through his nose and out the back of his head. He collapsed on top of the desk, then he slid off and hit the floor. Flames quickly swallowed his body. The planks of wood over the window snapped and fell apart. The fire followed a vine across the exterior of the house. The old building was engulfed.

"Carrie!" Keith shouted as he limped towards the door. "Allie!"

His eyes widened as a bloodcurdling shriek emerged from the room. He shot the padlock off, then he tackled the door. The smoke from the fire undulated into the bedroom, but he saw everything clearly.

A ray of sunshine entered the room through the open window, dawning on Riley and Carrie—*a divine light.* Bloody planks of old, withering wood littered the floor under the window.

Carrie lay on her back while Riley sat on her stomach. His thumbs were in her eye sockets, like fingers in a bowling ball. Her eyes were crushed, damaged beyond repair. He lifted her head up an inch, then he slammed the back of her head against the floor. Carrie whimpered and trembled, conscious but weak. Her entire head was covered in blood. Her survival was a miracle.

Keith shot at Riley. The bullet struck Riley's hip. It became trapped in his broken bone. Another bullet hit the floor beside Carrie. Keith lowered his weapon. He could have hit his daughter with a through-and-through shot. He couldn't take the risk.

Panting, Riley kissed Carrie's lips, then he said, "Die, you little cunt. Don't fight it. If you live, I'll kill you and the rest of your family."

He reeled away from her, blood oozing out of his hip. He jumped through the window, dodging a hail of bullets from Keith's pistol. He slid across the shingle roof, giggling like a child. He stopped on the gutter, then he scooted along the edge of the roof. He headed to the front of the house. He planned on dropping onto the Lincoln and speeding away.

Keith aimed at him through the window. *Come on, come on,* he told himself, *take the shot.* He shot once, but he missed. He shot at him again, but the bullet struck a shingle. Blankets of smoke billowed out of the window, obscuring his vision. He shot at him once more. The bullet whizzed past Riley's head. It only fueled his sinister laughter.

"Goddammit!" Keith barked. "You're not go–"

He kicked and swung as he was pulled away from the window. He aimed his pistol at his attacker, but he stopped before he could pull the trigger. Through the smoke, he found Gerald holding onto him.

Gerald said, "You didn't come here for him. You came for them."

Keith snapped out of his rage-induced trance. A lust for vengeance consumed him. He remembered the purpose of his mission: *rescue.*

He looked at Carrie, then at Allie. They looked dead. He stumbled towards them, tears in his eyes. He grabbed Carrie and pulled her onto his lap. She was brutalized, but she was still breathing. He grabbed Allie's forearm, but he didn't pull her towards him. The room was hot due to the approaching fire, each breath felt like a drag of a cigarette, but her skin was frigid.

Gerald noticed Keith's hesitation. He spotted Allie's pale face, discolored lips, broken limbs, and motionless body, too. Excluding the victims of their investigation, Gerald had discovered two dead bodies throughout his career: a teenager who ran away from a rehabilitation center only to be murdered days later by a pimp, and a neglected elderly woman who rotted in her apartment for weeks.

"Keith," he said in a soft, understanding voice. "She's gone, but I won't let you forget her. I'll carry her out. Okay? Can you carry Carrie?"

His bottom lip trembling, Keith stuttered, "A–Allie, baby. Wha–What happened to you?"

"*Keith,* this place is burning. Carrie is still alive. We need to get her out of here before she suffocates. Can you do that for me?"

Keith blinked erratically as he glanced at Gerald. He looked down at Carrie. She coughed and whined, like an injured, frightened pup.

"Dad–Dad... Daddy," she croaked out.

Keith said, "Yes, baby, *yes*. It's daddy. Daddy's here now."

Carrie reached for his face, trying to follow the sound of his voice. She said, "I–I can't... see you. Wh–Why?"

"You... Your... I... I'm sorry, baby."

His tears plopped on her cheeks. He used his tears to wipe some of the blood away with his thumb. It was the least he could do to comfort his daughter. A loud *crack* and a *snap* echoed over the roaring fire. The house cried as it burned.

Gerald patted his shoulder and said, "I won't let this girl die because you can't move. She deserves another chance to live. Lisa deserves to see them again. If you can't carry her, I will."

Keith broke out of his self-pity. He nodded at Gerald, as if to say: *I can do this.* He lifted Carrie from the ground. He held her like a bride on her wedding day as he limped out of the room. His gunshot wounds were aggravated by the extra weight, but it couldn't stop him. Nothing could stop him from rescuing his daughter.

With Allie in his arms, Gerald followed him through the smoke. He left the blanket over her body to protect Keith from seeing her mangled body. Keith nearly lost his footing as he walked down the stairs. Another *cracking* sound roared through the house.

They exited through the front door. Keith fell to one knee on the porch, exhausted. Gerald gave him a gentle shove—*you can do it, keep moving!* They walked off the porch and approached a tree some fifteen meters away from the house.

Keith sat with his back against the tree. He placed Carrie's head on his lap and coddled her. Gerald lay Allie's dead body beside him. Keith pulled her onto his lap as well.

Gerald said, "Whatever you do, don't take that blanket off her. Not yet, Keith. You're not ready for that. You understand me?" Keith nodded reluctantly. Gerald pulled his cell phone out and said, "Wait here, brother. I'm... I'm going to call for help. My assistant, Briana, she knows where we are. I told her everything. The cavalry will be here soon. Just... help her hang on."

He held the phone over his head and ran around in circles, searching for reception in the empty woodland.

Keith watched as the house burned. He heard the second floor collapsing into the first story. Flames consumed the exterior of the house while clouds of black smoke swallowed the clear, sunny sky. He noticed the empty driveway. His daughters' tormentor escaped his clutches. He sobbed and repeatedly apologized to his daughters. He saved Carrie, but he failed to rescue Allison. The burden of regret and failure sat on his shoulders.

He whispered, "I was too slow... I was too slow. I'm sorry, girls. I don't deserve to be your... your father.

What happened to you? Why did this have to happen to you? Oh, God, why? God… Why?"

Chapter Twenty-Six

April 3, 2019

Over twenty-two years passed since the incident in Montaño. After agreeing to a plea deal, Keith served fifteen years in the Penitentiary of New Mexico. Gerald's testimony, as well as the special circumstances surrounding the murders, also helped him secure a lenient sentence. Prosecutors weren't eager to imprison a local hero after all.

After the trial, which lasted six months, Lisa moved to Los Angeles, California with Carrie. Carrie voluntarily enrolled in an inpatient rehabilitation facility to treat her post-traumatic stress disorder and participate in physical therapy and mobility training. She never recovered her eyesight, but, even without her vision, she never forgot the images of her murdered sister and best friend. She remembered the good, the bad, and the sad.

Riley haunted her every waking and sleeping moment. His laughter rang in her ears at random times of the day. She often felt the urge to shove a screwdriver in her ears to stop the laughter—to finally forget the vile man who destroyed her life. She still dreamed and, in her dreams, she saw Riley, a man with a realistic wolf head, and a pudgy man with a realistic pig head. Rehab helped, but it couldn't fix it all.

After his release from prison, Keith spent five

years searching for the laughing man who harmed his daughters. Carrie gave him a name: *Steven Carter.* He investigated every Steven Carter in New Mexico, but he couldn't link a single one to the abandoned house. He never saw the killer's face, either, so he couldn't identify him. Carrie's descriptions were too vague for a positive confirmation.

Ashamed of his failures, Keith avoided his family, but he moved to Los Angeles to stay close to them. He watched them grow, heal, and expand. Carrie suffered from her mental and physical scars, but she didn't allow them to define her. She married a man named Doug Mitchell. They were attempting to adopt a child, hoping her past trauma wouldn't negatively affect their chances. They lived with Lisa, but they planned on moving to their own home.

Keith was hailed as a hero in Montaño and across the country, but employers were skeptical of hiring him due to his violent past. Fortunately, Gerald also achieved nationwide fame and praise thanks to his involvement in the investigation. He grew his business, hiring more investigators and research assistants, acquiring the latest technology, and opening offices across the country. He opened a private security firm in Los Angeles County: *Greenwood Security.*

Keith worked for Greenwood Security, guarding clients and their properties. At sunset, he sat in the living room of an empty Malibu beach house. He watched the sun descend beyond the horizon, painting the sky with oranges, pinks, blues, and purples. It was an uneventful day on the surface. But a whirlpool of tragic memories swirled in his mind.

Allie, Allie, Allie.

His cell phone vibrated in his pocket, but he didn't notice it. He stared at his reflection on the glass—a sad, middle-aged man. He gained some weight since the incident, his belly protruding forward, and his hair grayed. Depression took a toll on his psyche. It had been decades since his last smile. The phone rang again. His eyes on the sunset and his mind on his daughter, he answered the call.

He said, "Keith Klein, how can I help you?"

"Keith!" Lisa shouted.

Keith leaned forward in his seat. He felt the panic in his wife's voice and heard a woman sobbing in the background.

"What's wrong? What happened?"

"Carrie is having a–a–a meltdown! God, we've been trying to reach you for almost an hour! Listen, listen, I'm going to take her to the rehab center or a clinic."

"Is she hurt?"

"No, not... not physically."

Pacing back and forth in the living room, Keith asked, "Then what happened?"

"I don't know how to explain it. She... She... I don't know, she heard something and it, like, it triggered her! She's having a bad panic attack."

"Triggered? Triggered... Wait there. Give her some water and try to keep her calm. Take her to a clinic if she starts hyperventilating. I'm going to be right there."

Doubt laced into her voice, Lisa responded, "Keith, I think I should take her now. She's really–"

"Wait for me. Please, Lisa, I'll be right there."

He disconnected from the call and checked his phone—two missed calls and three text messages from Doug. He rushed out of the house, then he sped to Lisa's home.

***

Lisa opened the front door. Keith barged into the home without saying a word. He entered the living room. Carrie sat on a recliner, sunglasses covering her sealed eyelids. She sniveled and trembled and whispered—*horrified.* She didn't grow much since the incident, stopping at five-two, and her hair stayed as brown as milk chocolate. Doug crouched in front of her, her hands clasped in his. He whispered words of comfort at her.

Keith asked, "Carrie, honey, what happened?"

"Dad? Dad, is that you?" Carrie asked as she turned towards the direction of his voice.

"Yeah... Yeah, it's me. Dad... Daddy's here," Keith said. Doug stood up and moved to the side of the recliner, unwilling to release his wife's hand. Keith knelt down in front of her and asked, "What's wrong, honey?"

Carrie smiled. She treated her father like a hero, despite his own self-hatred. His voice always calmed her. Her lacrimal glands still functioned, allowing tears to wet her cheeks. Her smile broke as her lips shook. She pointed ahead. She memorized every nook and cranny of the house, the furniture was arranged specifically for her, so she knew a high-definition television was mounted on the wall.

She said, "Dad, the man… There was a… a… Shit, there was a talk show on TV, then a commercial. A…"

Keith said, "It's okay, honey. Take your time."

Carrie took a deep breath. She covered her mouth with both hands and sobbed. Doug rubbed her back.

"It was a movie trailer," Carrie said before releasing a loud sigh. "And… And the man in the trailer… He… He did this to me and he… he killed Allie."

Keith was stunned by the news. He looked at Doug, then at Lisa, and then at the television, which was turned off.

Carrie said, "I know you don't believe me. Mom, Doug… no one wants to believe me, but it's the truth. He… He had the same laugh. I swear, it was exactly the same."

Doug said, "It was some movie about a sad clown or something. I think it was called 'A Miserable Existence.' The character loses his job, then his girlfriend, and then his mother. He, uh… He goes crazy and… I don't know, it was just a movie trailer. He laughs at the end. It sounded like a clown's laughter, you know?"

"That wasn't a clown's laugh!" Carrie shouted. "It was *his* laugh. It was the man from the house, dad. I never forgot the way he laughed at me. It was evil. *Real. Evil.* He was a… a strong guy with blue eyes. He had this bright blonde hair, almost white. His face was very... square. Like... Like... angular, you know? I cut him, dad. I sliced his lip open. I'll never forget him... never... never..."

Doug rubbed her shoulder while Lisa held her hand. Lisa recommended a visit to the clinic, fearing she might have been suffering from an 'episode.' Doug was willing to do anything to help Carrie.

Keith walked to the center of the room. He stared at the television as he thought about Carrie's description. On his phone, he searched: *A Miserable Existence.* He read a news article about the film. Doug's explanation checked out. Then he searched the cast, browsing the profiles of each actor. He stopped on a 'Riley Watts.'

Now, Riley's hair was beach blonde. There were older pictures of him in his profile, though. In his pictures from the late nineties and early two thousands, his hair was platinum blonde—*almost white.* His eyes were a vibrant blue color. His face was slim, strong and angular. There was a scar on his upper lip. It resembled a microform cleft lip.

Keith read Riley's biography, which was written by his publicist, on the website.

"Born in 1970, first role in 1998, rose to stardom as a heartthrob, developed his skill to become a versatile actor," he whispered. "Critically acclaimed, nominated for multiple Golden Globes, working on his directorial debut... A social, economic, and climate activist fighting for the rights of every person, animal, and tree on the planet... Anti-war, anti-hate..."

Riley sounded like the perfect man. His publicist

sold him as a talented, hardworking, and caring actor. Keith didn't trust the snake oil salesman, though. He trusted his daughter. He watched the movie trailer on his cell phone.

"Stop," Lisa said as she glared at him. "I told you, Keith, it's a trigger."

Keith lowered the volume and walked away from them. At the end of the trailer, as the title card faded in—*A Miserable Existence*—he heard Riley's cackle. He replayed the clip. Then he played it one more time while holding the phone's speaker up to his ear. He remembered the young man's laughter as he slid across the roof of the abandoned house.

"It is him," he whispered, awed.

He walked out of the house. Lisa and Doug called out to him, but he ignored them. He paced across the lawn as he read the name on his cell phone: *Gerald Greenwood.* Gerald was now investigating the disappearances of multiple teenage girls in the New York City area. It was a high-profile case, his involvement was condemned by authorities, but he refused to quit. Ever since he discovered Allie's dead body, he dedicated his life to saving young girls from predators, traffickers, and serial killers.

He dialed his number. His heartbeat was louder than the tone. The call connected.

Keith said, "Gerald, it's Keith."

"I know, I know. I can read the caller ID," Gerald responded, smiling in his New York City office. "How are you doing, Keith? How can I help you? Did you finish up the–"

"I'm sorry, I'm not calling for chit-chat or business. I have something, um... something urgent to talk to you about."

"Urgent? What is it?"

"It's about 1996. About us. About Carrie. About Allie's killer."

A dead silence followed, as if each man held their breath.

Gerald said, "I'm listening."

"You won't believe me, but I think I know Steven Carter's true identity."

"Well, who do you think he is?"

"He's an actor. His name is Riley Watts. Before you tell me I'm batshit, Carrie described him to the T, Gerald. I verified it myself. His hairstyle back in the nineties, the scar on his lip, and his damn laughter gave him away. I trust my daughter and I trust myself. This is the guy. He *killed* Allie. He took *everything* from Carrie."

The silence returned for fifteen seconds. The sound of rustling papers and creaking wood emerged from Gerald's line.

Gerald said, "Riley Watts is a famous actor. Very popular with the ladies, and very popular with the men, too. He's a fan favorite. He's up for some pretty big roles in the next few years. And he's won many awards for his philanthropic work."

"I read about that. It doesn't mean he's—"

"A good guy," Gerald said, finishing his sentence. "I know. I have some files on him. I'm not sure how much research you've done on him, but he has quite the history."

Keith looked into the living room through a window. Carrie cried, but she found some comfort in her family. Lisa was angry at Keith, misinterpreting his contemplative behavior for selfishness.

"What did you find?" he asked as he watched his daughter.

"The big, obvious one? Well, in 2002, he was accused of appearing in a pornographic video with a minor. The teenage girl—fifteen or sixteen, I believe—refused to testify. The video wasn't the best quality, either, so the jury questioned his involvement. He was found not guilty on all charges. Thanks to some great publicity and some strong performances, it was forgotten. Who wants to believe their favorite performer is a child predator, huh? And, it's funny that you mention 1996. A lot of his history before that year appears to have been erased, except for some articles about his playboy lifestyle. He's always been surrounded by younger women, though. That's undeniable. Legal but young. Very young."

"That's enough for me. I know you have a lot of people out here in LA. And, since you have a file on this asshole and you have employees guarding houses across the county, I know you have his address. You mind handing it over?"

Gerald sighed, then he said, "That might not be the best idea. This guy has had a dark, mysterious past, but I don't know if he deserves your brand of 'punishment,' Keith. I mean, he's been tried and exonerated. I think he's hiding something, but I can't put him in your crosshairs if you're going to try to kill him. The guy is wealthy, too. He's richer than ever before thanks to his dad's wealth and his own. I'd go after him myself, but it's hard. Money changes everything because it buys everything."

"I was right in 1996. I'm right today, too. He deserves what's coming to him. If it makes you feel better, I'll let him talk before I do anything rash. If I believe him, I'll walk away. If I don't... I'll do something rash. But if I'm right, then he deserves to be punished. He... He took my sweet Allie from us. Carrie hasn't been the same since then, either. I need to find the truth and... No, fuck that. I need vengeance if I'm ever going to put this to rest and move on. Help me out, man. One last time."

Gerald felt guilty for two reasons: because he became wealthy off of the suffering of the Klein and Page families, and because he murdered a woman in a crack house and he was never punished for it. Yet, he trusted Keith's intuition. His investigation methods, influenced by desperation, were brutal, but he was correct. He owed him closure.

He said, "Answer the phone."

"What?"

The call disconnected. Keith stared down at the phone. A minute passed, then two. He thought about calling back, but Gerald's cryptic message meant something. The phone rang. The caller ID read: *Unknown.*

"Hello?" he answered.

A woman responded, "3600 Point Drive,

Hollywood Hills. A three-story gated mansion. Party tonight. Normal security. Be careful."

"3600 Point Dri–"

Mid-sentence, the woman disconnected from the call. Keith memorized the address. They didn't have to explain it to him. Gerald asked one of his research assistants to call him anonymously so he wouldn't be linked to the information. A party was set for that night at Riley's mansion in Hollywood Hills. He left the house without saying a word to his family. He was ready to exact his revenge.

Chapter Twenty-Seven

Into the Wolves' Den

Parked on the side of the road, Keith sat in his black SUV. Down the street, a three-story mansion stood at the end of the cul-de-sac. With floor-to-ceiling windows, the modern building showcased three-hundred-degree panoramic views of the mountains, the ocean, and the city. The outdoor deck had an infinity pool overlooking Los Angeles. The closest neighbor was a quarter-mile away, separated by swaths of foliage and tall trees.

A party was supposed to be occurring, but he couldn't hear any loud music and he didn't see any vehicles in the driveway. However, through the floor-to-ceiling windows, he saw a few figures wandering the house. They appeared to be trying to avoid the windows—*avoiding the limelight*. He couldn't identify any of them. There was no red carpet, no fleet of limousines, and no army of personal assistants and publicists.

It wasn't a party. It was a gathering.

A *secret* gathering.

Keith cruised past the front gate. He saw a man in a suit standing behind the iron bars. He wore an earpiece, so he assumed he was part of Riley's security detail. He was the only guard in the driveway. Keith took a right, followed the squiggly road up the hill, he took another right, and then another. He ended up where he started. He checked his seat belt, the straps on his bulletproof vest, the pistol in his waistband, and the revolver in his ankle holster.

(A suppressor, which was illegal in California, was attached to his pistol. It couldn't mute the gunfire, but it slightly dampened the sound.)

"This is for Carrie, Allie, and Brooke, you son of a bitch," he whispered as he turned off the headlights.

He stomped on the gas pedal. The car hit sixty miles per hour in less than seven seconds. His clammy palms slid across the steering wheel as he reached eighty miles per hour. His heart pounded like thunder, louder than the purring engine. The guard's eyes widened upon spotting the speeding vehicle. He placed one finger on his earpiece and reached for the pistol under his coat. Before he could say a word, the car hit the gate.

The gate burst open, doors exploding off their hinges and screeching against the pavement. The car hit the guard. The bumper snapped his legs at the knees, pushing his kneecaps behind his body. The bones popped out and tore through his pants. The momentum tossed his torso over the hood. His pelvic bones were *obliterated* upon impact. He screamed for less than three seconds, then the car crashed into a pillar between the garage doors.

The guard's legs were snapped back into place. His ass hit the pillar, which further damaged his pelvis. His back—from the small of his back to the back of his head—also hit the pillar. His back was bruised, his skull was cracked, and his neck was fractured. He collapsed into himself, his torso somehow sinking into his pelvis, as if his spine had turned into a Slinky and his flesh into jelly. He fell over the crushed hood of the car—*dead.*

Keith popped the airbag with a stab of his knife. Blood dripped out of his nose, staining his lips and chin. He exited the car, but he staggered right away. He was disoriented by the crash. He grabbed his duffel bag and a shotgun from the backseat, drew his pistol, and then stumbled across the front lawn. The dew on each blade of grass shimmered with the moonlight. He stopped as he reached the walkway. He aimed up at the double door entrance. The crash was loud, but security guards didn't swarm him.

"You… You're waiting for me, aren't you?" he muttered, out of breath.

He crept onto the porch while aiming his pistol at the doors. He heard voices and footsteps inside of the house. The footsteps approached the entrance.

Keith shot at the doors seven times—three through the left, four through the right, all near the center. The footsteps sped up, then the doors rattled. A man howled in pain inside of the house. He was shot, he lost control of himself, and he crashed into the doors. Women shrieked and men chattered in a panic behind him. The doors rattled again as the man teetered away.

Keith kicked the door—one, two, *three times*. The door on the left swung open, taking a chunk of the other door with it. Another man in a suit and an earpiece staggered around the entrance hall, his back to the intruder. He was shot twice in the stomach. He covered the wounds with his hands, but he couldn't stop the excessive bleeding. He left a trail of blood behind him—a crimson river on a shiny, luxurious white marble floor.

The guard turned around. His face was red and veiny, much like his eyes. He reached for the pistol in his holster.

Keith shot him with the pistol as he walked into the house, the shotgun in his left hand. The first bullet severed his index finger at the knuckle and the second round hit his chest. The guard collapsed in a puddle of his own blood.

Keith took a quick glance around, searching for any other guards. The cascading stairs wrapped around the gray walls in the entrance hall, leading all the way up to the third floor. He saw a shirtless man running into a bedroom on the second floor. He didn't see any guards above him.

He approached the downed guard. He was still alive, wheezing and squirming. He aimed the pistol at his face.

"I don't know if you're guilty, but I do know that you're in the wrong place at the wrong time," Keith said. "Collateral damage. I can't have you shooting me in the back, kid. I'm sorry."

"Wa–Wa–Wa–"

Keith shot him in the head. The bullet entered through his nose and exited through the back of his skull. Blood and brains erupted from the exit wound and splashed across the clean floor, like chunky beef stew from a fallen bowl.

A scream and a gunshot roared through the entrance hall. The bullet struck the door behind him. Keith turned and blindly returned fire. A guard stood in a hallway, squeezing the trigger of his pistol as quickly as possible. Most of the bullets struck the walls and door. One bullet hit Keith's chest. The bulletproof vest caught the bullet, but the impact caused him to stagger back.

Keith emptied his magazine, firing seven bullets at the guard. The guard was hit in the right shin, the right thigh, the pelvis, and his right arm. The other bullets hit the wall. The pistol fell out of his hand and he fell to his injured knee, blood squirting out of all of his wounds. He reached for the pistol with his left hand. *One more shot, I can kill him*—he was injured but motivated.

But Keith was *less* injured and *more* motivated. He reloaded his pistol, then he lurched forward and shot at the guard—*chest, chest, neck.* The guard fell back, holding his neck with both hands as if he were attempting to strangle himself. Keith slid to a stop and leaned against the wall. He locked eyes with the guard. The guard raised one hand at him and begged for mercy.

Keith sighed, then he said, "Fuck, I'm only here for Riley, you dumb motherfuckers. I don't want to kill you all, but I will if you get in my fucking way! You hear me?!"

People screamed and ran around the house. They heard him loud and clear.

Keith shot the guard, sending the bullet through his hand and into his head. He went down the hallway. A man ran through the doorway to his left. He instinctively shot him, striking his leg and hip. The man collapsed in the hall. He crab-walked through the parallel doorway.

The older gentleman shouted, "Wait, wait! I–I'm just the butler! The butler, you hear?! Mis–Mister Watts and those perverts are down the hall!"

"Don't fucking move," Keith hissed.

"O–O–Okay."

Keith looked through the doorway. It led to a butler's pantry and a kitchen. He peeked through the opposite doorway. It was a dining room. He heard whispers all around him, but he was only interested in Riley Watts. According to the butler, he was down the hall with 'those perverts.' So, he followed the corridor until he emerged in a banquet hall.

To his left, a double staircase led to the second floor and then another staircase led to the third floor. To his far right, ceiling-height windows opened up to the outdoor deck. Carts and tables with platters of cheese and seafood and desserts and other delicacies were scattered across the room. The home looked expensive, but it was barely furnished.

The banquet hall was filled with people. Four nude, malnourished teenagers—two males, two females—sat on their knees at the bottom of the staircases, each chained by their necks to a separate handrail. Their kneecaps were red and blue. Their lips were pale and black bags hung under their bloodshot eyes.

One of the girls had zoned out. She was there, but she wasn't *there.* She left her body during her torture.

Other nude teenagers stood beside the food carts and pedestal tables, chained by their necks to the handles of the carts and legs of the tables. They were forced to wear those shackles like bowties. The teenagers looked frightened, despondent, and even ashamed. They came in every skin color—pale to dark—but none of them appeared to be from the United States. They were imported from countries around the globe.

Mexico. Venezuela. Belize. Russia. China. South Africa.

There was a total of eighteen teenagers in the banquet hall. Most of them couldn't communicate with each other due to the language barriers. They couldn't communicate with their captors, either. Yet, growing up in a world full of cruelty and perversion, they knew exactly why they were there. They were victims of human trafficking, sold like cattle by other humans.

Keith clenched his jaw as he examined the other people in the room. He counted twenty-seven—then twenty-eight, and then twenty-nine. There were more people outside, cowering while searching for a way out. The guests wore animal masks. Some of the masks covered their entire heads, others shielded the top-half of their faces.

They were nude, and they came in all shapes and sizes—tall and short, strong and flabby, smooth and wrinkly, and everything in between. Judging from their figures, most of them were in their early forties to their late seventies. But, regardless of their age or physical appearance, *all* of them were deviants.

An elderly woman stood on her knees near one of the carts. Her breasts sagged onto her belly and her belly sagged over her crotch. Webs of blue veins ran across her wrinkly, milky skin. She wore a rabbit masquerade mask covering the top-half of her face while revealing her beady blue eyes and short gray hair. A flaccid dick in her mouth, she performed fellatio on one of the prisoners.

The teenager whimpered while holding a plate full of cheese. He was not aroused by the sexual act. He was disgusted, embarrassed, and sad.

At the other side of the room, a fat middle-aged man in a pig mask held a female prisoner over one of the carts and thrust into her. In fact, even after hearing the gunfire and seeing Keith with his own eyes, he continued to rape the prisoner. He slowed his thrusting, he was surprised and frightened, but he didn't pull out of her. Maybe it was the shock, maybe it was his unquenchable depravity.

Everyone stared at him, frozen in fear.

Keith approached the only clothed woman in the room—the elderly housekeeper. She knelt beside the hallway, cleaning a puddle of dark—almost orange—urine with a towel. He aimed the gun at her head.

He said, "Get out. Call the cops in five minutes. Give them this address and tell them there's an ongoing hostage situation occurring at this mansion. Don't tell them about the shooting. Tell them that I want to negotiate."

Keith had no intentions of negotiating. He was buying time. He figured the police would arrive sooner or later, but they would raid the house immediately if they were called to an active shooter scene. A hostage situation was different, though. In a hostage situation, the police would try to defuse the situation while strategically maneuvering around the crime scene for the perfect shot at the suspect before going in with their guns blazing.

The housekeeper stood up with her hands raised. She sidestepped away from Keith, then she ran down the corridor.

Keith walked towards the center of the room and said, "If any of you move, I'll start shooting indiscriminately. I'm armed with two handguns and a shotgun. I have more weapons in my bag. I can't kill all of you, but I can definitely injure most of you. I doubt you want to get caught with your pants down... Well, without any pants *whatsoever* out there in the cold, surrounded by nosy neighbors, stalking paparazzi, and an army of police. With these kids here, it's not a good look. Not at all. So, stay where you are."

He stopped beside the elderly woman and her young male prisoner. She still had his penis in her mouth.

"Take his dick out of your filthy mouth, woman," Keith hissed.

The woman cocked her head back, allowing the

flaccid penis to fall out of her toothless mouth. Without taking her eyes off the shooter, she reached for her dentures on the cart.

She stammered, "I–I–I–I–"

Keith shot her through the left eye. Held together by veins and bloody goo, pieces of her ruptured eye hung over her mask and dangled down to her cheek like hard-boiled egg whites attached together by runny yolk. Bits of her brain and blood splashed onto the floor. She fell to her side and crashed into the cart. The cart tipped over, plates *clanking* and wine glasses *shattering* on the floor. The teenager had to crouch because of the chain.

Keith turned around and shot at the fat rapist—who continued to thrust despite the elderly woman's murder—behind the other food cart. Three bullets tore into his stomach and one entered his chest. The young girl screamed as his warm blood sprayed onto her back. The man fell back, hitting the floor with a loud *thud*. He writhed in pain, he muttered indistinctly, and he stroked his erect penis. He was determined to ejaculate one more time.

The victim grabbed a silver-plated platter from the cart. She mounted the man's chest, restricting his ability to masturbate. Her labia against her chest was enough to keep him aroused, though. She growled and she screamed as she swung the sturdy platter at his head. The vibrating *thud* of each blow echoed through the banquet hall. The damage wasn't visible due to his mask, but she could see his flickering eyelids and some blood on his forehead. She felt his convulsions on her legs, too. She beat him into shock.

And she didn't stop. The guests and prisoners watched in silence.

The platter banging like a war drum in the background, Keith said, "My name is Keith Klein and I'm from Montaño, New Mexico. I'm here for a Mr. Riley Watts. So, here's what we're going to do. You can point him out, walk out of here, and *try* to get away from the cops. We can have you remove your masks one-by-one until I find him. In this case, since you'd be wasting my time, I'd have to kill you if you're *not* him. Or, I can start shooting all of you until I find him. What's it going to be?"

There was no response, only thuds and grunts.

Keith said, "Well, Option One is obviously off the table. I'd like to save some ammunition in case of surprises, so I won't shoot all of you… *yet.* That leaves Option Two. Take your masks off when I tell you to. If you try to run or if you try to fight back or if you ignore me, I'll shoot your legs and your genitals. I won't kill you. No, I'll let you live so you can face the consequences… and the public. Understood? Good."

He aimed the pistol at a man with a plastic horse mask. He saw the sweat glistening on his neck, beads rolling down to his hairy chest. He waved the gun at him, motioning his demands—*take it off, now.* The guest breathed heavily as he reached for the mask, his entire arm shaking. He grabbed a fistful of the mask's Kanekalon hair, then he yanked it off his head. He was a dark-haired man with bushy eyebrows and a trimmed beard.

Keith's mouth hung open. He recognized him as Jon Aston, an actor on a popular television show about a lawyer working with violent drug cartels. He played the lead role, filling the shoes of Samuel Ford. His character was intelligent but conniving, pacifistic but prone to violence, full of answers but always asking questions. Jon was a respected man in Hollywood as well. His career was blossoming thanks to his performance as Samuel.

You're a monster, just like the rest of these people, Keith thought. *I should have expected this. Riley has friends, doesn't he? And friends share common interests. Friends keep secrets. Friends 'play' together. You're not the only famous bastard in the bunch, are you?*

Forcing a smile, Jon said, "I wasn't even supposed to be here tonight, sir. Riley is over–"

Keith shot him right between the eyes. Some of the guests gasped as Jon hit the floor. It finally hit them: they were going to die if they didn't cooperate.

Keith moved to the woman next to him—a redhead with a curvy figure. A bull mask shielded the top-half of her face. She couldn't have been Riley Watts, but he needed the truth.

He grabbed one of the mask's horns and yanked it off her face. He recognized her, too—*Elizabeth Jones*. She starred in a show about a pair of detectives investigating a serial killer targeting homeless people in Los Angeles. The show was applauded for bringing light to the homelessness epidemic in California without exploiting it. She was praised for her philanthropic efforts as well.

He shot her in the throat before she could say a word. She gripped her neck with both hands and staggered back, eyes clenched shut as pain shot down her spine and blood up her throat. She croaked what sounded like: *help!* She fell to her knees and shuffled forward. She collapsed in front of a man with a wolf mask.

Keith lost his temper. He went from person-to-person, removing masks and executing deviants. He found well-known actors, actresses, businessmen, businesswomen, retired athletes, news anchors, socialites, and even a politician. Collectively, the guests were worth more than the rest of the city's lower-and-middle-class residents. He unloaded his magazine, killing twelve more people in less than three minutes. A man tried to run out of the banquet hall, but a shotgun blast riddled his back with pellets before he could escape.

Keith stopped in front of the man with the wolf mask. He was a lean, muscular man. He couldn't see his face through the mask, but, by looking at his eyes, he knew the enigmatic man was smirking at him. He pressed the muzzle of the shotgun against his chest, then he took the mask off his head. He took a step back and examined him.

Blue eyes—*check.*
Blonde hair—*check.*
Scarred lip—*check.*
"Riley Watts," Keith said.
"In the flesh," the man responded with a grin, his

arms outstretched. "You didn't have to kill all of those people to find me, you know?"

"Oh, I didn't? Then why didn't you reveal yourself when this *cunt* was dying at your feet, choking on her own blood?"

"Simple: I wanted to watch her die."

Keith huffed and sneered at him. He expected such a selfish, cruel answer, though. The man was accused of torturing his daughters. His history of abuse was buried by good publicity, but he couldn't deny the obvious facts in the banquet hall. He owned the mansion, he hosted the party, and he purchased the prisoners as sex slaves. He earned his punishment.

"Have you ever heard of The Troubles, Mr. Watts?" Keith asked.

Still smirking, Riley responded, "Nope."

"You haven't heard of kneecapping, either, have you?"

"*Nope.*"

"I'll have to explain it to you."

"Be my guest, but please remember: the cops are on their way to arrest you. I'll be paying them off as soon as we're finished, so if you have something important to say, tonight's your one and only night. I'm happy to give you the floor, Mr. Klein. I know I've been haunting you for decades. Oh, yes, I remember *that* day. It was the best rush of my life. I suppose some people would call it a 'high,' wouldn't they? The highest high in this world."

Keith smiled and said, "I'm glad you remember me. Now I won't have to waste time explaining why you have to die tonight."

He shot at Riley's left kneecap as the man snickered. The close-range shotgun blast mangled his knee, digging a dark, bloody crater into his kneecap. The pellets severed his arteries, tore through his ligaments and tendons, and broke his bones. His tendons and ligaments—white but covered in blood—hung *out* of the wound. His leg gave out and he tumbled to the floor, howling in pain and giggling with joy at the same time.

Keith said, "The Troubles was a conflict in Northern Ireland. I won't give you a history lesson. What good is history to a dying man, huh? All you have to know is: during that period of violence, paramilitaries used this method to punish drug dealers and child molesters like yourself." He pointed at his bloody knee and said, "That's kneecapping right there. But it wasn't just one knee. In fact, it was more than the knees. Much more. They shot their knees, their ankles, and their elbows. And they called it a six-pack."

Holding his breath, Riley said, "I don't... need a... six-pack. I've got one... already." He cackled as he tapped his firm, defined abs. He said, "I love this shit, man. I can... I can play a paraplegic now and none of those sensitive bastards can complain a–about 'appropriation.' Thank you for... for supporting my career. My biggest fan."

As Riley laughed, Keith shot him again. He shot him in his right kneecap. While Riley held his hands over the fresh wound, Keith shot at his right ankle.

Most of the pellets ricocheted off the floor and hit the neighboring cart, but a few went through his flesh and shattered his bones. His left ankle wasn't as fortunate. The third shotgun blast was direct. His left foot hung from his ankle, dangling like a pendulum. It was connected by a bloody ligament and his heel cord. The rest of his ankle was splattered on the floor—skin, ligaments, bones, and blood.

Riley bawled. He screamed until he was lightheaded. The blood and gore didn't make him woozy, though. He grew accustomed to it.

He stammered, "You–You–You–"

Keith shot at his left elbow. The pellets entered the side of his arm at an angle. Some pellets even penetrated his abdomen and one hit the floor. Riley grabbed his injured elbow with his right hand. His left leg, along with his nearly severed foot, hit the floor. The burning pain in his ankle intensified, flowing from his ankle to his injured kneecap and from his kneecap to his crotch. His other leg didn't fare much better.

Keith aimed at his uninjured elbow. He pulled the trigger, but he was out of ammunition. He reloaded the shotgun, one shell at a time.

During the shooting, some of the guests crept out of the banquet hall. A nude man in the infinity pool jumped from the outdoor deck. He rolled down a hill until he disappeared in the trees and bushes. The young woman continued to beat her rapist's head with a bent platter. The sharp edge of the platter ripped his mask and sliced the man's forehead open.

His head—mask included—was drenched in blood. She stopped beating him as Keith reloaded.

Keith aimed the shotgun at Riley's right elbow. He said, "You're never going to play a paraplegic because you're not getting out of here alive."

Fading in and out of consciousness, Riley said, "Kill… Kill me… If you don't… you'll make me… make me the most famous, celebrated man in the world. You've already made me a–a martyr…"

"Even if you survived, you think they're going to celebrate a pedophile like you?"

"They won't… They won't ever know about this party, you imbecile. I paid… I paid them. The…" He cackled deliriously, then, with a full breath of air, he shouted, "The police chief was here! He was here!"

"That's too bad. I have a man outside who's going to blow the lid off this. He was just waiting for a positive confirmation. So, whether I die or live, he knows the truth and he'll tell the world."

"Fuck… you…"

Keith shot his other elbow at point-blank range. The powerful blast severed his arm at the elbow. Blood spouted out of his arm like water from a drinking fountain. Riley fainted. His mind was strong, he knew all about pain and suffering, but the human body could only handle so much. He lay in a puddle of his own blood, twitching.

The sound of emergency sirens, squealing wheels, and loud engines emerged outside.

"The rest of you can leave now," Keith said as he watched Riley. "Leave the kids and go out through the front door. Tell them about the 'hostage' situation. If you say anything else, my friend outside will make sure your identities are revealed, even if you already paid someone off. Now leave before I change my mind."

The nude guests were reluctant. An army of police waited for them outside. And, as with every major crime in Hollywood, news reporters, paparazzi, and amateur crime scene photographers surely followed. The men and women exited the house with their hands up. The people in the pool left a trail of water behind them. As instructed, they all exited through the front door.

Keith crouched and slapped Riley's cheek until he awoke. Riley's eyes rolled, pupils dilated due to the pain and fear coursing through his body.

"What happened?" he asked in a weak, shaking voice.

"Don't act stupid now. You know what you did and you know what I'm doing. I wish I could torture you for seventeen days and nights. That's how long my daughters were missing, so I always thought that would be the most... 'appropriate' revenge. But it looks like we're out of time. So, what's the most painful way to die? Hmm? You're the expert, aren't you? What should I do to you?"

"What are you... What..."

"I'm kidding, Riley. I already know what I'm going to do to you. You see, I gave you a 'six-pack' because you did something similar to my baby. Allie's arms and legs were broken during her stay at your house.

What did you do to my sweet Carrie?"

"I–I... I didn't..."

"You gouged her eyes out. So, let's follow the rules of vengeance. An eye for an eye, as they say."

He pulled a stainless-steel spoon out of his duffel bag. He held Riley's eye open, then he slowly inserted the spoon under his eyeball. He wiggled the spoon in his eye socket—up and down, up and down, *up and down.* Riley's nostrils flared with each long, painful exhale. Blood and tears rolled down his cheek. He touched Keith with the bloody nub at the end of his right arm. He reached for him with his other arm, too, but it fell limp on his stomach before he could touch him.

He winced as a popping sound came out of his eye socket. The muscles attached to his eye snapped. The eye popped out of his skull, blood filling the gap underneath it.

Riley fainted again as Keith grabbed the eye with his bare fingers. He tugged on the eye while pushing the spoon upward. He heard a *crackling* sound, then a loud *pop*. The optic nerve and the other muscles attached to his eye were severed. He pulled it out of the socket, blood dripping from the torn arteries and nerves. Then he dropped it into Riley's mouth.

Riley hacked, his head swinging from side to side. Vomit erupted from his mouth—cheese, wine, blood, and an eyeball.

Keith said, "Now you're feeling *true* pain, *true* fear. I see it in your eyes... Well, I see it in your eye. I saw it in so many people back in 1996. Jim, Alvin, a crackhead, your buddies at the house. They were all scared to die. Is that what you're scared of? Death?"

Riley breathed deeply, then he panted, then he whispered something, and then he closed his good eye. Within seconds, he stopped breathing and his head fell to the side.

"Dead already?" Keith whispered. He stood up and said, "You were weaker than I thought."

He walked away from the body—one, two, *three steps*. Riley lifted his head from the floor, coughing and giggling. He licked the bloody vomit off his lips, then he smirked at Keith. Keith glared at him, his shoulders rising with each deep breath. Then he returned the smirk. Riley stopped smiling. His eye said something along the lines of: *what the fuck? Why are you smiling, too?*

Keith crouched beside him and said, "You're dying, but you're still trying to beat me at this... this game. You want to have the last laugh, you're trying to get under my skin, but I know you're scared. It's over, kid. This... This wonderful life your father created for you... It ends tonight and I'll get the last laugh."

Rage burning in his eye, Riley responded, "*Fuck you.* I... I'm not scared of... of anything."

"You're not laughing anymore, are you?"

"Fuck you..."

Keith pulled the knife out of his pocket. He grabbed Riley's flaccid penis by the glans. Riley reached for Keith's arms, but he was too weak to move. Keith casually sawed into the base of his penis until he severed it. He threw it at Riley's face. The bloody slug hit his jaw, then it fell to the floor beside his head. Riley looked at it, mouth ajar. He couldn't scream, he could only hold his breath. He was experiencing shock and grief, as if he had just received news of the death of a loved one.

Keith grabbed a fistful of his hair and dragged him across the banquet hall. Thanks to his blood and sweat, he slid across the floor with little effort. Riley unleashed one final bloodcurdling scream. He watched as blood squirted out of his crotch, joining the bloody trail behind him. Keith pulled him up three stairs. Riley's left ankle hit the sharp edge of a stair. The impact was enough to cut off his dangling foot. It stayed at the bottom of the stairs.

"She... She was right," he croaked out, barely audible. "Daddy saved you, daddy got me..."

The cool breeze touched his warm, moist skin as he slid across the outdoor deck. He was dragged into the infinity pool. Clouds of blood billowed out in the water. Most of the pool turned red in less than thirty seconds. The water reached Keith's waist while Riley floated across the surface of the pool on his back.

Keith placed both hands on Riley's face, then he pushed him down. He held him underwater and counted each passing second. The bloody water bubbled and sloshed, but Riley barely moved. He felt his struggle, though—his fluttering lips, his trembling nose, his twitching head. He stood there for five minutes, ensuring the man who tortured his daughters died in a slow, prolonged, and painful process.

Drowning wasn't peaceful or painless. First, the water poured into Riley's lungs, causing him to cough and retch. His body reacted by forcing his vocal cords to spasm and seal off his airway. So, the water filled his stomach instead. He felt a painful knot in his abdomen while his lungs were deprived of oxygen. The excruciating pain and the slow suffocation sent his mind into a panic.

His vision—already damaged by the removal of his eye—faded to black. The vibrant color vanished from his lips. His lungs were set ablaze, growing hotter while his limbs became numb. His heart hit his ribcage like a rubber ball hitting a wall during a game of racquetball. He felt like his chest would burst open at any second. Then he lost his hearing in both ears.

He heard his own voice in his head: *please, I'm not ready to die!* But he felt like he was floating away from his body. For a second, he entered a world between life and death. He saw Keith holding his head underwater, eyes burning with determination. Then it all went black. He stopped moving. He passed away in his expensive pool—dickless, footless, armless, *lifeless*.

Keith whispered, "You're lucky. This was the easy way out for you, punk."

He slogged his way out of the pool. He saw the red and blue emergency lights beyond the home's gate and the neighboring trees. He heard the police chatter in front of the house. The cops surrounded the home, securing the premises while waiting for the SWAT team to suit up and raid the house. He returned to the banquet hall. He spotted an elderly butler hurrying up the stairs, a key-ring jingling in his hand. Some of the teenagers yelled in different languages while hurling plates of food at him.

Keith aimed the shotgun at him and said, "Don't move, motherfucker." The butler stopped towards the center of the stairs with his hands up and the teenagers stopped shouting. As he approached him, Keith asked, "Where are you going?"

The man stuttered, "I–I'm... I–I can't say."

"And why is that?" Keith asked as he walked up the steps slowly.

"Be–Because... I–I'm not... I'm sorry. I'm just doing my job. Please don't kill me. I–I never wanted to work here, but I... I couldn't get out and we needed the money at home. I–I'm not like them, I swear."

Keith tapped the man's back with the muzzle of the shotgun. He said, "Well, you're not naked and you're not wearing a mask, so I assume you're not one of them. You are complicit, but that's not a reason for me to kill you right now. You're not going to turn around and try to shoot me, are you?"

"No! No, sir! I'm not armed!"

"Good, good. So, cooperate and I'll let you walk out of the front door. Where were you going in such a hurry?"

The butler sighed, then he said, "Mr. Paul Watts is upstairs in the master bedroom. He was... having a 'session' when you entered the house. His 'subjects,' as he calls them, refused to release him from his handcuffs because they thought you were a cop. They haven't harmed him yet because they're scared of being punished, but they're trying to stop anyone from releasing him. I'm supposed to get him out of there."

Keith nodded and asked, "Where's his bedroom?"

"The third floor. It's... It's a penthouse up there. He's handcuffed to his bed. The kids... Those poor kids are chained to the walls around the bed. I'm sorry. I shouldn't have allowed this to happen."

Keith took the keys from him and said, "Yeah, you're right. So, go out there and make things right. Be careful, though: they bought some cops. Go to a journalist after you've been questioned and tell them everything. An independent journalist, okay? I'll handle Paul Watts. Which key does what?"

"The gold key opens the penthouse. The small silver keys unlock the handcuffs."

"Got it. Now get out of here."

The butler walked down the stairs, hands up in fear and head down in shame. The teenagers shouted at him, throwing food at his back.

Keith went up the stairs. He ignored the ruckus in the bedrooms on the second floor. He wished he could have saved everyone, but he was running out of time. *The cops will get to them soon,* he told himself, *they can punish the rest of them, but Paul deserves my punishment.* He headed up to the third floor. At the top of the stairs, a short hallway led to a double-door entrance.

He opened the doors with the gold key. He found himself in a lavish penthouse, glass walls revealing a gorgeous view of the city, the mountains, and the ocean. The furniture was elegant—sable sectional sofas, matching leather recliners, a 98-inch 8K television, a grand piano, a long dining table with gold flatware on top, a bar with bottles of finely aged wine and whiskey, a small kitchen, sculptures and paintings by modern artists.

Through the door to his left, he could see a spacious walk-in shower, a hot tub with a view of the city, and a sauna. The ball-shaped toilet looked like it was transported through time—*futuristic.*

He heard a man muttering through a door to his left. He pushed the door open and peeked inside. Motorized roller shades covered the floor-to-ceiling windows, leaving the room dimly lit by one lamp and a few candles.

A seventy-nine-year-old man lay on a large bed, ankles and wrists cuffed to the bedposts. His small, shriveled penis was hidden by a wild bush of white pubic hair. His frail torso, flabby and wrinkled, was covered in matching hair. Liver spots spread across his hands, arms, shoulders, and face. His hair was slicked back, thin and white.

Keith recognized him because of his eyes—his vibrant, deviant blue eyes. The man was Riley's father, Paul Watts.

Two nude teenagers—a male and a female—stood at each side of the bed. The young man held a lamp, ready to strike Paul's head at a moment's notice. The young woman held a pillow, eager to suffocate her captor.

Keith entered the room, raising one hand at the teenagers. He said, "Don't worry. I'm not going to hurt you."

With a Spanish accent, furious and frightened at the same time, the girl said, "You can hurt me, but I'll kill him first."

"I said I'm *not* going to hurt you. I'm not going to help him, either. I'm here to punish him."

Paul glared at him and asked, "Who the hell are you? Where's Edwin? Where are the police?!"

"The police are outside," Keith responded. He dropped his duffel bag beside the bed. He said, "But they won't be here for a while. They're probably calling your landline, hoping to negotiate. We both know that's not going to happen."

"Wha–What? I… I didn't… Where did you… Listen, whoever you are, I have money. You're here, you… you clearly mean business, so you know who I am. I can pay you and I can make this go away."

"You can't make this go away," Keith said as he looked through his bag. "Your boy, Riley Watts, tortured my daughters. He killed my youngest when she was eight. You helped him get away with it. I already killed him. Now it's time to deal with you."

"You… You killed my son?"

Keith pulled a hammer out of the bag. He nodded at the young woman and wagged the hammer at Paul's face. The prisoner understood him. She placed the pillow over Paul's face. Paul's muffled scream barely escaped the room.

Keith swung the hammer at Paul's left hand. His

old, weak bones shattered with each blow. His metacarpals broke first. Then his phalanges snapped like twigs. After four blows, his wrist was dislocated. His ring and middle fingers were pushed back—and they stayed that way. His palm turned blue and purple. His knuckles were cut, blood dripping onto the expensive cotton sateen bed sheets.

"Take it off," Keith said through his gritted teeth. "Move it!"

The teenager removed the pillow, eyes wide with terror. She teetered away from the bed. She nearly reached the corner of the room, but the shackle around her ankle stopped her.

Gasping for air, Paul said, "You... You slimy fuck... You'll... die... out... there."

Keith shook the hammer at Paul's face and asked, "Do you know what your son did? Of course you do. You taught him, didn't you?!" He swung the hammer at the right side of Paul's rib cage. As Paul coughed and wheezed, Keith shouted, "You've been doing this for decades! These are kids, you sick motherfucker! *Kids!*"

He hammered away at Paul's rib cage, playing his ribs like a xylophone. His ribs *popped* and *cracked.* One of the bones snapped upward, causing a lump to protrude from his chest. Paul bounced and croaked. Blood sprinkled from his mouth, staining his trimmed goatee. He spoke indistinctly, looking at everything in the room with bulging eyes as if he were in a surreal nightmare. The pain sent him into a delirious state.

Petechiae and circular red marks—the size of the hammer's face—covered his rosy chest. The area around his right nipple was already bruised.

Keith set the hammer down beside Paul's torso, then he exited the room. Despite the pain and the handcuffs, Paul reached for the hammer with his broken hand. His entire arm wobbled while the bedpost barely groaned. He heard the running water, banging cabinets, and clinking flatware in the penthouse. He knew Keith was planning something for him. He was a master of torture, he was a masochist, but he could only handle so much pain.

Five minutes later, he heard Keith's footsteps in the penthouse. He held his breath. He would rather suffocate than suffer.

Keith returned to the room. In his left hand, the flatware was bundled together in a tablecloth. In his right hand, he held a bucket of water. Steam rose from the surface of the water. He sat the bucket down beside the bed, then he unrolled the tablecloth on the mattress. He grabbed one of the seven gold forks. He thrust the fork into Paul's stomach, which forced him to gasp for air. The four stab wounds from the tines were shallow but deep enough to scrape his internal organs.

"I could rip you open with a knife, but I want this to last," Keith said. "It takes more force to stab someone with a fork. I think it hurts more, too."

"I–I'm an old, *old* man," Paul cried. "You can–can't do this to me."

"That won't work on me. You can't guilt me, you

can't shame me," Keith responded. He stabbed his thigh with another fork. As Paul whimpered, Keith said, "You deserve this, just like your son."

He pulled the fork out, then he stabbed him again. Since Paul was a thin man, the tines penetrated his femoral artery. It wasn't pulled out. He thrust the third fork into his stomach. The fourth fork went through his left nipple, two of the tines cutting through his areola. He stabbed his chest three times with the fifth fork, then he left it protruding from his pectoral muscle. The sixth fork was thrust into his shoulder. The seventh fork was used to stab his stomach one more time.

Keith glanced over at the window upon hearing a muffled announcement over a loudspeaker. It was a hostage negotiator. He warned the remaining people in the house to surrender. Since the calls for negotiations were ignored, the SWAT team was preparing to raid the home. Paul screamed, tears rolling down his face. He was a deviant, like his son, but he was also a coward. He played the role of a victim because he wanted to survive. He didn't laugh in the face of death because he wanted to live forever.

Keith said, "Shut your mouth, you sick bastard." He lifted the bucket from the floor. He shouted, "Shut up!"

Keith dumped half of the bucket's boiling water on Paul's head. The feathers of steam rose from his scalded face. His skin peeled, turning his nose, cheeks, and forehead pink. As Paul convulsed, Keith dripped more of the boiling water on his forehead.

The water cascaded across his face. His forehead became blood-red while the rest of his skin continued to peel. Some of his hair fell from his scalp.

"How does that feel?!" Keith barked. He threw the empty bucket aside and shouted, "This is hell! This is what I hope you'll feel for the rest of eternity!"

The male prisoner dropped the lamp and turned around. The young woman covered her face with her hands. The prisoners dreamt of vengeance, but their minds weren't ready for the extreme violence.

From the first floor, a police officer shouted, "Police! Police! Put your hands up!"

"Goddammit," Keith muttered.

He grabbed a bottle of pepper spray. He looked at the prisoners. He wanted to warn them, but they wouldn't spare a glance. He covered his mouth with his elbow, then he shot the whole bottle of pepper spray at Paul's face. When used properly, pepper spray caused temporary blindness while inflaming the mucus membranes of the eyes, nose, and throat. It caused an intense and immediate burning sensation.

On an open wound, the pain was amplified a thousandfold.

Paul's face was peeling due to the boiling water. His entire face was an open wound. He felt the powerful burning sensation from his forehead to his toes. It felt as if his face were set on fire. Bloody tears oozed out of his sealed, crimson eyelids. Mucus bubbled out of his nostrils. Saliva foamed out of his mouth. His face became swollen. He felt his brain pounding against his skull, as if his heart had moved from his chest to his head. He tried to scream, but he could only cough.

"Police!" an officer yelled from the second floor. "Don't move!"

Keith coughed violently as he searched for another torture device. A box cutter, a skinning knife, a screwdriver, a crowbar, a taser, a box of matches, and a coil of rope sat in his bag. He was out of time, though. He considered shooting Paul, but he wanted him to suffer. He didn't want the police to gun him down, either. He sighed in disappointment.

Coughing between his sentences, Keith said, "I'm sorry, Mr. Watts... I guess our playtime is over... I wish I could have had a few more minutes with you, but... Oh well." He grabbed the handle of the fork sticking out of his thigh. He leaned closer to Paul's unrecognizable face and said, "This was for Allie Klein, Carrie Klein, Lisa Klein, Brooke Page... and every person you ever hurt through your actions. They'll let me out again, and I'll make sure every Wolves' Den burns to the ground... You have my word on that."

He wiggled the fork and ruptured the artery, then he pulled it out. A continuous flow of blood shot out of his thigh, splashing on his other leg. Paul stopped screaming. A chill spread across his body as his hot blood was siphoned out of him. The shackles rattled as he twitched. He fainted in eighteen seconds, goops of foamy blood and saliva rolling out of his mouth. Death was certain.

"Police!" a cop shouted in the penthouse.

Keith threw the fork aside. He raised his hands over his head, turned around, and fell to his knees. The cop—wearing a suit of armor, a helmet, and a face mask—entered the bedroom. He aimed a riot shotgun and a flashlight at Keith.

He yelled, "Don't move! Keep your hands up! Don't–"

His eyes widened as he examined the nude elderly man chained to the bed. The stream of blood slowed to a steady trickle. Feathers of steam blossomed from his burnt face. His chest was motionless. He shone the light at the naked teenagers crouched in the corners of the room. He turned his attention to Keith, baffled.

Keith chuckled and cried at the same time. He didn't shed tears of joy, though. His eyes told a story of tragedy and vengeance, sadness and hatred, redemption and failure. He got the last laugh, but it wasn't as sweet as he had imagined. Surrounded by mayhem, he could only think about Lisa, Carrie, and Allie.

Join the Mailing List!

Did you enjoy this disturbing trip into the Wolves' Den? Are you a fan of dark, provocative books that push the boundaries? If so, you should sign up for my mailing list! I'm *not* writing a sequel to this book, but I've written several similar books in the past and I'll be releasing more dark, disturbing books in the future. I am an author of extreme horror. If you like disturbing, violent, nasty, provocative, and thought-provoking horror books, I think you'll enjoy my work. And I release books very frequently!

By signing up for my mailing list, you'll be the first to know about my newest books, my massive book sales, and other important news. You'll usually receive one email per month. You might receive two or three during some busy months, and you might receive none during others. Either way, you have my word: I will *never* spam you. The process is fast, easy, and free, so visit this link to sign-up: http://eepurl.com/bNl1CP.

Dear Reader,

Thank you for reading *Into the Wolves' Den.* As of August 15, 2019 (the release date of this novel), this is my longest book ever. According to my manuscript, it is approximately 70,000 words long, excluding this letter. Wow! I really hope it didn't drag. If you're reading this, then you made it to the end—or you skipped to the end to feverishly hunt for my contact information so you can send hate mail. If you're part of the latter group, you'll find all of those details at the end of this letter. This book featured a lot of disturbing scenes, I pushed a lot of boundaries, so I won't blame you if you were *a little* offended. But, like I always say in these letters, please remember: it's just a book.

Into the Wolves' Den was inspired by a photograph—a series of photographs, actually. These pictures supposedly originated on the deep web. They involved adults wearing animal masks standing beside weeping, terrified children. Real or fake, I don't know the story behind these pictures, but they left an impact on me. They sent my mind down a rabbit hole of what-if scenarios. What if those masked adults kidnapped those kids? What if they were using those children to produce illegal videos or selling those kids to child predators? What if they were part of a network of violent people who sold depravity for a living?

After completing the first draft of this book, I found specific cases that resembled the events in this novel. I stumbled upon those cases by coincidence, I was reading more deep web horror stories in search of inspiration, but it really hit me hard. I started to think: *what if those pictures were authentic?* It made my story, a work of fiction, feel real. And that scared me. I actually considered removing some scenes because it was just too close to home. Monsters like Allen and Riley exist. As a matter of fact, those real-world monsters are worse than the characters portrayed in this book.

The story was also inspired by the usual suspects: Jack Ketchum, the New French Extremity movement in film, and brutal revenge movies like 'I Saw the Devil.'

I originally planned on ending this book on Chapter 25. Keith and Gerald would have rescued Carrie and Riley would have escaped. The end. It felt too sudden and unfulfilling, though. So, I added a long, 'epic' conclusion. I treated this book like a horror epic, so it deserved an epic ending, right? I wanted to reveal the secret society, bring justice to the victims, and leave some hope for the future. No,

I'm not currently working on a sequel. But, maybe someday in the future, I'll burn another Wolves' Den down. It depends mostly on your feedback, so...

If you enjoyed this book, *please* leave a review on Amazon.com. (Or your local Amazon store if you're one of my wonderful international readers!) Feel free to leave reviews on Goodreads and Bookbub, too. Everything helps! Like I always say, your reviews help me improve, they help me choose my next projects, and they help other readers find my books. When more people read my books, that gives me the resources to write *more* books. The money helps, there's no denying that, but your reviews and your kind messages also motivate me. I smile every time I get a message from one of you, and it gets me pumped up to write the next book. *You* are the reason I'm still doing this. Thank you for that. (And sorry about taking so long to respond to some of your messages. I really need to work on that!)

Need help writing your review? You can try answering questions like these: did you enjoy the story? Was it too disturbing, just right, or not violent enough for an extreme horror book? Was the book too long? Were you satisfied by the ending? Would you like to read a sequel in the future? Your review can be long and detailed or short and to the point. Either way, it's very, very helpful.

I'm writing this letter on June 10, 2019. I am currently working on a small library of violent, nasty, and provocative horror novels. I am also trying to juggle my personal life with my *long* work hours. In August, when this book hit shelves, I'll be in Tokyo, Japan again. I'll be there from August 1st to September 14th. As usual, I'll be working during my stay. I'll also be spending time with my girlfriend, who is Japanese. (I'm pretty sure I've mentioned that before.) Things are going well for me, fortunately. I plan on moving to Japan by May or June of 2020, so I'm working very hard these days. I've already thanked you a few times in this letter. But I have to do it again: *thank you.* Thank you for reading my books, for liking my Facebook page, for signing-up for my newsletter, for keeping in touch, for motivating me, for changing my life for the better. Sorry, I didn't mean to get sappy in this book, but I had to say it!

If you enjoyed this book, please visit my Amazon's author page and check out my other novels. I frequently release new books—at least eight to twelve books a year! I am an extreme horror author, I like to focus on 'human horror,' but I enjoy blending mystery and thriller elements into my books, too. I've also dabbled in other genres/subgenres, including supernatural and psychological horror. At the end of the day, regardless of genre, my writing is meant to disturb and provoke. My last release was a tribute to the cannibal horror movies of the 70s and 80s titled *Cannibal Jungle.* My next book is about an obsessive girlfriend who tortures her former lover—emotionally and physically. The book will be titled *Maneater* and it will be out in September 2019. You don't want to miss it. Once again, thanks for reading!

Until our next venture into the dark and disturbing,
Jon Athan

P.S. If you have any questions or comments, or if you're an aspiring author who needs *some* help, feel free to contact me directly using my business email: info@jon-athan.com. You can also contact me through Twitter @Jonny_Athan or my Facebook page.

Printed in Great Britain
by Amazon